CX. INFORMATION CENTER
FINE ARTS & PERFORMING ARTS
CHICAGO PUBLIC LIBRARY
00 SOUTH STATE STREET.
CHICAGO · 6060~

D1462074

Lying in the Middle

MUSIC IN AMERICAN LIFE

*A list of books in the series appears
at the end of this book.*

Lying in the Middle

Musical Theater and Belief at the Heart of America

JAKE JOHNSON

UNIVERSITY OF ILLINOIS PRESS
Urbana, Chicago, and Springfield

© 2021 by the Board of Trustees
of the University of Illinois
All rights reserved
1 2 3 4 5 C P 5 4 3 2 1
∞ This book is printed on acid-free paper.

Publication supported by a grant from the General Fund of
the American Musicological Society, supported in part by the
National Endowment for the Humanities and the Andrew W.
Mellon Foundation.

Portions of chapter 5, "Everything Old Is New Again," were
originally published as "'That's Where They Knew Me When':
Oklahoma Senior Follies and the Narrative of Decline," in
American Music (Summer 2016): 243–62.
Portions of chapter 6, "Mezza Voce," were originally published
as "Building the Broadway Voice," in *The Oxford Handbook of Voice
Studies*, ed. Nina Sun Eidsheim and Katherine Meizel (2019),
475–91. Reproduced by permission of Oxford University Press.

Library of Congress Cataloging-in-Publication Data
Names: Johnson, Jake, 1984– author.
Title: Lying in the middle : musical theater and belief at the heart
    of America / Jake Johnson.
Description: Urbana : University of Illinois Press, 2021. | Series:
    Music in American life | Includes bibliographical references
    and index.
Identifiers: LCCN 2021005311 (print) | LCCN 2021005312 (ebook)
    | ISBN 9780252043925 (cloth) | ISBN 9780252085994
    (paperback) | ISBN 9780252052859 (ebook)
Subjects: LCSH: Musicals—United States—History and
    criticism. | Musicals—Middle West—History and criticism.
    | Musicals—Social aspects—Middle West. | Musicals—
    Oklahoma—Oklahoma City—History and criticism.
Classification: LCC ML2054 .J64 2021 (print) | LCC ML2054
    (ebook) | DDC 782.1/40973—dc23
LC record available at https://lccn.loc.gov/2021005311
LC ebook record available at https://lccn.loc.gov/2021005312

For Cora and Magnolia
and all the better worlds of your imagining

. . . Come, my friends,
'Tis not too late to seek a newer world.
Push off, and sitting well in order smite
The sounding furrows; for my purpose holds
To sail beyond the sunset, and the baths
Of all the western stars, until I die.
It may be that the gulfs will wash us down:
It may be we shall touch the Happy Isles,
And see the great Achilles, whom we knew.
Tho' much is taken, much abides; and tho'
We are not now that strength which in old days
Moved earth and heaven, that which we are, we are;
One equal temper of heroic hearts,
Made weak by time and fate, but strong in will
To strive, to seek, to find, and not to yield.

—Lord Alfred Tennyson, "Ulysses"

*   *   *

"Somewhere is better than anywhere."

—Flannery O'Connor

Contents

A Brief History of This Book   ix

1   Stories Out of Place   1

2   Re-Placing the American Musical   12

3   Fundamentalism, Produced   27

4   Biblically Accurate   50

5   Everything Old Is New Again   68

6   Mezza Voce   92

7   The Afterlives of Truth and Musicals   112

Notes   127

Bibliography   143

Index   153

A Brief History of This Book

"Your great mistake is to act the drama / as if you were alone," begins David Whyte's poem "Everything Is Waiting for You."

> Put down the weight of your aloneness and ease into
> the conversation. The kettle is singing
> even as it pours you a drink, the cooking pots
> have left their arrogant aloofness and
> seen the good in you at last. All the birds
> and creatures of the world are unutterably
> themselves. Everything is waiting for you.

As lonely as book writing can seem, I know I didn't act this drama alone. I appreciate the poetry of a book caught between its debts. The bibliography at the back is a bunch of people, places, and ideas I plucked from the wild and pressed into form in these pages. It is lengthy enough and will have to do as a space where we all agree that influence and impression gave birth to what lies in this book. But I want to point out a few significant scholarly minds, ideas, people, spaces, and things whose role in this drama deserves to be part of this opening gambit.

Writing a book about deception can be a trick in itself, furtive and untoward in its seeming straightforwardness. Same for musicals. Alexander Nemerov's question—"What if I were an artist and scholarship was my medium?"—gave me permission to make a book as playful as its subject but as serious as its effects. I wrote much of *Lying in the Middle* while writing an experimental biography of music patron Betty Freeman; it probably couldn't be helped that I would work out my thoughts about expanded networks, far-flung places outside the borders of conventional narratives, and agency while attending to both projects. While these companioned books appear to have little in common, they grew to maturity alongside each other, swapping clothes and sharing a bedroom in my mind, vying for my unequal attention, and slowly starting to become their own selves even as their genetics betray their individuality.

I count myself fortunate to be working in a subfield of popular music studies that includes so many wonderful scholars and even better humans. John Koegel has been an important champion of my work and a true friend as has Raymond Knapp, who enabled a symposium in 2019 that brought together some of these scholars in musical theater and popular music studies more broadly. That conversation afforded me a longer lease on some of the issues wrought out in this book. I need to acknowledge the crackerjack team of scholars who made that conversation happen: Masi Asari, Amy Coddington, Nina Sun Eidsheim, Robert Fink, Daniel Goldmark, Raymond Knapp, Mitchell Morris, Shana L. Redmond, Holley Replogle-Wong, Oliver Wang, and Elizabeth L. Wollman.

Investigating the lived experience of musicals required a new set of approaches and skill sets. Whether they were aware of it or not, I drew mightily from peers and scholars more fluent in ethnography and whose methods I admire. Philip Bohlman, Joshua Kalin Busman, Melvin Butler, Judah M. Cohen, Joanna Dee Das, Amy Derogatis, Pamela Klassen, Andrew Mall, Andrea Most, David Savran, Isaac Weiner, Stacy Wolf, and Elizabeth L. Wollman all figured into my thinking as I worked through this project. Although while writing this book I was coeditor with Judah Cohen of a special issue of *Studies in Musical Theatre* on ethnography and musicals, I feel a debt of gratitude for those authors who in their work taught me about the often loving work being done to better understand the place of musicals among local communities. An abundance of thanks to Monique Giroux, Julie Hagen, Jiyoon Jung, Helena Marinho, Millie Taylor, Jennifer Thomas, Joseph Toltz, and Stacy Wolf for their contributions and to Judah, Dominic Symonds, and George Burrows for modeling kind and erudite editorial decision making.

This book wouldn't be possible without the cooperation and patience of the communities represented in its pages. I wish to thank especially the cast and creative team of the Oklahoma Senior Follies for being willing to discuss, evaluate, and analyze their own workings in musical theater. My visit to Sight & Sound Theatres in Branson, Missouri, was impeccably managed and kindly facilitated by Megan Rolofson. Also, my warmest thanks to the wonderful team at the University of Illinois Press, especially Julie Laut for her enthusiasm and Laurie Matheson, who saw potential in this project early on and helped bring it to life. Laurie's Music in American Life series at the press is a lasting legacy in American music studies. I am honored to have my work included there.

This book picks up a thread that my first book left dangling. In *Mormons, Musical Theater, and Belonging in America* (2019), I worked through a good deal of this framework, nourished and parlayed primarily by my community at UCLA. Those friends and scholars include Olivia Bloechl, Patrick Bonczyk, Kerry Brunson, Caitlin Carlos, Patrick J. Craven, Peggy Davis, Nina Eidsheim, Robert Fink, Pheaross Graham, Leigh Harris, Mark Kligman, Raymond Knapp, Kacie Morgan, Mitchell Morris, Tiffany Naiman, Tara Prescott-Johnson, Shana Redmond, Arreanna Rostosky, Helen Rowe, Jessica Schwartz, Schuyler Wheldon, Morgan Woolsey, and many others. This community gave license to radical thinking and welcomed a way of writing that could parallel and intersect with conventional narratives. Although the particulars of this project came into greater clarity since leaving that program, the UCLA community's fingerprints remain part of what I see through my window into the world.

After arriving at Oklahoma City University, I was welcomed into a different kind of community. It is a rare fortune to be in the middle of my work as both practitioner and scholar. Students and faculty at the Wanda L. Bass School of Music have gifted me a network of challenges that have made me and this project all the better. After years of teaching historiographical mysteries—that *what* is true is far less interesting than *how it came to be* true—I finally had to come to terms with what those words mean. My students have pushed back on formative ideas I once thought inescapable and brought me back to the drawing board time after time. Their tough act makes me question possibly everything, a confusion I welcome as a gift.

There is probably a sociological imperative to discover in the mutual birth of my teaching career and this book: redrawing the boundaries around music curriculum in the twenty-first century and reconceptualizing the work of musicals in America became, in hindsight, more and more the same project. I must thank my teaching load for this book. Being forced every day to work through values and ideas and to search for time to write and think perhaps counterintuitively gave me the greatest space to work with. I have learned to loosen my gritted teeth when speaking of my position's demands. As the saying in my family goes, while many have it worse than me, none have it better.

Amid the unusual turns of my career, I have also carved out a space at Oklahoma City University where I have been able to revisit other performative skill sets. My work as a vocal coach and musical director, in fact, helped shape much of these chapters. I have maintained over the last several years a wonderful and quirky coaching studio. Students who come through my door have pretended to entertain musicological canvassing of their repertoire or of musical theater and place. There are many to thank, but I especially want to mention Trey Baker, Megan Carpenter, Brandon Dallmann, Troy Freeman, Claire Greenberg, Anh-Mai Kearney, Kaden Mahle, Gillian O'Daniel, Laura Leigh Turner, and Ally Zahringer. The future of musical theater is not only talented, but it's super smart and clever to boot.

Working in regional theaters has given me a wonderful circle of friends and colleagues, including Michael Baron, Matthew Cypress-Banks, Eric Grigg, Brian Hamilton, David Andrews Rogers, and Ashley Stover Wells at Lyric Theater of Oklahoma and Wayne Bryan, Josh Larsen, and Nancy Reeves at Music Theatre of Wichita.

Finally, my community in Oklahoma City includes a vibrant group of scholars and teachers I have enjoyed learning from and with. Of these, I count Christa Bentley, James Chang, Bill Christensen, Courtney Crouse, David Easley, Beth Fleming, Eric Frei, Erik Heine, David Herendeen, Kelly Holst, Katy Kinard, Chuck Koslowske, Catherine McDaniel, Jan McDaniel, Karen Miller, Melissa Plamann, Sarah Sarver, and Autumn West as especially hardworking, kind, and resourceful people in my life. We are a large music school with small school resources, and I am always amazed what my colleagues are able to make out of so very little.

The good vibes of my compatriots outside the bounds of the Bass Music Center are also felt throughout these pages. Many thanks to Tracy Floreani and Lisa Wolfe, especially, for being wise guides in navigating scholarship within a rigorous teaching institution, and for Jennifer Saltzstein, Michael Lee, Zoe Sherinian, and Kenneth Haltman at the University of Oklahoma for the guidance, appreciation, and abundance of good-natured fun I have enjoyed over these last many years. It's good to be back among you.

I am grateful that the Society for American Music found this project, even in its infancy, worth supporting. The Virgil Thomson Award helped ease the burden of completing this book during a time when the burdens were significant, money low, and mental bandwidth thinning. I thank Mathew Campbell for making my musical examples look beautiful, and Rebekah Bruce Parker for her deft help in transcribing them.

I knew of musicals most of my life not because of Broadway but because my parents and small community made sure they were part of my life. As my argument goes, I owe them more than I could ever repay.

I also owe a measure to the sunny southern plains and opulent windows to perch and work. My front porch earns a line here for its pleasurable company and my dim work office for its pushing me out into the world. To my daughters, who came upon a love for theater and all the possibilities it entertains honestly, I dedicate this book. And to my wife, BrieAnn Lund Johnson, for continually shaping and reshaping our great drama together—you are the truest thing I know.

Lying in the Middle

CHAPTER 1

Stories Out of Place

This is a book about stories out of place. Some call them lies; others call them musicals. I suggest that both can make us better: that every gesture toward the ineffable, the unreal, or the untrue is a nod toward a world that does not yet exist, a vehicle for wishing that ought to be kept in good working order. The book you are reading is such a wish. The book I have written for you, if it is to do anything good at all, must also be a lie. *Call me Ishmael*—I cannot be trusted.

More to the point, *Lying in the Middle* is about musicals, a particular kind of lying. Musicals are a hot commodity at the moment, if we are to judge by economic reports of Broadway and Hollywood. Musicals are also an active force outside these commercial centers, as I argue throughout. Surely one metric for measuring any artifactual success is its potential for eliciting and enticing deceit. The general buzz around this form of deception casts urgency upon knowing better what work musicals perform for the deceived and the deceiver.

Individuals lie for all sorts of reasons, big and small; the lies that groups tell themselves with musicals, on the other hand, unsettle the fabric of reality in much more significant ways. We can look to communities who engage in theatrical deception as models for building our own alternate reality—a world with more satisfying answers to the kind of questions our actual world has yet to ask. Lies of this sort are often symbolic, usually religiously so. They can do real harm; don't get me wrong. But their agreed-upon weightlessness permits such deceptions a pass into the figurative. In this way, deceptions engage a safety release valve, a release in the direction of new ways of being. Lots of things can encourage lies; musicals enable and embody our belief in them.

Our work here, then, is to locate musical theater in its most prevalent and potent form, which is to say, in its liveness and its locality. Musicals are an everywhere phenomenon. They sustain and promote values particular to communities who in turn perform themselves through the musical stage. I am following an emergent group of scholars in gazing beyond America's commercial centers of the art form—Broadway and Hollywood—to better understand how the musical works and what kind of work it produces. I have a suspicion, a hunch, guiding this book: we don't yet understand the potency of musical theater. If we wish to name that power for what it is, we have to follow Stacy Wolf's gaze and look "beyond Broadway."[1] To tweak Rudyard Kipling's adage, I ask in this book what any of us knows of Broadway who only Broadway knows.

Between Truth and Fiction

Which is maybe another way of asking what anyone knows about truth. I am not alone in relishing the power of musicals to construct fantasy and alternate worlds. Even casual observers of the musical have noted its predilection for escapism and hapless joy. Musical theater fans have become something of apologists on this front, echoing to one degree or another Oscar Hammerstein's sheepish admission that, well, *somebody* has to say things are okay in the world.[2] Even ancient theater, caught in the orbit of shamanistic religion, was driven by spectacle to illustrate, as Mircea Eliade writes, the world "in which *everything seems possible*, where the dead return to life and the living die only to live again, where one can disappear and reappear instantaneously, where the 'laws of nature' are abolished, and a certain superhuman 'freedom' is exemplified and made dazzlingly *present*."[3] As much as Friedrich Holländer attempted to repurpose the cabaret during the Weimar Era as a blessedly unreal space ("Truth is hard and tough as nails / That's why we need fairy tales"), or to the degree that campy assignations proliferate in today's Broadway musical theater as a meta-language speaking beyond the stage, the theater and its defenders for better or worse have had to come to terms with its place outside of reality.[4]

And yet precisely because of the way musicals lie to us, they perform a demonstrably important work for modern audiences. I have argued before that through musical stages communities both transform the profane into the sacred and enliven the sacred through the profane. In fact, Johan Huizinga's theories of play constitute pretend as an essential tool for socializing, preparing for battle, partnership, work, or leisure. So central is play to human sociality, Huizinga defines the modern human experience as that of Homo Ludens—Man the Player.[5] More recently, Jill Dolan explains that theater—a form of pretend—gives people the "affective possibilities of 'doings' that gesture toward a much better world."[6] This feeling of action, even if only a ruse safely performed onstage, is nonetheless palpably important for movement toward a more ideal world—however that may come to be defined. In her 2005 book *Utopia in Performance*, Dolan defines theater's affective fantasy space as "utopian performatives," a phrase that speaks as much to the desire for a better world as to the impossibility of ever inhabiting it.

Dolan is not wrong. Or perhaps she was more right in the Bush II years than today. In retrospect, utopia seems a fitting descriptor for what theater at times seeks to accomplish. Today, however, the aspirations of theater to show a way forward are lost in the mists of disbelief that cast doubt on whether a way even exists. When faced with the enormous weight and pressure of political insurrections rife with widespread disruptive glee, to say nothing of an impending climate disaster so consequential and far-reaching that minds fail to comprehend it, escape is all the more needed and yet all the more distrusted. In this moment, audiences aren't hiring theater to transport them to utopia; they are hiring theater to make the present dystopia more real. It is difficult to know which *topia* we ought to be tilting. When truth lacks currency, we must turn to lies to return us to reality.

In his 1891 essay "The Decay of Lying," Oscar Wilde attempts to invigorate the art of lying, reversing the entrenched Romantic position that art imitates life by claiming that life, in fact, is the one doing the imitating. Life follows art, and if our art cannot freely imagine new worlds, then life itself will likewise be empty of creativity and thought, impoverished of possibility. Wilde goes so far as to say that America's industriousness, commercialism, and subsequent lack of imaginative power are due to the prevailing myth that its founding father and homegrown hero simply could not tell a lie. "And it is not too much to say," he adds, "that the story of George Washington and the cherry-tree has done more harm, and in a shorter space of time, than any other moral tale in the whole of literature."[7] Lying is an art. Periodically, Americans forget that—they lay their axe at the root of deceit but end up whirling in circles in a wild swing-and-miss.

But I am less interested in the lies people tell for individual and personal reasons, except to say that the impulse to fabricate or fudge the truth in the immediate and everyday spheres of our lives is firmly attached to how collective, or group, lies so easily take hold. To lie is to create a new, not-yet-existent world; lying, in fact, and as Wilde makes clear, is a *creative* endeavor. Journalist

Dan Ariely points out as much when in his study of deception he discovers that creative people are more likely than others to bend the truth or act in outright dishonest ways. The reason, he explains, is the creative mind's insatiable appetite for narrative. "We're storytelling creatures by nature," he writes, "and we tell ourselves story after story until we come up with an explanation that we like and that sounds reasonable enough to believe. And when the story portrays us in a more glowing and positive light, so much the better."[8]

Ah, the unearned afterglow of knowing you are right. The catch, it seems, is that we can be so good at explaining away our own dishonest behavior or sidestepping that time when we took the bait and spread false information that we soon forget an act of deception ever took place at all, even when confronted with our deception. (Mark Twain's affirmative "lying is universal—we *all* do it" is of strange comfort.[9]) Ariely again:

> Putting our creative minds to work can help us come up with a narrative that lets us have our cake and eat it too, and create stories in which we're always the hero, never the villain. If the key to our dishonesty is our ability to think of ourselves as honest and moral people while at the same time benefitting from cheating, creativity can help us tell better stories—stories that allow us to be even more dishonest but still think of ourselves as wonderfully honest people.[10]

I suspect many think of themselves as "wonderfully honest people." Each of us is so often the hero of our own story. Those same people may even believe that the world's known liars—politicians, actors, and others—are of a different class of people than they. Yet we can all imagine daily acts of fictive transgression: flattering a friend with news they want to hear or a doctor administering a placebo drug to a worrisome patient, for instance. Social scientists call these "prosocial lies," and studies suggest that displays of altruism and benevolence, even if built on deception, encourage trust more than honesty.[11] "Individuals trust people who help others," write Emma E. Levine and Maurice E. Schweitzer, "even when that help involves deception and when that help is self-serving."[12] In other words, while a social mandate on lying suggests it is universally wrong, lying is frequently allowed—admired, even—if we believe it is in the service of creating a better world. Creativity begets dishonesty, and honesty can never be pure.

Purity is actually an operative concept, which is why I turn to established discourse on purity rites in anthropology and sociology to help explain the work of deception. First, Mary Douglas's claim in *Purity and Danger* that dirt is simply matter out of place is of singular importance in my study.[13] By "out of place," Douglas means that dirt operates as a symbol—of pollution or what is taboo, for instance. It isn't dirt so much as a community that makes dirt *dirty*.

We might think of deception similarly; lying is an act of imagining that irks because of its storied out-of-placeness. Think back to the examples of prosocial lies I described earlier. The very qualifier any of us might cast upon, say, flattering a boss with untruths—a *small* lie, a *little white* lie, and so on—implies a social contract that allows lies in principle but only conditionally. Immanuel Kant famously concluded that lying could never be a vehicle for social good, which is why these small lies are so pesky if lying is *always* a principle of violation, and yet they clearly are doing good, maybe even preventing harm.[14] In this regard, lying itself may not be a transgression, but lies in a particular manner or for a particular cause may wrinkle the social fabric. Following Douglas, I suggest lies are misjudged for their potential to rattle our cages in creative and useful ways. They are simply stories out of place.

Deception, therefore, is an index of storytelling, of narratives that pass up and down the social classes. I am interested in the kind of tools and beliefs that enable a group or community's dallying with the untrue. Douglas's work on what has been dubbed the "Grid-Group model of cultural theory" illuminates this difference (see fig. 1.1).[15] On one axis of the model lies the *Group* dimension, which describes strong or weak bonds of connectivity among people. People in "high" Group identity easily define and police themselves, while those in "low" Group identity are more individualized and find it difficult to manage or care about collective resources. On the other axis, *Grid* explains how difference permeates group identity, allowing for varied roles and perspectives. In "low" Grid, people are more or less interchangeable with one another in work and other activities, with people largely independent of others since most everyone else is just like them. On the other end, "high" Grid describes communities with distinct roles and levels of accountability, where people rely on experts with skills and profiles unlike their own.

Environments where Group identity is weak and the Grid dimension reflects interpersonal differences Douglas describes as *Fatalistic*. Communities with strong Group bonds amid many interpersonal differences are *Collectivist*. When Grid dynamics reflect greater homogeneity within a weaker Group bond, communities exhibit greater *Individualism*. Finally, strong Group bonds within homogenous Grid dynamics produce *Egalitarianism*.

Drawing from Douglas's model, I make the case that a post-truth climate survives best in a Fatalistic culture. Current populist uprisings in the West, especially in America, suggest that Group bonds are weak amid many varied and competing interpersonal dynamics—a Fatalistic environment where people have little in common and so are suspicious of everything but deception itself. Aloof and capricious, those living in this environment are plagued with uncertainty, isolation, imbalances of power, and despotic leadership. Individuals are

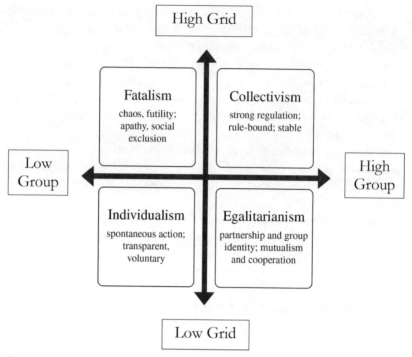

Figure 1.1: Grid-Group model of cultural theory

on their own, and groups construct weak narratives. Economic advantage is masked as empathy. Apathy and narratives of meritocracy mutually ensure that Group bonds weaken under increasing disfavor toward the "have nots." Such an environment is stagnated and lacks direction; with facts devalued, truth claims fracture and falsities congeal, dislodging truth as a virtue and opening the space for creative solutions to managing stronger Group bonds. Lying is one of those solutions.

Musicals, on the other hand, so often dramatize a group of people transitioning from Fatalism to ultimately become a strong Egalitarian community. Reconciliation dominates the storyline almost at all costs. As plots carry communities from disorder and chaos into a world of clarity and unity, musicals enact strong *moral* values rather than central laws to govern that transition. In the musical *Oklahoma!*, for example, we meet a community rattled with discord between the cattle workers and the farmers. Their beef is with the law, a question of fences and water rights. The symbolic union of the two factions with Laurey and Curly's marriage—a marriage that is enabled by the death of the community's social pariah (and Curly's main rival), Jud, and the subsequent kangaroo court erasing Curly's role in the death—leads to a unified future where law takes a backseat to the community's preferred values, values they (with the help of Aunt Eller's pistol) clearly plan to manage collectively. A similar scenario plays out in *The Music Man*. The known swindler Harold Hill and the reclusive librarian Marian Paroo unite a community in music making, despite the long con game Professor Hill employs as his gimmick.

The high-Group and low-Grid dynamic of Egalitarianism can easily be romanticized onstage as an ideal utopia, though many have been quick to point out that such a community takes shape at a significant cost. In both of the examples I provide here, people must be erased or expunged from the community for the high-Group dynamic to be sustained. In *Oklahoma!* the low-class and racialized farmhand Jud, who Andrea Most refers to as a "sacrificial scapegoat," presents a threat to the community's unification; in *The Music Man* the women of River City, Iowa, who were all along working toward building an arts culture in their town, are reduced to mere prattle after Professor Hill sweeps in to do the same.[16] The tidy Egalitarianism of musicals need not be examined as a carbon-copy ideal. Rather, the path toward such a transformation reveals a key value that musicals speak of our times: radical change often turns on the axis of duplicity, cleverness, and sometimes outright deception.

My argument, then, is that Fatalistic societies need *more* out-of-place stories to dislodge from the ennui of neoliberalism, corruption, social inequity, impending climate disasters, and so on; that the solution to these complex problems is, paradoxically, *less* truth—through, finally, a reading of René Girard's concept of the scapegoat.[17] Violence is a natural condition of humanity, Girard claims, though over time that violence had to be mitigated against larger communities and enemies of different sorts. Violence has to be managed. Modern communities now enacting social pacifism (as mandated by a police state) require periodic acts of symbolic violence to release pent-up tension, and these acts of violence are perpetrated upon scapegoats, often (though not always) in the realm of the religious. Scapegoats ensure maximal violent release with the least amount of societal trauma.

Lying is a similarly disruptive act that shocks a social system into change. Rampant dishonesty might come in moments of clearest crisis. Max Weber makes this connection neatly: religious charisma has its own form of rationality and is typically associable with egalitarian cultures.[18] Just as religion enables violence through controlled and regulated rituals, such as the worship of and partaking in the death of Jesus, so too must lying be managed and conditioned so that it can offer the most usefulness with the least disruptive effects.

As an example, I'm reminded that insensitive and racist musical depictions of marginalized communities on American stages ("coon songs," ethnic novelty songs, or the Irish in blackface, for example) may have diffused real violence toward such communities, "substituting travesty for assault and battery," as Raymond Knapp and Mitchell Morris suggest.[19] Girard's concept of the scapegoat is clearly at play in such a scenario. Even in lying about a racialized population—in this case, by perpetuating exaggerated depictions and stereotypes—the musical stage can translate violence into a world of even incremental stability. It may be a devil's bargain to choose defamation over violence, but musicals in these cases don't make the rules of injustice so much as they point to a rule book hidden away elsewhere, out of place.

Musicals are clearly being enlisted for such work. More than other forms of escapist entertainment, musicals concoct worlds where song and dance erupt out of nowhere, shattering the familiar and common, raising our eyebrows at their radical unreality. Even more, as my examples of Jud in *Oklahoma!* and the women of River City in *The Music Man* illustrate, musicals can and do eagerly scapegoat outsiders in order to achieve peaceful ends—a practice that is not without alarm. The push toward fantasy may invite some and repulse others, but musical theater's aesthetic is not the point here. What this book uncovers is how these platforms of radical fiction enable slight fictions—consensual lies, deceptions that are genuine—to shift the values of the community enmeshed within its production. The draw toward the musical may have never been for its honesty, these chapters show, but rather for its enabling of specific modes of *dis*honesty. The way the musical invites prosocial fantasy into a community conditions our value of untruth. Musicals channel the need for a scapegoat of deception without which untruths would prove greatly disastrous, run amok and without borders. Musicals are a ticket to unsettling a Fatalistic culture; whatever web of deception musicals spin, we need to deepen the tangles and not cut them away.

Piecing Together Our Stories

I am charmed by Will Ashon's approach to storytelling. Don't think of this as a book, he says; think of it instead as a historiographical jigsaw puzzle—a story dumped in your lap, its pieces upside down, scattered and turned sideways, out of place and in need of direction. Puzzles and history take shape with fits and starts. The story begins with what first catches your eye or a pattern that seems easiest to match. Maybe you start with the flat edges along the border. Maybe you pick out that odd shape and start there. If you stick with the game long enough, you will eventually arrive at a complete image, though our exact paths toward that finish may never be retraced and the journey will necessarily look different from one person to the next. Remember, this uncertainty is part of the fun. "There is a real value to being lost," Ashon says.[20]

Making new maps is my goal here, though I suspect I may be a lousy cartographer. The following chapters are as much a decentered strategy as they are cohesive. Read cover to cover, this book tells one story. Read piecemeal, quite another. If you follow the instructions as laid out in the chapter order, you may come to similar conclusions that I have about musicals and deception. But I can't help your relationship with stories. Misplace them. Read the book upside down and inside out, twist and squeeze if you can get away with it.

Like the musicals and lies I write about, this book may be out of place. Chapter 2 is a twinned introduction for this book. "Re-Placing the American Musical" regroups my pass-through here and shows the paths musical theater took through the Middle to arrive at the Broadway theater district.

The nexus of deception and plausible deniability is in many ways the religious experience. The next two chapters scan closely to two religious communities to investigate the power that musical theater holds within fundamentalism. Juxtaposing, in chapter 3, "Fundamentalism, Produced," a production of *The Sound of Music* by a polygamous fundamentalist community in rural Arizona, with, in chapter 4, "Biblically Accurate," the original musical *Samson* at the evangelical Christian Sight & Sound Theatres in Branson, Missouri, this pair of chapters seeks to understand the modes of piety and devotion performers use to navigate their faith on and through the musical stage. I look at the place musicals hold in these two communities and ask how and for what purposes musicals are useful in recreating these experiences.

The next two chapters deal with bodies and voices. This pairing showcases less feverish examples of belief, but they are important nonetheless to illustrate how piercing some of musical theater's hard-shell conventions can reveal the believing heart animating those practices. Whereas aging or aged voices in popular music are often revered as authentic, musical theater performers who are growing older face an industry that is largely uninterested in positive representations of aging. Musical theater sustains a persistent correlation between aging and deterioration. The Senior Follies movement is designed to counter this decline narrative by granting value and purpose to aging performers through a Ziegfeld-inspired musical revue. In chapter 5, "Everything Old Is New Again," I draw on my work as musical director of the Oklahoma Senior Follies to highlight the effects the movement has had on Oklahoma City audiences and performers. As I argue in that chapter, the Senior Follies movement not only engages the narrative of decline but also undoes conventions of musical theater that have coupled aging with disability or invisibility. Chapter 6, "Mezza Voce," observes that many of the performers on Broadway today are products of collegiate training programs in the middle of America, located sometimes thousands of miles from Times Square. The chapter uses interviews, close listening, and my own experience working as a vocal coach in several of these musical theater programs to suggest that inasmuch as these programs train young students to use "their own voice" to meet a wide variety of musical styles on Broadway today, the industry nonetheless brands a *particular* vocal sound at the expense of the unique voice promised them in their training—a vocal ideal that has something to say about the future of democracy and political expediency.

The final chapter, "The Afterlives of Truth and Musicals," asks what the world might look like if we attend to the predictions of this book. What happens to lying, I ask, when we increase the depths of our deceit? And what becomes of musicals when we re-place them from their commercial centers? What can our musicals do if we no longer recognize their work as being fiction? If we displace lying for truth, have we also displaced something essentially human in the process? I leave readers with a few examples for how an end to truth might still involve musical theater.

Lying in the Middle pulls these stories out of the middle of America into a discussion of truth, authenticity, and, ultimately, representation. As my broadest argument is that musicals are an everywhere phenomenon, these case studies are, of course, far from exhaustive. I have chosen them for a number of reasons, but broad representation of community, regional, or touring theater is not one of them. This book alone cannot contend with the breadth of musical life among underrepresented communities across the Americas, and I hope people continue to write about and study theater making that is happening in unsuspecting corners of the country. Nor do I take these several chapters to explain *theater* so much as I use them as explanatory models for various modes of deception that musicals afford communities not often associated with the genre.

Rather, I have assembled these particular communities to glimpse a more nuanced and slightly off-kilter reality among majority populations. It is an important fact that the communities studied here are mostly white and that theater making throughout America belongs to groups of all backgrounds and lived expressions. I note in the following chapter how American musical theater develops because of and in response to hosts of ethnic, racial, religious, classed, and regional theater making in this country. While the communities I study here are wildly different from one another in ways the singularity of race cannot register, it is nonetheless true that many, most, in these chapters navigate the world with visible privilege and often parlay that privilege in their theatrical work. And yet they also find in theater a space for contending with the inevitability of change, the immutability of their autonomy, power, and mythologies. Theater has proven to be a useful space for mitigating social change among immigrants, ethnic populations, and disempowered people of the past; it no less finds work contending with social dynamism still today, including among white communities of people who feel their way of life is threatened and look to musicals to help contain that threat. Narratives of redemption can be discovered among many kinds of people. This book is not to say those narratives are proscriptive, but it also isn't designed to simply echo well-spoken social narratives elsewhere.

Musicology is "anything you can get away *with*," says Phil Ford; it's also everything musicologists try to get away *from*, say I.[21] Now is as good a time as any to bring this up, because this book is a musicological narrative, and musicology's narratives are valuable *for what they leave out*. I take sociologist Randall Collins at his word when he explains that the most endearing and long-lasting books are those that miss the mark; failed books—books that tell half-truths, spin incomplete stories, or otherwise run aground—are more apt to linger in future work because the requirement of our labors is first to have something to belabor.[22] Books that are bold in their blunders give us quixotic windmills for tilting, a map liable to lead us astray. There is, after all, real value to being lost.

Lying in the Middle is such a story out of place, a far-off windmill that could be anything. So if this book can spin something worthwhile, it must be a lie.

But I already told you that.

CHAPTER 2

Re-Placing the American Musical

Musical theater tells lies, to begin with. There is no doubt whatsoever about that. But the story so often told *about* musicals is also untrue—that is, that New York is where musicals of any significance, if significance is to be found, happen. The story presumes that:

- the musical is an almost exclusively commercial form;
- the musical reaches its apotheosis at Times Square and its surroundings; and
- the musical is a middlebrow commentary *about* America rather than a practice everyday Americans use to imagine and recreate that idea of America.

Such a narrative sleight of hand disappears the bulk of musical theater practice with smoke and mirrors. Musical theater is actually an everywhere genre, despite the spirited deception of theater districts. Ebenezer Scrooge could name this trick for what it is: there is more of gravy than of grave about such a tall tale.

This chapter takes a second sweep past the opening chapter to situate musicals alongside deception. Musicals exist in the middle of all our concerns about America. They also easily take shape in communities centered elsewhere in the country. If we are to understand musicals on their own terms—and make better use of the lies they afford us—then we have to be willing to see them working at a distance. Musicals happen to be about the Middle. They are stories out of place.

Here I map out a history of the American musical that admits its out-of-placeness. Musicals must be "re-placed," I suggest—reimagined as practices not only in major coastal cities but as conditional and everywhere performances of America itself. Sound and place are twinned geographies we must attend to in these pages. "Places I love come back to me like music," Sara Teasdale hums.[1] *The hills are alive with the sound of music*, a nun sings as she twirls.

Our story lies in the Middle.

It starts with me.

Musicals and the Middle

I come from the Middle. I was born in a rural hospital in Hughes County, Oklahoma—just a few miles from where my maternal and paternal families had settled generations earlier. Most of my life I was told that I was one of the last to be born there, that the small hospital stopped delivering babies shortly after I was born. I now know that story wasn't entirely true, and folks are still debuting on the world's stage by way of Holdenville General Hospital.

Half-truth or not, the idea of being the last person born into a way of life has shaped much of who I became. Caught between old customs and new ideas, rural assuredness and urban complexity, religious hubris and cultural humility, my life has weathered an identity that seems both wholly comfortable and anxiously unsettled with itself. There comes a restless Zen with being caught in the in-between. I am the Middle and the Middle is me.

In more ways than one, this book is about life in the Middle. Not my life, but the life of a quintessentially American style of performance—the life musicals give and the lives it shapes among those who live and work in the middle of the country. *Why musicals?* I ask of them. *What kind of work do musicals do for you?* For me, this line of questioning has proven helpful in investigating the formation of American identity through musical theater for three related reasons:

- Unlike most popular music styles, musicals have been neither primarily nor traditionally top-down, media-dependent, so
- musical theater is a decentralized mode of music making, existing everywhere among many types of communities, which means
- musicals reveal through liveness local values among a host of American populations.

My earlier book, *Mormons, Musical Theater, and Belonging in America*, situates musical theater as a central theological tenet of Mormonism and a significant means for that faith's cultural assimilation in America. This book scans even closer to see how embedded musical theater is in the fabric of America. It ultimately makes a case for why its fictions are important to the drape of America's future.

Musicals are widespread and everywhere. At the same time, however, musicals are a nomadic and unsettled style—they exist in the Middle. Few take them seriously anyway. Their campiness and jazz-hands stylizing set musicals apart as sometimes painfully unreal, especially when compared to other styles of popular music that more forcibly insist on their authenticity.[2] While musical theater *is* a branch of popular music—a significant siphon of popular music styles, even—it often is not the kind of popular music most people call to mind with the word "popular." Those who do take musicals seriously often find themselves inhabiting a shadowy in-between space.[3]

This book is an attempt at shadow busting. My choice of title speaks to the three dimensions of musical theater that this book highlights: *Lying in the Middle* refers at once to place, centrality, and duplicity. First, each chapter follows a community and its musical theater practices in the middle of the country, making this a project of geography. Second, and as these case studies suggest, musicals fulfill a central role in identity formation among those living in this part of the country. Musicals are an essential vehicle for conceptualizing American values, whatever those may be or however they are defined. And, finally, the title draws attention to the duplicitous quality of musicals in forming those values.

While "lying in the middle" semantically tackles all three elements of how musicals work, the remaining part of this book's title, "Musical Theater and Belief at the Heart of America," more directly implicates musicals in the kind of work they actually do among these communities. Heart is pulse, the animator. It gives nutrients and takes away refuse. It is in the Middle—literally located centrally in the body but also caught in the middle of all other essential bodily processes. Even more, heart speaks for the whole, representing the very fibers and throbbing tissue of identity. The heart is where we so often turn to find our truest self, the original pulse that animates a belief in who we are and where we belong. It is, finally, an apt metaphor for the grit, drive, and sincere optimism that animates America's favorite stories about itself.

This book tries to capture how musical theater attends to all of these qualities—reverberating throughout the entire country as a long-lasting tradition of otherworld building.

My glance away from Broadway begins with a closer look at Broadway itself. The middle of the country has been a fixation of New York musicals for decades. Some of the most lasting and penetrating musicals ever written are set within parts of the country that have since been dubbed "flyover," including *The Music*

Man, State Fair, The Bridges of Madison County, The Wizard of Oz, Annie Get Your Gun, The Best Little Whorehouse in Texas, and *Oklahoma!* Scholars have pointed out that apple-pie America has traditionally been imagined strongest in the Middle; for a genre that solidified during America's mid-twentieth-century ascent to global superpower, it is unsurprising that many of its most beloved stories are imagined at the heart of the country.

A certain *kind* of country, that is. Although America's Middle includes some of its largest and fastest-growing urban areas, the Middle of musical theater's imagination is persistently a "rural idyll"—the proscriptive rather than descriptive America of the imagined frontier past. Rural America is a strategy for a show, not a reality. Cara Wood notes that any depiction of Middle America on stage or in film "tells us more about the preferences and fantasies of their creators and audiences than about the 'real' of historical Midwest."[4] Musicals may play a significant role in strongly romanticizing life in the Middle but not without a careful curating of fantasy in an effort to appease urban malaise elsewhere.

Which is not to say that it is immediately clear why musicals are such a fixture of the swirling Middle that Allen Ginsburg dubbed the "vortex" of the nation.[5] In fact, for communities in the Middle looking for an effective delivery system, musicals seem a remarkably bad idea. They are patently fake, known to be cold to sincerity and simplicity, and require immodest resources to pull off. Even more, Broadway musicals court a reputation for the flashy, crass, and exotic, and were designed to entertain white liberal audiences in New York— qualities that are hardly resonant with standards immediately associable with the American Middle.

In important ways, this blurry quick glance clarifies after a more steadied stare. The Middle, in fact, enjoys a reputation as both heart and backbone of American values but also as the itchy rash tormenting the nation at night. John Steinbeck romanticized their plight and Woody Guthrie loaded his guitar weapon full of their stories and took aim at capitalist exploitation, but Okies and others fleeing the horrors of the Dust Bowl found little sympathy from almost any direction they turned. Once upon a time, western Missouri was viewed as the edge of the world. Only a few generations passed before those who traveled west through the country's back door would look behind them with a sneer of resentment. Modern animosity toward the Middle in recent decades has been tracked through politics, as historian Thomas Frank's broadside and bitterly polemic *What's the Matter with Kansas?* attempted in 2004. The people of the Middle, according to Frank, continually make political decisions that are not in their best interest and in the process spoil things for the rest of us. "If this is the place where America goes looking for its national soul," he claims, "then this is where America finds that its soul, after stewing in the primal resentment of the backlash, has gone all sour and wrong."[6]

Frank's trenchant analysis illuminates the Middle's magnetisms for populists of all stripes, which is to say its penchant for dreamers and robust displays of overwhelming sameness. Like the patiently flexing landscape itself, the region's populations appear at first glance to be pridefully homogenous. "The Midwest is largely a social system based on everybody looking and acting like everybody else," writes Richard C. Longworth, a fact not lost on outsiders looking in. While the Middle often bandies repute as a bastion of white preservation, if not outright supremacy, that reputation may not be fully earned. Measured by metrics other than race, communities in the Middle have their own social pariahs, majority blocks, ethnic vibrancy, and well-policed values just as they exist in other pockets of the country. Nonetheless, optics afford a more common story about life in the Middle as racially—and therefore determinatively—homogenous.

In any case, the demographic density is shifting weight under new economic pressures. Globalization has emptied pockets of the region quite dramatically, creating an opportunity for those who are willing to relocate to and try their hand in the Middle. Migrant workers with darker-colored skin have begun settling in the homes and jobs once occupied by the region's white rural workers who themselves descended from migrants drawn to the area for opportunities that less hearty souls passed by. The center may be "the whitest part of America," to use Longworth's words, but only because the previous generation's migrant workers largely came there from European nations.[7] Migration, impermanence, and ethnic volatility are as much the defining features of those living in the Middle as the deep roots, traditional middle-class values, and stability so frequently paraded about by people who only occasionally peer into the Middle from other parts of the country.

Migration, impermanence, and ethnic volatility are also the defining features of a musical style so heavily commercialized and centered in coastal cities and yet blushing with intrigue toward the Middle. Whatever makes the Middle enticing to Broadway is what helped make Broadway in the first place.

Hiring Musicals

McDonald's customers were buying milkshakes for breakfast. The company's top-shelf marketing teams wanted to know why: Why were most milkshakes purchased by people on their way to work in the morning?

A milkshake, it turns out, was optimal commuter food. Its caloric density, slow and thick slurping fun, and one-handed hold were all wins for commuters looking for less messy and longer-lasting food options on their morning drive. We might say the milkshake was being *hired* to do a job that a competitor food—say, a doughnut or breakfast sandwich—couldn't do as well. In focusing too narrowly on how customers were predicted to act, McDonald's marketers neglected to consider what motivates customer decisions in the first place: the job a product is being hired to do for them.

Harvard business professor Clayton M. Christensen uses this story in his book *Competing against Luck* to illustrate a point about consumption habits.[8] I find it productive when applied to popular music. One way of understanding music is through studying the ways and places in which music is supposed to matter. Within what Christensen calls the jobs-to-be-done framework, however, it is the function of music, not necessarily its intended use or expected locale, that motivates listeners and performers. Such an economic framework props up an ongoing multidisciplinary strategy to decenter the agency of objects and "artifacts" from their intended use.[9] Rather than asking why people listen to Judy Garland, for instance, a more focused question might ask what job causes someone to hire Judy Garland's voice. And of all the competitor voices available, what causes someone to hire Judy Garland's voice for that job in particular?

My work tilts a similar line of questioning toward musical theater, a genre that carries a reputation as one of the most undervalued and kitschy musical styles in America. Musicals are boundless and workaday, in recent years even spilling the banks of popular culture, and yet musical theater scholarship has remained outside the purview of most popular music studies. The musical is consistently used by communities of all stripes to do ambitious and serious work in spite of—or precisely because of—its overwhelming unreality. This marginal and also central piece of Americana seems to me such a curiosity. To adapt art historian Alexander Nemerov's cunning phrase, I want to show what a musical does that it does not know it is doing.[10] In short, I keep afloat the lingering and obvious, yet also seldom considered, question: *Why musicals?*

A thoughtful response requires looking askance at the way the musical has come to be defined. New York City remains, in both the popular imagination and in many critical studies, the most significant place where musicals happen. However, most people consume musicals not primarily as Broadway performances but rather through an astonishingly rich variety of musical productions on national tours, cruise ships, film and television, and theme parks, or the amateur venues of junior and senior high schools, community theater, and regional pageants. A few leading scholars have drawn attention to musical theater practices and traditions outside of—and preliminary to—Times Square.[11]

Yet by far most research and teaching of the American musical continues to be centered on Broadway and its primary audiences of New York City tourists.

We need a new map, a new geography, of musical theater that can account for the American musical's far reach. This project seeks to "re-place" the American musical by highlighting the lived experience of musical theater in other locations and with other purposes than those near Times Square. I take the position that musical theater is a style that cuts across social groups and demographics in a way that few other genres can; musical theater is therefore a useful lens into various social behaviors, even those among crowds gathering for shows in atypical locales. Acknowledging the important yet understudied place musicals keep in communities large and small across America, this project shifts the focus of musical theater scholarship away from Broadway and investigates how and for what job people hire musicals to do things.

A fair word of warning, however. Upturning rocks along this less-trodden path is a task that is not exclusively value-positive. As Pierre Bourdieu reminds us, historicizing the past is fundamentally a discovery of what labor went into disguising and hiding that past.[12] Turning toward the way musicals are practiced and employed in the Middle expands greatly what we know about the kind of work musicals perform, though we would be wise to situate that work as labor enlisted for the efforts of both good and evil.

In our current political climate, in which consumers are fixated on the perceived urban-rural divide and U.S.-international relations, it seems especially important for popular music scholars to turn critical attention to musical and dramatic practices outside of familiar institutions and explore the ways that American musical theater matters to communities far removed from Broadway. In broadening the focus of musical theater scholarship to include everyday lived experiences with and of musicals, my work charges the discipline to investigate the musical more robustly with ethnographic methods. Musicals are entangled with a number of modes of dissemination, such as sheet music, recordings, and radio and television broadcasts, though musical theater is distinct among popular music genres for largely developing a different relationship with mass media—a fact that admits of liveness and variegated experiences among audiences. By foregrounding the fluidity and interchangeability of musicals in everyday use, this book spins within the "ethnographic turn" of popular music studies and pivots outward to communities and people out of place.

Along the way, this book shows how communities across the middle of the United States use musical theater to construct a past that is more in favor with their present. I am careful to point out here that reconstructing the past is not the only reason musicals have gained traction in these or other parts of the country, nor are musicals the only means for fooling ourselves. Audiences gather around musical theater for a variety of purposes, some hard to pin down, and likely no single reason ultimately explains why musical theater has achieved such prominence in the lives of these communities. Nonetheless, I find it rewarding and revealing to re-place musical theater more closely at the center of discussions about this geographic region, religion, aging, and geopolitics, because its place among these communities and purposes has been downplayed or ignored for so long. It is also precisely among communities like these where current post-truth and well-spun fictions of our political and economic world find significant traction. The American musical may not be central to American values such as these, but it nonetheless is caught up in the middle of each of these processes. This and the remaining chapters ask *why* and *how* this middle-ness works to create worlds of central concern to us all.

America's Center Stages

As they were for many of those I encountered in writing this book, musicals were a formative part of my childhood in the Middle. My family watched film musicals on our television, of course, but live musicals within driving distance were also a part of my growing-up years. I saw and was a part of middle school and high school productions in my small remote town. As I learned to play piano for church, I accompanied singers during services with moralizing show tunes like "You'll Never Walk Alone" from *Carousel* and *The Sound of Music*'s "Climb Ev'ry Mountain." One of my earliest memories of musicals, in fact, was attending a production of *Oklahoma!* mounted by a now defunct theater company near Tulsa called Discoveryland. This company put on exactly two shows every summer— *Oklahoma!* and *Seven Brides for Seven Brothers*. The most memorable moment for me was singing Ado Annie's flirtatious "I Cain't Say No" on car rides, which, come to think of it, must have sent a chill from the backseat all the way down my mom's spine. I think I just liked the tune; the meaning of Ado Annie's song (for both Will Parker and me) wouldn't be appreciated until much later.

   I offer this biographical detour to illustrate musical theater's deep tussle with America's material and spiritual values, what Ian Hodder calls "entanglement."[13] What plans and purposes arose and fell for my younger self to meet in the Middle with musicals those many years ago? How did musicals become centralized and codified among these people? In what ways have communities like my own been shaped—knowingly or unknowingly, performed and naturalized—by the musical stage? In what ways are musicals shaping values in such places even now?

The reign of the musical stage in the United States is convoluted and syn-thetic—a fanciful, frightened, and only recently wholesome practice among the nation's widest margins of inhabitants. From its mischievous and debauched work in blackface minstrelsy to its milking of sentimentality and structure out of operetta to stylistic shavings taken from a number of antecedents such as burlesque, vaudeville, and Yiddish theater, what qualifies as musical theater today contains a bundle of active, inactive, and less-active genetic strands that nonetheless weave together musical theater's wide and tangled net in America. We now know better than ever how musical theater engaged a wide range of individuals and communities. Alexander Saxton notes that minstrelsy emerged as a flavor of Jacksonian ideology near upstate New York, consequently the same region and time out of which homegrown American religious traditions such as Mormonism were born (see chapter 3).[14] More recently, Raymond Knapp expands Saxton's claims to suggest minstrelsy's rise and reign among Ameri-can entertainment venues held lasting power not only as an engine for racism (which it was) but as a significant system of class critique.[15]

The beginnings of the genre lay bare the fact that middlebrow trappings take hold not simply, or even because of, aesthetic value; rather, musicals were born *into* and *as* a system of critique—sustaining contrarian worldviews that require big imaginations, big lies.

A musical form of such veracity channels predictable power holders but also fuels a wide range of critique from an astonishingly wide variety of people. While much of the scholarly attention is directed toward major commercial centers for theater, including Boston, New York, and Los Angeles, there is a growing awareness among scholars of how musical theater figures within a number of communities previously thought of as being off the beaten path. Musicals intersect with religion, immigration, and politics, for instance, and a common theme among the chapters in this book is that these intersections in modest, everyday productions throughout the country often result in greater inclusivity, representation, and theatrical perspectives than seen in major commercial cen-ters, where efforts to diversify are measured against a bottom line. Here I keep to an unsophisticated observation: when scholars begin asking new questions of stage music, we will get different answers. Katherine Preston's recent work, for instance, shows how most theatrical companies were managed by women who discovered an open market for vernacular operas (the generic term used to describe most sung theater) "without the pretensions and high prices of the fashionable foreign-language troupes."[16] And as Michael Pisani illustrates in *Music for the Melodramatic Theatre in Nineteenth-Century London and New York*, these nineteenth-century dramas were performed regularly and promiscuously.[17]

Another promiscuous form of musical theater in the nineteenth and twentieth centuries was the pageant-masque. Often enormously elaborate and spectacular, these outdoor pageants drew large crowds to the Middle, and elsewhere in the United States, to celebrate big agendas and events. In the summer of 1914, one of the largest pageants in America took shape in St. Louis, Missouri. Spearheaded by local civic icon Luther Ely Smith—who in later years propped up the St. Louis Municipal Opera Theatre, or "The Muny" for short—*The Pageant and Masque of St. Louis* displayed more than seventy-five hundred local performers reenacting the city's past, present, and idealized future for an opening-night audience of seventy-five thousand. The performance was carefully calculated. At the time a major trading center and the fourth largest city in the United States, St. Louis's reputation had suffered after the Civil War, preserved as a backward-looking relic of a shameful Southern past. A musical drama could help invigorate civic pride and bring positive attention to the city. In *American Historical Pageantry*, David Glassberg shows how progressive leaders in the region's midsize cities saw pageants as a dramatic means of not only injecting vitality into wilting regional centers but also publicizing and cementing progressive municipal reform. For Smith and others in St. Louis, this meant getting citizens on board with a new city charter, a free bridge to span the Mississippi River, and a large downtown plaza as part of the ambitious "City Beautiful" plans.[18]

The ambitions of these Progressive Era musical pageants laid the foundation for municipal support of musical theater in the coming decades. Pageantry in America has since fallen out of fashion—with notable exceptions, including *Texas Outdoor Musical* in the Palo Duro Canyon State Park in Canyon, Texas; the Ramona Pageant in Hemet, California; and the Great Passion Play in Eureka Springs, Arkansas—but St. Louis remains something of a theatrical touchstone in America. The Muny is now one of the largest outdoor summer stock theaters in the country, regularly employing vocal talent from the musical theater training centers dotting the Middle (see chapter 6).

Middle cities like St. Louis regularly brought in pageant directors, traveling shows, and traded in theatrical markets from the coasts rather fluidly. Vaudeville troupes likewise traveled to the Middle corners of America, finding willing audiences with loose change in their pockets. Burlesque and minstrel shows stretched even to the farthest reaches of the country, popping up in Utah Territory, for instance, in 1871 with locally flavored operettas like the Mormonized version of Jacques Offenbach's *Blue Beard* put on by Lydia Thompson's burlesque troupe. Many now historic theaters stand apart in America's small towns, mere fossils of a once vibrant theatrical trade between big cities and communities in the Middle.

Some of this trade eventually slowed, halted probably more by the invention of the talkies than by the twinned economic and ecological disasters of the Depression and the Dust Bowl. Film redefined live theater. Sound films only exasperated the musical's unreality, making the sung numbers in films like *The Wizard of Oz* "seem an artificial intrusion," technicolored and vibrant, reliant on what Raymond Knapp dubs a "Musically Enhanced Reality Mode."[19] Dorothy Gale was wrong about one thing: she really was in Kansas, but also Minnesota, and Oregon, and Georgia. Musicals had always been everywhere, and film made them *everywhere* everywhere.

Audiences adjusted to this enhanced reality; musicals remained quite popular in the Middle, as they had been long before Hollywood got involved. David Saltz reminds us that "theater survives in an age of film and video precisely because the reality of the theater event matters"—that, in its purest sense, the stage carries power for its ability to make the unreal seem real.[20] The new century may have brought new technologies that created the commercial centers of Broadway and Hollywood, but those technologies galvanized already familiar and well-trodden channels between coastal cities and a much broader audience between them.

New technology did make this larger-than-life genre small enough to squeeze into tight places. In his engaging study of how Broadway musicals made their way into American homes, Laurence Maslon notes that show tunes are for the most part "public performances experienced in private spaces."[21] Musical theater took route from Broadway to Main Street via recordings, dance orchestras, sheet music, and, later, radio and television (enabled by Ed Sullivan, an unlikely ambassador to Broadway, among others). Importantly, Maslon's study shows how the musical trafficked both ways. Beginning in 1935, NBC's radio (and later television) program *Your Hit Parade* discovered the kinds of song and songwriting styles everyday Americans most appreciated and, in turn, siphoned those preferences back into new Broadway hits.

By now the middle of the country was casting glances to both coasts for its entertainment. Musicals themselves became displaced in the bicoastal process. I discuss in the following chapter the growing importance of Hollywood in broadcasting American values to the Middle, but a simple anecdote reveals how fuzzy that signal could be: musical theater dynamos such as Bing Crosby, Dinah Shore, Frank Sinatra, and Judy Garland popularized and helped shape the Broadway show like few others in history while never actually appearing in a Broadway musical. Broadway, despite its Times Square address, was already an idea out of place.

Steve Young and Sport Murphy's quirky but fascinating book, *Everything's Coming Up Profits: The Golden Age of Industrial Musicals*, bumps the needle in further discovering the place of musicals in America. Commissioned by corporations such as GE, Ford, and IBM, "industrial musicals" made training and selling products more fun. Even more, they helped assuage the ennui of corporate life by romanticizing or more blatantly distorting the commonplace work life. "Industrial show vets attest to the power of a song to bring tears to the eyes of hardened salesmen and middle managers," Young and Murphy write, "especially if the message affirmed the value of their daily battles and the glory they could bring to themselves, their families, their company, and America."[22]

Even in New York, musicals were always more than Times Square. Musical shows had been closely threaded with ethnic communities since the early nineteenth century, particularly within immigrant pockets of Manhattan and the surrounding boroughs but also elsewhere in the United States. White ethnic groups such as Jews and the Irish famously practiced theatrical postures, including blackface minstrelsy, to encourage a social uplift.[23] But musical theater owes a great deal to the vibrancy of ethnic theater throughout America, and America owes something of its shape to ethnic theater as well. John Koegel's comprehensive account of German immigrant theater in New York and Sabine Haenni's broader study of New York City's ethnic "amusements" during America's industrial age showcase how, in Haenni's words, "sites of leisure became sites of virtual mobility."[24] Musicals, in more ways than one, *moved* America.

This kind of mobility was true in communities outside of New York City, of course, both then and now. Nineteenth-century German immigrants brought theatrical styles to places like Cincinnati, Ohio, and transnational adoptees in the upper Midwest invigorate Korean theater in cities like Milwaukee and Minneapolis today.[25] As much as these ethnic theaters set the pace for Broadway's commercial ascension, musicals were doing important work for immigrants in other parts of the country, even if the historical narrative of musical theater has largely ignored it.

Nicolás Kanellos, for instance, uses his 1990 book, *A History of Hispanic Theatre in the United States: Origins to 1940*, to correct the scholarly impression that "such a theatre did not exist."[26] Focusing on case studies in Los Angeles, San Antonio, Tampa, New York, Tucson, New Mexico, and the greater Midwest, Kanellos insists that by examining this presumed nonexistent theatrical form, we find communities with "the ability to create art even under the most trying of circumstances, social and cultural cohesiveness and national pride in the face of racial and class pressures, [and] cultural continuity and adaptability in a foreign land." Kanellos adds that theater was "without a doubt the most popular and culturally relevant artistic form in Hispanic communities throughout the United States."[27] It was common for communities everywhere to siphon politics and local issues through the musical stage. Almost three decades later, John Koegel's subsequent investigation of Spanish-speaking theater in Southern California makes this explicit as he shows that the term *revista*, employed by impresarios such as Romualdo Tirado during the 1920s and 1930s, refers to both a musical revue and a newspaper.[28]

As musicological studies have adapted to a borderless conceptualization of America, the work of musicals has likewise become better defined. The Cuban zarzuela, for instance, as Susan Thomas has shown, "participated in a growing quest to define national identity, at a time when that identity was undergoing tumultuous change."[29] Andrew A. Cashner's work adds to our understanding of early modern theater among Mexican religious communities circulating *villancicos* while undergoing colonial exchange.[30] And Nancy Yunhwa Rao paints a provocative picture of the musical stage in her magisterial book on Chinese theaters in North America. "In spatial and symbolic terms the largest gathering places in the community," Rao writes, "the theaters by default served as important public spaces which forged a unified voice. Warrior operas about loyalty or heart-wrenching family dramas about filial obligation shared the stage with community rallies for patriotic, political, or social causes, and the sense of duty and passion connected them."[31] Musicals exist outside of America's borders, and important studies of musical theater's development in Korea, Germany, Japan, and China, among other places, while not central to my concerns here, likewise bear witness to the rising stock that musical theater enjoys around the world.[32]

Disrupting conventional narratives can be hard, dangerous work, and no less for musical theater. Rao reminds us that doing so "requires that we release these theaters from their repressed silence and perpetual invisibility, as well as separate them from the myths about them."[33]

Separate from the myths. Re-place the stories. Stories out of place.

These are the conditions of this book. Clearly, scholars have been actively mining many theatrical encounters from a number of disciplinary outlooks. I mentioned here only a few representative cases but do so in order to acknowledge the breadth of work on musicals, the centrality that musicals occupy among communities otherwise quite different from one another, and the possibility that musicals afford scholars invested in deciphering social practices writ large. *Lying in the Middle* is not the first study to pursue this issue and joins a robust group of mindful scholars and practitioners who have been at this chase for a while now.

Conclusion

The work of storytelling all over the planet has been increasingly managed by American musical theater. Musicals in turn use these stories to manage our belief in what worlds are possible. The animating question in this book is thus one of ontology: What can be true if it can't be imagined? As I staked out earlier, I take this imaginative work to be patently religious in nature; it is no secret theater's parlay with religiosity. I mean this in two ways: first, and as much of my earlier work has shown, musicals are readily associable with religious communities of all stripes and creeds, and, second, musicals themselves are religious texts covered in a thin veneer of entertainment.[34] I might even modify Friedrich Kittler's taut observation that all entertainment is a misuse of military equipment to conclude that all musicals are misused religion.[35] At the very least, musicals are religion out of place.

What I present overtly now and thread through the rest of the book is that musical theater's willful engagement with unreality at once implicates itself as religious even as that unreality flirts with and flits against the truth. They are both, in the modern age, *liminal*—in-between, a Middle space. Religion and musicals alike are largely uninvested in the world as it is, equally and persistently inviting its disciples to worlds yet to come. A cynic might claim religious leaders do this through lying; a musical theater fan might readily admit the same.

I'll argue that they would both be right, though I should add that my indictments against religion and musicals as lies come in the spirit of admiration not condemnation. Religion and musicals in some ways share complementary goals. As musicals increasingly are employed by communities represented in this book to slow the creep of modernity, this performance often takes shape around a framework of belief. Historian Leigh Eric Schmidt's study of how the senses became disciplined through the Enlightenment tilts our ears closer to belief. During the Enlightenment, Schmidt claims, hearing became a marginalized tool of navigating truth and reason; the prevailing proto-scientific dogma of the time prized sight over most other senses.[36] Religion, the mystical, and the superstitious likewise were pushed to the margins of social authority, as has, incidentally, the practice of listening—in Schmidt's words, we all unknowingly suffer from "hearing loss." The subsequent "untuning of the sky," as John Hollander puts it, carries consequence even today.[37] If religious expression requires a willingness to engage some degree of mystery and the unknowable, the space for such thought grows increasingly limited under scientific and reasoned narratives, and that desire for uncertainty either gets channeled elsewhere or disappears altogether.

I suggest the former and that musicals are one of these channels, a carrier of religiosity and belief in so many ways and yet, most profoundly in this post-truth moment, as a heaven-sent transmitter of uncertainty, untrue claims, and enchanted alternatives to reality.[38] Musicals, I believe, own up to their religiosity best not with reconciliatory themes or moralizing plots or even happy-ever-afters, although my sense is that these are all important. Rather, musicals are at their most religious in their invitation to dispose of the current world in favor of a new one. We miss that work if musical theater is believed to be important in only one way. Assuming too little of musicals, we misjudge their powerful belief in worlds out of reach. Musicals lie in the middle of our appeals to a better life *out there*. Re-placing the musical helps retune the skies.

CHAPTER 3

Fundamentalism, Produced

We watch a captain with seven children haltingly pronounce his love for his children's governess. In a quiet moment, he calls to her from across the room, asking if she will join his family. She demurs at first but is even then unable to calm her voice, quivering with excitement: "Yes, of course I will. Right away, in fact, if not sooner."

The orchestra has taken its cue and begins the underscoring that musical theater fans and detractors alike know is a song introduction in disguise. With eyebrows raised, we watch the captain step forward to join her, the music tracing a love song. Flanking him on one side is the governess-turned-fiancée, Maria, but there's another woman on his other side, smiling, with arms outstretched.

Wait—Who is she?

Anyone watching must recognize by now that this scene is playing out quite unusually, a curious departure from *The Sound of Music* we thought we knew. The orchestral strains heard earlier—music that aficionados might presume belonged to the romantic duet "Something Good" that Richard Rodgers added to the 1965 film version—turn out to belong to a different musical entirely, the opening verse from *Chitty Chitty Bang Bang*'s paternal song "You Two," the Sherman Brothers tune that Dick Van Dyke's eccentric widower character Caractacus Potts sings to his two young children:

Could be
We three

Get along so famously,
'Cause you two
Have me,
And I have you two, too.

That's right. The captain before us who we once knew to be a militant widower who falls for a nun is actually not a widower at all but a married man seeking Maria as a *second* wife, who then leads these two women in a song originally directed toward the young children of another onstage widower from another musical entirely. The scenario is dizzying. But the song works perfectly.

The scene just described unfolds during the dramatic climax of a 1994 production of *The Sound of Music* put on by a polygamous community known as the Fundamentalist Church of Jesus Christ of Latter-day Saints (FLDS for short) who live along the rugged border between Utah and Arizona. I hesitate calling it a *production* of *The Sound of Music* since it both is and isn't that show; in fact, the architects of this production dubbed it *The Re-Sound of Music*, a clever title that pays homage to its model while suggesting that where it departs materially and dramatically is meant as an *upgrade* rather than a parody. The title also suggests a restatement of the original—an echo reverberating through the surrounding desert canyons what initially bounced off the skyscraper facades of faraway New York City.

Anyone who has ever been to an amateur musical production is probably familiar with this kind of adaptation: changing the song's key to fit the voices available, taking out entire scenes altogether, or, as in this case, substituting unfitting material from one musical with an outlier tune that makes more sense with that production. Plots and songs in lasting shows develop a tolerance for being interchanged or even done away with, at least as measured by the demands of local theater. But even larger markets, where the financial and artistic stakes can be considerably higher (and the penalties for unlicensed productions much steeper), can fall for misconstruing a musical's intentions. Laurence Maslon writes how the limited space on 78 records meant rearranging the original songs of *Oklahoma!*, eliminating some of the darker moments like Jud Frye's brooding and rape-fantasy number "Lonely Room," and completely turning the musical inside out in order to fit on its original record release. "Devoid of these numbers," he writes, "the listeners of the original album set might mistake *Oklahoma!* for a purely upbeat, optimistic story of romantic couples and their feudin', fightin', and makin' up in the end."[1] Maybe anything worth its salt in popular culture generally includes some kind of failsafe, a remarkable ability to adapt in the wilds of commodification, like lizards regenerating a lost tail or clownfish switching sex organs willy-nilly. Musicals are rather organic in that way, even if their adaptations sometimes result in unexpected evolutions.

This technique is an example of what some call "textual poaching"—that is, atomizing objects in their original form and piecing them together for a new or reconfigured purpose.[2] With its face turned toward the fractured and broken, poaching may seem a postmodern exercise; in fact, it isn't an altogether new or modern technique. Literary theorist Mikhail Bakhtin pointed out the multiple styles of language (or "heteroglossia") within any author's work, clouding the waters of single authorship and literary authority that so often is employed as a cudgel against adaptivity. This opened space for scholars to rediscover the sometimes surprising ways our seemingly impenetrable artworks have been broken apart and put to use. Lawrence Levine's telling of the remarkable fluidity of Shakespearean plays in early America is just one recognition that theater is very commonly modified to reflect local needs and purposes.[3]

This process has become increasingly familiar in recent years, however, especially as popular culture moved from passive consumption modes (e.g., print, television, and film) to active consumption modes via social media and the internet. From underground fanzines to mashups on the television show *Glee*, textual poaching has become institutionalized as a practice of making the general more specific and the distanced more immediate.

Musical theater is a particularly potent space for textual poaching. Often, as is the case in Colorado City, communities use the loose narratives of familiar musicals to reinvent the past and help them make sense of a future that is largely a lie. Musicals are at face value about pretense, which may make them gimmicky, but it also makes them highly effective remedies against the creep of modernity and globalization. Fundamentalism is also a concoction of loose narratives employed and reemployed over time to exact political power out of religious fragments. If one mode of deception is disguising half-truths as full ones, then musical theater and religious fundamentalism offer each other a rich space of mutually beneficial storytelling. This chapter lifts the hood on both musicals and fundamentalism to better understand how musicals work for this community poaching from the Middle—along the way, recalibrating the current narrative of Broadway musical theater as an inherently progressive platform to ask what, exactly, these progressive values defend against.

Polygamy as American Theater

I first learned of *The Re-Sound of Music* after stumbling upon amateur video recordings posted on YouTube by a former member of the FLDS. The home videos capture the halcyon days enjoyed by the polygamous faction of the mainstream Mormon Church in the years leading up to the irascible leadership of Warren Jeffs, a man perhaps best known for establishing the Yearning for Zion Ranch in Eldorado, Texas, which was raided by Texas law enforcement agents in 2008. The raid eventually led to Jeffs's arrest and his serving a life sentence for two felony counts of child sexual assault. Perhaps understandably, the FLDS community today remains distrusting of strangers. I mostly rely on these home videos to tell the story of this production, much like an archaeologist pieces together a narrative from mere bone fragments and shards of pottery.

Tara Westover's celebrated memoir, *Educated*, while not a record of the FLDS in particular, does offer one contemporaneous example of musical theater among religious fundamentalist families in the Intermountain West. Westover grew up in rural Idaho. She found refuge and acceptance in joining productions of *Annie*, performing vicariously through the redheaded orphan a version of familial normalcy that gave a rare moment of acceptance and kindness from her doomsday and prepper father. It also gave Westover the confidence of a strong-willed girl caught in the charms of a loving Daddy Warbucks. "If I didn't have anything to say," she remembers, "at least Annie did."[4]

The grainy video of our production is corroborated by former FLDS member Carolyn Jessop's 2007 memoir, titled *Escape*, which also places *The Re-Sound of Music* in a broader musical and social context. Jessop explains that a play or program was put on at the end of every year to honor then prophet Merril Jessop's birthday. *The Re-Sound of Music* was one of these.

Every year around Merril's birthday on December 27 the family would perform a play or put on a program in his honor. His daughters usually took charge and orchestrated everything. For Merril's birthday in 1994 one of his daughters did a new version of *The Sound of Music*.

In those pre–Warren Jeffs years, we still watched movies and listened to the radio. Some families had TVs and their children watched videos. We were all familiar with *The Sound of Music*. Our extravaganza was going to be staged, in honor of Merril, at the community center, which could hold a thousand people. Margaret's version of the musical was based on several polygamous families. She wrote parts for every child in Merril's family, and by then there were more than forty. Margaret called it *The Resound of Music*.

I was pregnant with my fifth child and was too weak from morning sickness to take part. In our version, Maria was a nanny sent from one large polygamous family to another. Captain Von Trapp was not a widower but a married man with a large family. He had recently been introduced to the principle of plural marriage and was thinking about joining the FLDS. He hired Maria because he respected her father and knew he needed her to take care of his very large family.

These two large families created parts for many of his children. But then Margaret needed parts for sons and daughters-in-law. So there were characters in the script that seemed to wander in and out from nowhere.

Margaret dreamed of having an orchestra provide the music, but the reality was she was stuck with our little FLDS band. She dressed them up in formal wear so they looked like a professional orchestra, but when the band started playing the score from the real *Sound of Music* the audience laughed because they sounded so amateurish.

The gist of the plot was that everyone was trying to escape the Nazis and flee to America to join the work of God. The play ended with a musical talent show while German soldiers stood guard. Merril's sons-in-law played the Germans. After each talent number the actors pretended to flee to the mountains to escape. When the show ended everyone was hiking through the mountains to safety.[5]

There the record ends and we turn to the video itself for more answers. These video recordings preserve a time gone by, but an analysis of how the musical *works* may give an indication of the kind of religious work musical theater did and does, not only among the FLDS but also among disparate communities elsewhere in the United States. *The Re-Sound of Music* offers a lens through which to see how musical theater as practice and genre has penetrated and sustained parts of the country that are perhaps the most unassuming. The FLDS community, then and now likely one of the most estranged, misunderstood, and insular communities in the United States, surprisingly found relevance and interest in, of all things, American musical theater. I am intrigued by how piecing together various stories, songs, and conventions of what are largely (if not completely) film musicals, the FLDS community could claim something "American" about themselves, if only on their own terms. This patchwork of film musicals reveals the musical as intrinsically flexible and accessible, strung together with electric wires and connected with technological materials to communities around the country as common expressions of American-ness.

From 1871 to 1961, polygamy-themed musicals and musical dramas proliferated stages in the United States and London. Polygamy was central to these stories, though largely in specifically Mormon contexts. Many nineteenth-century Americans were both appalled and enthralled by Mormonism, and the seemingly cavalier sexual practices on America's frontier made the allure all the more salacious, if not politically hysterical, considering the waning yet still very much intact cultural policing during the Victorian era. Consequently,

Mormons were forcibly driven from place to place and increasingly became a favorite American pariah. As historian Patrick Mason argues, the cultural tide that heaved against Mormon practices like polygamy swelled shortly after the Civil War ended, when the eradication of polygamy became one of the first cultural missions of a now reunited America.[6] With Mormons by now mostly nestled out of reach in the faraway West, proxy harassment onstage and in the papers increased in fervor and humor toward Mormons and their unusual practices. No wonder, then, that a Mormon-themed adaptation of Jacques Offenbach's operetta *Blue Beard* appeared in 1871—connecting the infamous serial lady-killer with Mormon polygamists:

> Blue Beard is my name
> Polygamy's my fame
> For the girls I seal 'em quick,
> Mormonise them very slick.

Other productions followed, including *Deseret, or a Saint's Afflictions* in 1880, *The Mormons* in 1895, *The Wanderer, or a Mormon Wooing* in 1901, *The Girl from Utah* in 1913, and *His Little Widows* in 1917. Americans were fascinated by all things Mormon, especially as transmitted in popular culture venues like the musical stage, leading one *New York Times* reviewer of *His Little Widows* to opine, "Mormonism is just about the only religion that can be exploited in musical comedy."[7]

The pace of Mormon-themed shows slowed after World War I as the Mormon Church moved in 1890 to abandon its more controversial practices like polygamy in hopes of broader acceptance. By mid-century, ridicule toward Mormons had waned considerably. Lerner and Loewe's 1951 Broadway show, *Paint Your Wagon*, which featured a polygamist Mormon family as a comedic sidebar, was one of the last of its kind. In 1961 the NBC Opera Company mounted Leonard Kastle's television opera *Deseret*, which portrayed a more genteel side of Mormon prophet Brigham Young. These two productions show, within a decade of each other, the musical stage's empathetic shift in perspective toward Mormons.[8]

So why the sudden change in public perception of Mormonism generally, and polygamy more specifically? One explanation is that Americans were tuning in to the fact that mid-twentieth-century Mormons looked and acted quite different from their nineteenth-century counterparts. Nineteenth-century Mormonism, winks anthropologist Daymon Smith, celebrated a revolutionary, Marxist, warrior Jesus while modern Mormonism worships a pastel-colored Jesus holding sheep and conversing with children. Theatrical portrayals softened in response to Mormonism's tamer, more mainstream, American vibe.[9]

An allergy to governmental overreach may offer another explanation. On July 26, 1953, more than one hundred Arizona state police officers and soldiers from the national guard raided the Mormon fundamentalist compound in Short Creek, Arizona—a response to rumors about older men marrying younger women, which Arizona governor John Howard Pyle saw as an FLDS conspiracy amounting to white slavery. News of the raid, which came amid a period of intolerable deviancy in America (the Short Creek raid took place in the same week as the Korean Armistice Agreement and about a month after Julius and Ethel Rosenberg were executed for committing espionage), swiftly curtailed public ridicule of polygamy.[10] Americans read and watched news reports of polygamist families being torn asunder by American soldiers and police officers. The entire community, save a handful of individuals, were taken into custody, including 263 children. Public distaste for the terrifying scene led to the government's "hands off" approach to polygamy for the next fifty years. Seven years after the raid, the town was renamed Colorado City.

Musicals can't help but get caught up in these kinds of events. Mocking polygamists in *Paint Your Wagon* gets fewer laughs when your audiences have seen images of actual polygamists lose their homes and children. While the mercurial polygamist King Mongkut's death as the curtain closes on *The King and I* (Broadway 1951, film 1959) is meant to elicit imperialist cheers, it also unwittingly becomes framed within these larger discussions of polygamy in America. *Deseret*'s sympathetic portrayal of a benevolent and sage-like Brigham Young—who though still foregrounded as a polygamist nonetheless finds redemption at the end of the opera when he allows a new wife (his twenty-fifth) to leave and marry the man of her dreams—mirrors this strong reversal in public opinion toward polygamy. In fact, Young's identity as a polygamist in itself may have prompted sympathy among audiences in 1961, since *Deseret*'s empathetic treatment of polygamist outliers reimagined them as coeval with other character types associated within the broader folk history of American mythology, such as the maverick, the rugged frontiersman, or the seeker of religious freedom. All of this was taking place while the mainstream Mormon Church continued to distance itself from polygamy in an effort to gain greater middle-class acceptance.

Nonetheless, the FLDS community has maintained a fraught relationship with the United States. Ties were cut long before the Short Creek raid. FLDS leadership inherited early Mormon antagonism toward the U.S. federal government. Most nineteenth-century Mormons blamed the government for founder Joseph Smith's murder in 1844 and their forced exile into Mexican territory beginning in that year. Many saw the Civil War as divine penance for Mormon persecution.[11] Brigham Young's vengeful position against America, in which he encouraged his followers to pray for and expect devastation to befall the country that so severely mistreated them, was resurrected by fundamentalist sects of

Mormonism at the turn of the twentieth century when, after years of religious leaders sidestepping the issue, Mormon prophet Joseph F. Smith yielded to federal pressure and discontinued polygamy in 1904. Although polygamy is still upheld as a nascent ideological principle in mainstream Mormonism (Mormon apostle Bruce R. McConkie preached well into the middle of the century that the "holy practice" would continue upon Jesus Christ's return to earth), any Mormon who practices polygamy today is excommunicated—a position that confirms for many fundamentalists that the larger religious body has apostatized from the truth in its effort to appease mainstream America's falsehoods.[12] America is the Philistine giant in need of slaying. Many FLDS families purposely game the welfare system and reportedly engage in tax fraud in order to "bleed the beast."[13]

Warren Jeffs's leadership pushed the already insular community further into obscurity, often relying on theater to do so. Jeffs used media, story, and the stage to coerce and control his followers, at times acting childlike and humorous through theater. Stephen Singular describes Jeffs as being especially popular among children, playing games, sledding, and joking with them. Jeffs even did "slapstick imitations of Groucho Marx and Jerry Lewis, which left the kids roaring. He put on plays at the school and delivered long speeches to his captive audience, giving his voice a lulling, hypnotic quality, repeatedly driving home his central point: perfect obedience leads to perfect faith, perfect lives, and perfect people."[14]

Jeffs understood that theater derives from a popular culture that might challenge some of the community's most fundamentalist beliefs; Jeffs thus seems to have used comedy and theater strategically, on his own terms, and for specific purposes. He was exacting in his policing of the community and increasingly so over the years. Television and radio were banned, teenage girls were married off to men at his discretion, certain foods were abruptly forbidden, and people (especially young boys—future challengers, after all, for additional wives) who couldn't or wouldn't live up to his standards of perfect obedience were ousted from the community without regard to their well-being or education. Taught to fiercely distrust the outside world and that leaving the FLDS community is as egregious a sin as murder, these so-called Lost Boys, numbering between four hundred and a thousand, are caught between two competing and dangerous worlds. One of the more prominent Lost Boys, Brent W. Jeffs, nephew to Warren Jeffs and therefore of "royal blood," writes in his memoir about the fragile place even favored young men hold in the community: "Being born into the right family like I was is a good start—however, it may not be enough."[15]

In this regard, Warren Jeffs resembles his more infamous prophetic prede-cessor, Brigham Young. Young's hard-nosed leadership style also fit somewhat awkwardly with his championing of theater and song as important diversions from hardships that might otherwise sow seeds of discord among his followers. Brigham Young eventually became something of an impresario in the Salt Lake Valley, often appearing onstage in plays and skits even while upholding a dual reputation as both beloved and unflinching prophet, governor, military com-mander, and frontier lawman.[16] The fact that Jeffs inhabited similar personality and career traits and sought out opportunities to be onstage himself suggests that theater may play a larger role within theocracies than has been previously examined.

The Theater of Belief

Let me massage that provocation even more by suggesting that fundamental-ism requires the charisma and spirit of musical theater—if not the substance of musicals themselves—in order to recruit and sustain its membership. Others have already considered a connection between fundamentalism and art. In his book *When Art Disrupts Religion*, religion scholar Philip Salim Francis interrogates such an assertion by asking "Can art save us from fundamentalism?" Francis follows Christian evangelicals who move away from strict fundamentalist views once they are exposed to canonic selections of classic literature, drama, art, and music. He specifically studies young, college-age evangelicals who are assigned by left-leaning evangelical professors works by the likes of Shakespeare, Dos-toevsky, and Beethoven—all paragons of the Great Books movement—to see if art has the potential to "educate young minds out of any fundamentalist trap-pings they may have acquired thus far and to make them maximally resistant to the allure of fundamentalism in their bright futures."[17] In other words, Francis asks, once exposed to aesthetic objects or experiences that show a wider world of possibilities, are fundamentalists more or less likely to interrogate the more stringent parts of their belief systems in favor of moderation?

It's an intriguing question, no doubt, but one that seems tired and deeply flawed in conception. Francis's project is directing an old assumption about art toward a current political impasse where fundamentalists are presumably throwing roadblocks along the path of global progress. Yet, ironically, in Fran-cis's hands the question "Can art save us from fundamentalism?" becomes a fundamentalist missive itself, relying on romantic aesthetic values (here in the shape of Great European Masters) to conquer romantic religious values.

Furthermore, Francis's assertion skirts the artistic affinities of fundamentalist leaders. Warren Jeffs is not alone in claiming violent power from the whimsical stage. Charismatic religious leaders as a rule, particularly those proffering fundamentalism, share a love for the theatrical. A quick glance at prominent cult or fundamentalist leaders of the last several decades shows a strong predilection toward the musical stage:

- David Koresh composed music and enacted plays for his followers, the Branch Davidians. Amazingly, some scholars have even employed a musical metaphor to explain the deadly resolution to the standoff between the FBI and the Branch Davidians on April 19, 1993.[18]
- Saul B. Newton, whose psychosexual cult reportedly practiced pedophilia, absorbed into the Fourth Wall Political Theater (formerly the Fourth Wall Repertory Company), which created children's theatrical productions like the 1978 musical *The King of the Entire World*.
- Before leading the Heaven's Gate cult in mass suicide in 1997, Marshall Applewhite was a professional musician, once the chair of the music department at the University of Alabama and boasting a graduate degree in musical theater from the University of Colorado, Boulder. According to one news report, while in college Applewhite "played the lead in 'South Pacific' and 'Oklahoma' before moving to New York, and later to the Houston Grand Opera, to pursue a career in music."[19]
- Charles Manson counted among his core followers the musician and former actor Charles "Tex" Watson and former musician and adult film star Robert Beausoleil. Dennis Wilson of the Beach Boys came briefly into Manson's orbit in 1968, the year before Manson's "family" turned murderous. The Beach Boys recorded one of Manson's songs later that year, which they renamed "Never Learn Not to Love," and withheld crediting Manson as songwriter. The song's opening lyrics are a terrifying prophecy of Manson's murderous potential: "Cease to resist, come on say you love me / Give up your world, come on and be with me."[20]

These are just a few examples. If we were to expand this list to include individuals better known in the music world—including composers Erik Satie and his Metropolitan Church of Art of Jesus the Conductor, Richard Wagner's deification through universal drama, or Alexander Scriabin's theosophy, to say nothing of performers like R. Kelly or Michael Jackson, who maintained cult-like retreats (if not prisons) in more recent years—we start to see a pattern emerging. New ideas, radical ideas, that break form with established conventions require the breathing room of theatrical personas in order to make those stories seem closer to reality. A careful observer would have to admit that art, and especially theater, seems intimately entwined with fundamentalism, not innately at odds with it.

Theater does an essential work for fundamentalism, then, and probably in ways we haven't yet fully grasped. Surely fundamentalist thinking rattles Enlightenment's sabers, emerging precisely whenever and wherever religious mysticism and devotion ought to be in decline. Modernity's admixture of belief and reason has always been an unsettled one. As one nineteenth-century observer put it, the condition of modernity is to be afraid of ghosts even if you don't believe in them.[21]

Modernity, it seems, is the other side of fundamentalism's coin. "The world is accordingly divided," as Terry Eagleton puts it, "between those who believe too much and those who believe too little."[22] If there weren't already a space where truth could parry with fiction, it would be necessary under these conditions to invent one—which may in fact be exactly what happened. The musical stage invites a way of rethinking the past in order to reimagine a future big enough for religious values to enlist a place at the table, if not a theocratic throne at its head. This is certainly what composers Scriabin and, though less seriously, Satie had in mind. Dabbling in mysticism, composers and artists of the spectacular conjure worlds not yet in existence by first clinging to mythologies of the past. And aren't myths, as literary critic Frank Kermode writes, just fictions that have forgotten what they are?[23]

What I mean has little to do with similarities between theater and religious ritual (although those, of course, are significant enactments worthy of the gallons of ink spilled by scholars since Victor Turner) but rather points to a genetic inheritance shared by both musicals and American religion. In my book *Mormons, Musical Theater, and Belonging in America*, I argue that Mormonism and musicals were cut from the same ideological cloth. Joseph Smith assembled the nascent religion out of the same cultural whims of 1830 upstate New York from which Thomas Rice and other early white performers derived blackface minstrelsy. What unites American fundamentalist religion with American forms of stage entertainment most powerfully is the work of sustaining white America's place as the country's supreme cultural and social narrative. Not every aspect of musicals or religious fundamentalism necessarily indicates white supremacy, of course, but such a disposition is what binds the thing together. More to the point, an allegiance to white supremacist values is a masked concern with power structures in threat of being toppled. Smith and other nineteenth-century religious leaders enacted strong fundamentalist urges not out of thin air but through siphoning cultural themes around them and binding together powerful statements about the local.

Both Broadway musicals and fundamentalist religion retain iconic American status precisely for how well each showcases its "poached-ness"—the degree to which it is held together as an assemblage of this and that, its seams passionately on display while also vehemently denied.

Before going any further, this might be the place to check the knots, tighten our laces. Like other communities in the Middle, the FLDS's *The Re-Sound of Music* sutures a connection to America with small wires—connections between commercial centers like Broadway or Hollywood and their technological surrogates in faraway places, connections along strands of musical ideas, connections bound together loosely yet decidedly with wistful strings of stories about worlds unlike our own. Religion itself is held in place by these wires. "My faith is a great weight hung on a small wire," writes the poet Anne Sexton in her posthumous collection *The Awful Rowing toward God*, adding that a small wire is still enough to keep God in place—"just a thin vein, with blood pushing back and forth in it, and some love."[24]

Pay attention to the wires. See how the machinery works, and take note of the thin strands holding this and stories like it together. By the end, you may come to appreciate how much weight these small wires support and yet how they usually, somehow, are enough.

The Re-Sound of Music

The structure of *The Re-Sound of Music* shows a high level of sophistication for its poached-ness. The plot mostly follows its host story of the von Trapp family, departing with significance here and there. The climax of the piece I already described, where Maria joins the family as a second wife. But Maria's backstory melds intriguingly with the original here.

The show opens with Maria's large family gathering for a family meeting in their Austrian living room. Her father announces that Maria will begin work as a governess to raise money for the family to move to America. After two of Maria's brothers sing "Watch Your Footwork" from *The Happiest Millionaire*, the family sings together "The Sound of Music," confirming already that this is a show not about Maria but about a collective ideal. As Maria readies herself for the move, the family sings an unidentified song: "Just sing a little simple song / Even if your day goes wrong / It will keep you going strong and make you happy." The song's sentiment models both the FLDS community's motto of obedience and disposition ("Always keep sweet") and musical theater's dogma that singing is what makes a community work.

Maria sings Richard Rodgers's late addition to the film, "I've Got Confidence," as she transitions into the world of the von Trapp family (in this production renamed as the von Stadts). Immediately she encounters support and kindness from the household, a thematic departure from the austere scene in the film when Maria is welcomed reluctantly as just the latest in a long string of governesses to the family's troublesome children. The house staff here mirror the community Maria leaves in the original story, the nuns in the abbey. Sensibly, they proceed to sing *their* song, clucking their tongue for "a problem like Maria"—here the "problem" being not Maria's precociousness or sore-thumb presence, as the nuns relate, but rather a commitment among the staff to unite her with the captain. Evidently, the captain is looking to become a fundamentalist Mormon and the house staff are eager to play matchmaker on his behalf.

As both the title song and the family's tune predict, Maria enters the family as a songster. The original musical suggests that singing is the means by which estranged families can be reunited; the scene in the film where Captain von Trapp reaches for the guitar and sings a verse of "Edelweiss" is one representative moment, as that song is the hinge upon which his hardened heart turns sweet again. Musicals often use singing as a meta-concept. Of course, we expect characters to burst into song on stage and screen, but in shows like *The Sound of Music*, singing not only furthers the plot for the audience, but it also reveals to the characters something significant about their own story. Singing about singing makes for a common experience among musicals, sometimes laughably so, but the point that musicals make nonetheless is that the voice is the primary yardstick for measuring acceptance, belonging, and growth. This quality of musicals is sustained in *The Re-Sound of Music* when Maria shows the children how to sing by teaching them the basic fundamentals of music in "Do-Re-Mi." It is also a moralistic message drawn outward from the production. During the closing prayer offered after the production ends, Merril Jessop, prophet of the FLDS at the time, applaudingly remarks, "My father used to say if you can't say it, sing it."

At this point in the production, the captain asks Maria to join him as his second wife. The substitution of *Chitty Chitty Bang Bang*'s "You Two" in place of "Something Good" may be one of the more egregious instances of textual poaching in this show. It is a sophisticated move, admitting a familiarity with how musicals work and what makes them tick. This itself is rather remarkable since even before Warren Jeffs's austere leadership, the FLDS community existed in isolation from the rest of the world. There likely were no productions touring through Colorado City, Arizona, let alone FLDS groups traveling to see a musical on Broadway. Those who created *The Re-Sound of Music* presumably did so by watching film versions of shows—perhaps some sheet music circulated the town, and certainly radio broadcasts made their way to the commune on occasion, but likely that was it. Small wires.

This scene is remarkable, then, because of what it says about how musicals work. *Chitty Chitty Bang Bang* is representative of what Raymond Knapp calls "children's musicals" in that the show expels energy not to unite a romantic couple but rather to rescue a family in crisis. In the case of *Mary Poppins*, *Chitty Chitty Bang Bang*, and even *The Sound of Music*, that crisis involves a father in need of saving.[25] Even though the context and nature of the restored relationship in these musicals differ from the norm, the musical and dramatic structure of almost all musicals remains the same. "You Two" is originally a love song between a father and his children as is the father-daughter duet from *Annie*, "I Don't Need Anything but You." These love songs are meant to be restorative and are examples of a song "type," meaning these songs belong to a larger category of song that does similar kinds of work and, therefore, might be easily interchanged. The economy of musical theater does not differentiate between the two—a love song is a love song is a love song.

What gets a little icky is when a romantic love song gets swapped for a paternal love song, which is exactly what happens in *The Re-Sound of Music*. Shifting the focus of a child-child-father musical number to a wife-wife-husband musical number makes little difference to the overall *work* of the production but makes a world of difference in the *kind of work* the musical does. This production may be an extreme case, but it does not radically depart from how musicals transfer values. It takes little effort to make musicals mean something completely different from what many might imagine was their intention, which I think is part of the widespread bi-partisan interest in musicals. Fluidity helps make musicals adaptable and popular among a variety of groups, but it is also what makes musicals matter in ways that could fundamentally upset the moralistic apple cart out of which American musical theater was carved. All it takes is familiarity with how the genre works.

By replacing "Something Good" in this scene, the musical takes a different shape, molded on a wire frame that is bent and misshapen though still at work. "You Two" and "Something Good" are musically unalike, but because this show forces us to take a closer look, we can see that the tunes are in some ways inversions of one another. "Something Good" opens with a lyric implicating some good deed, despite a difficult childhood for Maria, as payment toward her sudden fortune as an in-love adult—"somewhere in my youth and childhood," she says, blushing, "I must have done something good." The Potts children in *Chitty Chitty Bang Bang* have no less a difficult childhood: motherless at the start, their schooling scattershot, and coming of age in what amounts to a junkyard. And yet they and their eccentric father are deeply in love and sing about their gratitude for one another's company. The musical strands from both songs cross

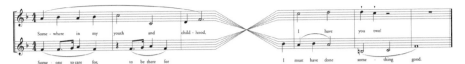

Example 3.1: Crossed wires. Substituting a father-child-child love song for the lover-lover love song changes very little of the show's structure but drastically changes its outcome. "Something Good," words and music by Richard Rodgers. "You Two," words and music by Robert B. Sherman and Richard M. Sherman.

and tangle (see example 3.1), but musically these crossed lines demonstrate the flip side of musical theater's love songs: the mutability of the form and ease with which musical values drift and twist outside the lines to craft something entirely different, something perhaps not altogether good. The very work the Colorado City community enacts with their production gets caught here in a web of musical meaning.

Because this production removes the baroness Elsa and therefore lacks a romantic challenger, *The Re-Sound of Music*'s architects instead create out of Max and Elsa the secondary romantic partners whose relationship mirrors that of Maria and the captain. In the original production, Max and Elsa do sing a duet, "How Can Love Survive?" (cut from the film version), which is a cynical portrayal of romance and wealth among effete society. Max's character represents Viennese bourgeois complicities in the rise of fascism in Austria; his identity as clearly Jewish and probably gay makes his complicity all the more egregious and the baroness's pursuit of his attention all the more calculated. Which is why when Max and Elsa (renamed Augusta here, for some reason) instead sing Tevye and Golde's love duet "Do You Love Me?" from *Fiddler on the Roof*, audiences are left with a different situation entirely. Not only does such a song placement make explicit Max's religious identity, but it also erases any question of possible sexual malfeasance.[26]

The captain plots to escape his military duties by enlisting his family for the Nazi talent competition. In this scenario, however, the German presence has been diluted, so the stakes seem considerably lower than in the original. This may be why the folksy song "Edelweiss," the emotional climax of the film, is eliminated. Instead, the now united family sings "Ten Feet Off the Ground" from the Disney television show *The One and Only, Genuine, Original Family Band* to celebrate, followed by a dance to the tune of "The Lonely Goatherd." With most of the dramatic tension removed in this production, *The Re-Sound of Music* could end there with little lost. Fascism is a neither serious nor clear ideological threat to these characters, and we know the family has intentions to leave for America of their own volition anyway. So when Nazi soldiers appear on stage throughout the show, they confirm rather than depart from or challenge this sentiment.

The final scene, however, takes the cake. In their best *Hogan's Heroes*–style German, the soldiers denounce Hitler and dramatically tear off their SS bands and Hitler-style mustaches. Their leader announces that they too are moving to America, and the troop marches through the auditorium singing "Yankee Doodle Dandy." Carolyn Jessop writes that one of these Nazi soldiers was played by Warren Jeffs himself, a poetic underscoring that you just can't make up. In her words, "The audience was laughing, unaware of the shadow falling across our community. It was the shadow of a totalitarian society that would one day consume every aspect of our lives and be under the control of Warren Jeffs."[27] The full company then moralizes the show by singing "Climb Ev'ry Mountain," closing the evening with conventional bouquets of flowers at the curtain call and an unconventional prayer to send everyone home. A quick glance at this re-sounded production's song list illuminates the sophisticated poaching at play; only a handful of songs (in bold below) are retained from *The Sound of Music*, and yet the story survives adaptation remarkably well.

"Watch Your Footwork" (*The Happiest Millionaire*)
"The Sound of Music"
"Just a Simple Song" (unknown origins)
"I Have Confidence"
"Maria"
"Do-Re-Mi"
"You Two" (*Chitty Chitty Bang Bang*)
"Do You Love Me?" (*Fiddler on the Roof*)
"Ten Feet Off the Ground" (*The One and Only, Genuine, Original Family Band*)
"Yankee Doodle Dandy" (*Yankee Doodle Dandy*)
"Climb Ev'ry Mountain"

Musicologist Raymond Knapp has suggested that *The Sound of Music*, like most musicals of this era, can't help tell a story of contemporary America. The whole notion of Nazis removing themselves to America only makes explicit what the original postwar production tries to hide—that "what is at stake in *The Sound of Music* is America's *nationhood*."[28] The FLDS community's restructuring the show to be about polygamists in America seems a stretch only when we think of the obvious content differences and accept that even the original version stretches the truth of these historical figures. But settled underneath its more outrageous pretension is the show's insistence that musicals are about America and those who understand them in this way are, by extension, American too.

Performing the Past

It seems bewildering, then, to learn that the fundamentalist Mormon community not only enjoys putting on musicals but also apparently has a firm enough understanding of how the genre works to be able to refashion one of the most iconic American cultural objects into a polygamous propaganda piece. Because American musical theater is such a fixture of American values and culture, and because polygamist communities still outfitted in nineteenth-century fashion are clearly *not* fixtures of America today, this meeting makes for a fascinating moment to explore exactly how malleable our Americanness is and ask why, of all things, musicals seem to play such a part in the molding.

It is one thing to craft a propagandist story of your own imagining. It is quite another to poach one from familiar objects. Because musicals are already flimsily tethered to history—this despite the prevalence of historical plots onstage as in musicals like *Evita*, *1776*, *Titanic*, and *Fiorello!* or on display with the current appetite for so-called bio-musicals such as *Jersey Boys* and *Tina: The Tina Turner Musical*, shows Elissa Harbert identifies as "history musicals"—they make the work of revision a relatively simple task.[29]

In its original form, *The Sound of Music* was already a problematic history musical. Devised liberally from Maria von Trapp's memoirs, the show's book turns the von Trapp family into emblems of antifascist sentiment while quietly eliminating Maria's own questionable anti-Semitism. It also dreams up an anti-Semitic Austria fighting for moral high ground against the tyrannical Nazis, as if Austria weren't already ideologically occupied by fascist thought long before the actual German occupation in 1938. Even more, the specter of an innocent Austria forced into violence by outsiders finds a poetic and perpendicular narrative in Maria's calming presence amid a family ruled by a tyrant father—a family, in Knapp's words, practically "Fascism *in nuce*" (in a nutshell).[30]

Musicals are rarely about the things they say they are about, and this is no less true of a musical about historical subjects. *The Sound of Music* produces the kind of heroes America needed in 1959—upright, principled, and in love with each other. And, as with any good musical, they needed to be in love with singing. No matter its setting in 1938 Austria, *The Sound of Music* is about America—especially New York City's America—caught in a different war where right and wrong were less defined. Musicals may never be able to tell the truth about the past, which makes skeptics wary yet all the more surprised when those shows make the past something new. Relevance seems key. "In order to succeed," Harbert observes, "history musicals must coax audiences to reflect on issues in their own time. When a history musical is relevant, critics and audiences feel they've become more personally connected to that history."[31] The present needs of history help remake the past, not the other way around.

In other words, we expect musicals to be flimsy and fictitious, but we also really seem to enjoy when at the same time they can reinvigorate our relationship with the past. This is especially the case if that version of the past sustains what are perceived to be truths today—even fabrications that show good, though selfish, intentions can still come to be accepted as desirable, "prosocial," lies.[32] The voice is central in this calculation. In musical theater, the moments of greatest emotional resonance and authentic honesty for characters come when they spontaneously break into song. These moments resonate exceptionally with audiences yet also constitute the most blatantly and infamously contrived moments, since they remind viewers that the conventions of musicals do not play out in the real world. As Lionel Trilling argued, sincerity becomes important to a society whenever a distinction can be made between a simulated self or selves and an actual or true self.[33] He suggests that this cleave first appears in the age of Shakespeare, where sincerity arises as a moral ideal to confirm one's true self, an attitude that, under scrutiny, is revealed to be a pose; Polonius's "to thine own self be true" admits there is a false self always available and that sincerity comes through an act of choosing one over another. Authenticity, then, which becomes a recognizable ideal in more recent history, convinces through performance. Trilling's point is that to *be* authentic or to *appear* sincere have different social meanings, yet both nevertheless are constructions rooted in duplicity. Whatever fantasy musicals perform through the voice, they succeed in part because of this tension between a hopeful belief in the true self and the modern-day skepticism that there may be no such thing.

A quick jaunt into a more recent history musical adds to the presumed values-making that deception offers us. *Hamilton* has become the most prominent example of Broadway's commitment to inclusivity. A studied glance, however, gives reason to doubt this is its real work. Despite an ethnically mixed cast, one might even conclude that the show maintains musical theater's political compromise by applying a fresh coat of liberalism over the familiar tale of a rich white man and the women who loved him. Middle-class pretentiousness was, for Susan Sontag, a hallmark of camp, and this seems especially pertinent in the case of *Hamilton*—a musical telling of one of the architects of America's middle class adored by people who identify as middle class or who identify as champions of the middle class. *Hamilton*'s conservative patina peeks through the liberal gloss when one considers that the show's characters are modeled on people who are actually responsible for creating the conditions of the contemporary underclass. The real Alexander Hamilton, despite (or perhaps to spite) his immigrant and orphan status, concocted a financial system that is designed to maintain inequalities of wealth. In one *New York Times* op-ed, Jason Frank and Isaac Kramnick caution against Lin-Manuel Miranda's cherry-picked depiction of Hamilton as a champion of immigrants or the underclass. "Hamilton," they argue, "with his contemptuous attitude toward the lower classes, was perfectly comfortable with the inegalitarian and antidemocratic implications of his economic vision. One has to wonder if the audiences in the Richard Rodgers Theatre would be as enthusiastic about a musical openly affirming such convictions."[34]

That seems as unlikely as audiences being appreciative of the stubborn anti-Semitism lurking in the background of the actual Maria von Trapp. Tidy histories have their charms. And that doesn't mean the fictionalized history is inauthentic; rather, actors attempting to gather history's power become "hyperhistorians," to use Freddie Rokem's term; their captured energy from the stage "validates the authenticity of the events that are depicted on the stage as historical events."[35] What passes as real or authentic is a decision based on energy or intensity of expression, a gut feeling. Just because musicals traipse in and out of reality willy-nilly doesn't mean they can't convey a sense of truth and with great force. They may in fact be better than the truth. In Scott Magelssen's words, getting history wrong or revealing on stage some daylight between actual events and imagined ones "can actually be more productive to discourse than blindly following the historical script."[36]

In pursuit of story, caricatures and myths are consequently more common in our musicals than historical actors and a commitment to truth. Kirsten Walsh and Adrian Currie have used these terms to challenge the philosophical narrative that history deserves an unbungled reputation, especially in classroom settings. Arguing for a "tempered respect for history," Walsh and Currie distinguish between licensed distortions of the past, or *caricatures*, and those that are not, which they dub *myths*. Mythmakers "distort the truth about the past on the justification that those distortions help us better understand the present," adding that "a caricature retains core truths, while a myth distorts them."[37] Using Walsh and Currie's language, we could determine that musicals that make a claim about the past are either purposely distorting history to make an important truth claim that otherwise might remain hidden, or that the distortion is intentionally doing a disservice to the past in order to construct a truth for today's purposes. *Hamilton*'s color-blind casting seems to be an intentional distortion of the past in order to make an important point about today—a caricature of the past; *The Re-Sound of Music*, on the other hand, is invested in mythmaking. In both cases the past is made disposable; the biggest difference seems only to be the speed with which it is tossed to the floor.

What the Deception Has Wrought

Despite the fantastical imaginings of *The Re-Sound of Music* as validation for an unconventional America, polygamy might be having a moment in this country. Popular culture's obsession with polygamy has switched perspectives but not intensity since nineteenth-century operettas lampooning Mormons. The television shows *Sister Wives* and *Big Love* helped bring polygamy into the larger discussion of nontraditional family units, including same-sex couples. Scholars like anthropologist Janet Bennion have called for decriminalizing polygamy in the name of radical feminism, claiming that legalizing polygamy would allow government and nongovernment agencies alike to monitor and better track the health and well-being of women in polygamous families.[38] Bennion believes that polygamists have become a convenient social pariah against middle-class self-righteousness. "By marginalizing polygamists," she writes, "we can reaffirm our values as monogamists, labeling ourselves more righteous or superior than the deviant group."[39]

Although many polygamists in the United States do not identify as Mormon or Mormon fundamentalists (the majority of American polygamists are Muslim), representations of polygamy in popular culture and media reinforce that such families and communities are largely white and religiously motivated.[40] Once viewers see that polygamy is already practiced by people who have normal jobs and experience typical family tensions, criminalizing it no longer carries the whiff of women's oppression. Instead, a growing body of activists in support of decriminalizing polygamy see it as a move *toward* a liberation of women. "It is my belief that forcing polygamous families to the fringes of society facilitates instances of abuse taking place outside the watchful eye of law enforcement," Bennion adds.[41] Pushing polygamy out of the dark corners, in other words, would do everyone some good.

The intervening years since *The Re-Sound of Music* might be a success story for polygamous families, but what will that mean for fundamentalism more broadly? Political and religious fundamentalism are on the quick rise. There remains a troubling sense that musical theater may unwittingly be aiding in fundamentalist work, perhaps complicit in its dangers and violence, despite its vaguely liberal narratives of acceptance and progress. What conclusions can we make about theater's deception and trickery that so easily enables charismatic individuals and makes their audiences grow in fervent support? Can musicals remain musicals without undoing the fantasy they protect?

Clearly there are times when the past needs to remain intact. As Francis Fukuyama pointed out in his *The End of History and the Last Man*, the project of history was all along a project marching liberalism toward modernity.[42] Fundamentalism of all stripes, not just the religious variety, is an imbalanced relationship with the past; musicals are a convenient way to correct that imbalance with a more facile historical perspective. The unforgiving and dynamic frustrations of the historical past, then, are anathema to fundamentalism, as the current post-truth, alternative-facts climate makes ever clear. Philip Salim Francis's opening salvo—"Can art save us from fundamentalism?"—seems more and more to be part of the problem, not a solution.

But fundamentalism, like musicals, is also a point of contact with a more meaningful world outside the fatalistic one we currently inhabit. "As long as there appears to be some immanent sense to things," Terry Eagleton notes, "one can always inquire after the source from which it springs."[43] God, truth, and meaningfulness can never be truly dead, *contrary to* Nietzsche, but rather exists always in the human *desire for those things to exist*—God's disappearance will come only with humanity's, to put it bluntly. This may be why musicals fly so effortlessly under the critical radar. Seemingly always about the comic resolution, musicals insist everything will work out all right and, unlike the tragic, have little traffic with suffering as a bargain between mortal and immortal beings.

What we might take from this situation of musicals and fundamentalism is that there is precious contact. If a channel has been opened between those accepting modernity and those challenging it, then it ought to be exploited for good. Musicals have currency among fundamentalists, and the kind of deception musicals offer is a fuel for fundamentalism's engine. For similar reasons, musicals are on the uptick in our world as well. Supposing more history musicals emerge, and carry their banner of fabrication into the farthest reaches of America, then the wires of communication are being laid across the wide-open spaces of the Middle. These may well be our lifelines. Most everyone wants to live in a world unlike the one we have now. Let the deception carry us further into the worlds of fierce imagining—the worlds of belief, the worlds of musicals, the worlds of the yet-to-become—and make use of the sharpest tool in our arsenal: big lies.

Conclusion

Perhaps most of us haven't appreciated enough just how wide-reaching these beloved but ostensibly innocuous musicals have been. Or how easily these shows can be deconstructed and then rebuilt to mean something else entirely. Arguably it is the fluidity and interchangeability of musicals that give them potency, especially outside of professional circuits. While Broadway is reluctant to adapt or meddle with even problematic themes from past shows in revivals, theater making on the ground in communities all over the country depends on the versatility of the form. Lyrics are changed, aging characters with few lines are more often than not played by less-experienced actors, and some scenes get scrapped entirely. It is not uncommon, for example, for Stephen Sondheim's dig at happy endings to be thwarted when local productions with limited resources decide to entirely cut the second act of *Into the Woods*, as is frequently done when performed in American high schools. The point seems to be more about fun making and experience than about provocation through high art, a sore point the musical theater community has nursed while also acknowledging that its middlebrow status is part of the charm and power.

But it is no doubt the wonder of transmission, of mobility, that strikes at the heart of this story. A community trying to keep out of reach nonetheless finds signal in the noise and sends back a message of belonging. Isn't this the real message of the Middle—that someone is out there, listening?

Near the end of his novel *The Topeka School*, Ben Lerner's autofictional character Adam Gordon returns to his hometown of Topeka, Kansas, to read his poems after winning a prestigious literary award. Memories of space and place haunt his visit. His parents' workplace, the progressive psychological center known as the Foundation, has churned for Adam a fanciful claim of communication—with oneself, among others, and across time. Before the speech, he experiences a transmission in the middle, from the middle of nowhere, maybe from the Middle itself:

> I imagined that all the speech that had ever been uttered at the Foundation was somehow still in the air, if only I could tune in, the way old radio broadcasts have started returning from space, where they've bounced off heavenly bodies made of ice, a ham radio operator picking up Herbert Morrison's *Hindenburg* disaster broadcast from 1937, the year of Fritz's birth, in 2014. Oh, the humanity, electromagnetic radiation falling back to earth. I shut my eyes and listened, but there was too much interference, noise from the Big Bang, the crackle of sparks, lightning, stars, a charged body beneath white silk, wires crossed.[44]

Crossed wires. Crossed stories. A five-lined musical tightrope on which to perform belonging and a song turned on its head to sell the story.

Something re-sounding implies it is going someplace new, maybe like these old radio broadcasts journeying back to where they came from. All we have is a grainy home video of the FLDS's production. Who knows how long even it will last? It's a fitting symbol for the fragility of the past and the potency of stories out of place.

Somewhere in the Middle a thin wire retunes the sky.

A song stirs.

Nothing comes from nothing. Nothing ever could.

CHAPTER 4

Biblically Accurate

In his autobiography, *The Seven Storey Mountain*, the Trappist monk and priest Thomas Merton recounts attending a play put on by African American children living in Harlem in the 1930s. "It was an experience that nearly tore me to pieces," he writes.

> All the parents of the children were there, sitting on benches, literally choked with emotion at the fact that their children should be acting in a play: but that was not the thing. For, as I say, they knew that the play was nothing, and that all the plays of the white people are more or less nothing. They were not taken in by that. Underneath it was something deep and wonderful and positive and true and overwhelming: their gratitude for even so small a sign of love as this, that someone should at least make some kind of gesture that said: "This sort of thing cannot make anybody happy, but it is a way of saying: 'I wish you were happy.'"[1]

Merton's recollections hinge meaningfully on how theater takes many forms, by many people, for many reasons. It is perhaps no surprise that Merton includes this ethnographic detail in his conversion memoir. Theater, and perhaps especially musical theater, shares one of religion's strongest characteristics: inviting audiences and participants alike to escape the trappings of the old world and glimpse worlds yet to come. But they alone can't bring happiness. Religion and theater are both, as Merton puts it, ways of saying *I wish you were happy*.

That wish often means setting aside what we feel is true in order to glimpse the truth that others gather from the musical stage. Authenticity has never been a musical's strong point. People congregate around musicals for other reasons. As in Merton's emotional response to the children's production, musicals tear to pieces whatever separates truth from fiction. The musical is a borderless nation among a people conditioned to dig fence posts.

Say your business was to tell the truth—to witness of a truth so cosmic that it required a large imagination to pull it together. Evangelical Christianity traffics in this kind of business. Sight & Sound Theatres in Branson, Missouri, produces original musicals about biblical stories at a spectacular level. As the branch campus of Sight & Sound Theatres' home base in Lancaster, Pennsylvania, Sight & Sound Theatres in Branson taps into a ready market of Christian tourists from around the region. Billed as "the live music capital of the world," Branson siphons much of that liveness into religious expression. Sight & Sound Theatres goes one step further in turning live music into a staged spectacle unlike anything else in the town or region.

It doesn't seem to bother anyone in Branson that musicals are the vehicle for translating Christian values and virtues. In some ways the religiosity of musicals plays easily into the hands of modern Christian principles. The moralistic fetish of resolving conflicts between good and evil can make musicals close cousins to sermons. This is perhaps truer of earlier eras in musical theater; Cole Porter described Richard Rodgers's music as having "a certain holiness about it," and Ian Bradley shows how Oscar Hammerstein's Protestant and liberal Jewish upbringing shaped his work's reconciliatory fantasies. The culture wars of the 1970s later ensnared *Jesus Christ Superstar*'s humanistic depictions of Jesus and his disciples.[2] But, regardless, musicals have intercepted religion and religion musicals in often mutually beneficial ways. Their twinned strategies of make-believe and mild but persistent anti-intellectualism give musicals a religious vibrancy that can't help but be made useful.

Play-acting is also at the center of Christian religious experience. In *Mere Christianity*, C. S. Lewis memorably explained that the Lord's Prayer was a way for Jesus to teach his followers how to pretend to be him; it was only by *pretending* to be the Son of God that you immediately realize you are, in fact, a mere mortal, and *that* is the humility that enables a firsthand experience of the Divine.[3] You must pass through duplicity before reaching something true and authentic. Dean Sell, a branding manager for Sight & Sound Theatres, told me that the "power of play" in theater allows us to experience the world as a child again. When you get people to feel like a child, he says, "something meaningful happens."[4] In abdicating religious experience to the playfulness of musicals, Sight & Sound Theatres, like Christianity writ large, echoes Martin Luther's praise of the prosocial lie from ages past: "What harm would it do, if a man told a good strong lie for the sake of the good and for the Christian church . . . a lie out of necessity, a useful lie, a helpful lie? Such lies would not be against God; He would accept them."[5]

This chapter takes a close look at how religious truths rest upon deception. It is not only fundamentalist sects that favor the imaginative world of musicals to do this work, as discussed in the previous chapter. Rather, a study of Sight & Sound Theatres reveals how the animating force behind false worlds and exaggerated depictions of the past is doing work for mainline Christianity no less than those communities on the fringes. What makes this study so compelling, I find, is how audiences come to believe the truth of what they see in these musicals, despite the fact of musical theater's unreliability as a medium and disclaimers by the Sight & Sound Theatres that what they are witnessing is creatively ahistorical. Nonetheless, what this chapter uncovers is the role that deception, play-acting, and exaggeration play within religious expression in modern times and how musicals construct and defend against the palisades of unreality within religion itself.

Walls Will Fall

I sit down next to Carl and Cathy, a couple in their early sixties from Fort Smith, Arkansas, who are in town to celebrate their honeymoon. We are on the back row of the floor seats. While a magician entertainer is onstage with a donkey and camel, priming the audience, I turn behind me and see steeply raked auditorium seating. The theater is impressively large. It holds over two thousand and tonight is almost at capacity.

Yet what you notice right away when you step into the Sight & Sound Theatres is the three-hundred-foot wraparound stage filled with massive set-pieces, which for this production include walls of faux rock rising as high as four stories. The sets are all controlled by GPS, the manager at my motel tells me when I check in later that night. As I think of it, I remember seeing only a handful of moments when cast members were clearly spinning or shifting around the set-pieces. With pieces of this size, it would likely be too bulky and heavy for a small group with even Samson-like strength to move. I am given a backstage tour later and told that the space behind, below, and surrounding the theater together are the exact dimensions of Noah's ark. In more ways than one, this show measures up to biblical proportions.

Cathy is a repeat visitor. She saw *Moses* here a few years before and tells me almost right away that what she appreciates most about Sight & Sound Theatres is that their shows are "biblically accurate." She tells me this just a few moments after the onstage magician, now mounted on the donkey, assures the audience that while this is a creative telling of the mighty Samson, it is rooted in the Bible. Cathy doesn't seem to mind this caveat, or that a stage musical is never accurate about much at all. As Isaiah, who played Samson that night, later told me, "Most of our guests are probably not theatergoers, so this would be their Broadway or regional theater," adding that "it's a plus for them that they are biblical stories."[6]

This is true for Cathy and Carl, neither of whom had been to many shows outside of those in Branson, and it squares with Sight & Sound Theatres' audience demographic: 25 percent of their audiences attend several live shows a year, another 25 percent attend Sight & Sound Theatres' productions exclusively, and the remaining 50 percent attend only two or three shows a year. These figures are from both the Lancaster, Pennsylvania, and Branson, Missouri, campuses combined, which, it bears pointing out, represent two very different populations. Eighty percent of Sight & Sound Theatres' audiences come within a three-hundred-mile radius of the theaters, and more than two times as many people live in the region surrounding Lancaster as that surrounding Branson. Those coming to Lancaster are pulled from nearby cities like New York, Philadelphia, and Washington, D.C. Audiences coming to Branson are sourced from rural areas and Middle cities like St. Louis, Kansas City, and Bentonville, Arkansas. A likely scenario is that the audiences gathered with me in Branson that night are much less familiar with live theater than their Lancaster counterparts.

That's why when Sight & Sound Theatres bills itself as the place "where the Bible comes to life," that work of conveying accuracy onstage may come to matter differently to people gathered with me that night like Cathy and Carl—audiences less familiar with musical theater's reputation as flippant or how the genre works to convey truth. As we'll come to learn, some stories need a little nudging to make them true for modern audiences.

And this is what most captivates me as I experience my first Sight & Sound Theatres production. It's hard not to be awed by the sheer scope of these shows. The sets, the costumes, the dozens of cast members, the horses, goats, and camels paraded through the aisles and onstage—they are all of a piece with the high production value that betrays its rather unassuming location in the heart of the country.

Branson is a small Ozark resort town that suddenly appears when driving between Fayetteville, Arkansas and Springfield, Missouri. It is a curious place.

The best way I can describe Branson is that it is the evangelical Christian (in) version of Las Vegas—stocked with hundreds of live shows representing an astonishing diversity of musical styles and locales, all bent toward audiences who are largely gathering from the surrounding region to be affirmed in their faith and to have a good time doing it. Despite a reputation as regional entertainment center, Branson's dusty, off-the-road persona resonates with its appeal as unencumbered by the corrupting influences of the world. Certainly part of this appeal is the beautiful and largely untamed natural surroundings, which make Branson's comparison with Las Vegas a revealing one; the fantastical mirages that both cities inspire in their visitors are directly linked with the sense of isolation, otherworldliness, and complete disappearance from the rest of reality. As Denise Von Glahn notes in her study of nature and American music, natural spaces rhyme with the belief that God holds "special promise for America," which in the center of the country retain the nineteenth-century outfitting of nature as "an uncontaminated laboratory."[7] It is through a mediated natural landscape that Las Vegas tourists feel an escape into something larger than themselves, and that translates into Branson's visitors gaining access to God and God's people.

Sight & Sound Theatres is in harmony with this ideal, packaging biblical stories that moralize widespread death and condemnation (including *Moses, Jonah, Noah, Daniel in the Lion's Den*, and *Samson*, with additional productions planned every few years) in the veneer of a genre that plays on resolution, if not outright happy endings. The marketing centerpiece to *Samson* is his suicidal destruction of the Philistine temple. Driving into Branson earlier that evening, I passed at least five large billboards advertising the show with catchy blurbs such as "Walls. Will. Fall." This was in line with how other productions here are promoted. Most posters advertising Sight & Sound's productions draw attention to those stories' central act of destruction, whether it's Moses parting the Red Sea, a sinking Jonah being swallowed whole by a whale, the hand of Jesus grasping that of a drowning Peter, or Samson pulling down the pillars of the Philistine temple. Theatergoers can even take their photo beneath a large sculpture indicative of these moments (see fig. 4.1). While I was here, lines quickly formed after the show so visitors could smile for posterity while precariously perched beneath the crumbling temple that Samson is tearing asunder.

This kind of spectacle is familiar in theater. Musicals depend on crisis and work toward resolution of that tension. It's also part of the fun. I think I might be disappointed in a musical about Moses that didn't in some way theatricalize the parting of the Red Sea, even if the other side of that story is the horrific deaths of thousands of Egyptian soldiers. An honest appraisal of the kinds of

Figure 4.1: A statue of Samson in the lobby of Sight & Sound Theatres. Photo by the author.

tension and resolution frequent among traditional musicals would recognize that theatrical resolution can often be an act of violence. In *Oklahoma!* Laurey and Curly are free to wed after Jud falls on his knife and dies. *The King and I* works as a show because the king's death enables progress. Even musicals as recent as *Hamilton* spin the death of a protagonist as a catalyst for remarkable change. As one review of the production notes, the moral of *Samson* is "that good can befall you even in the worst of circumstances," which is a curious answer to the question of what stories of destruction are meant to convey, but in the context of the genre it may not be all that unusual.[8] On the other hand, most audiences don't buy tickets to *Oklahoma!* because they want to watch Jud get run through (at least I hope not). Theatergoers at Sight & Sound Theatres are pulled into the seats for a number of reasons but not least because the theater assumes they are interested in what massive acts of destruction dramatized onstage can add to their personal narratives about redemption through Jesus Christ. As one actor told me, "They come to see the walls fall, but they also come to see *how* we do it."

This form of violent spectacle has proven a useful and creative evangelizing tool among Christians in other theatrical platforms. From "Hallo Witnessing" to the so-called Hell Houses set up during Halloween, churches around the country have for decades used haunted house–style theater to scare audiences into converting or reaffirming their place in the afterlife. ("Where haunted houses promise to scare the bejeezus out of you, Hell Houses aim to scare you to Jesus," as Ann Pellegrini neatly puts it.[9]) Depictions of violent scenarios like car accidents, abortions, or teen suicide are performed in such spaces by costumed actors as a form of shock doctrine. In *Violence and the Sacred*, René Girard argues that religion has helped quell violent urges through worship of scapegoats; in Hell Houses and other similar theatrical spaces, evangelicals ritually enact violence in order to draw the audience's attention to the scapegoat (in these cases, Jesus Christ) and "be saved"—saved, in other words, from a violent and never-ending torture in hell. Importantly, these Hell Houses are riffs on an established genre—the haunted house—that gifts Hell Houses an imprimatur of innocent make-believe and allows producers to direct that imagination toward a specific (and saved) end.

These venues certainly play into the region's appetite for Christian narratives, flying in the face of secular or scientific ones. Hank Willenbrink's study of Hell Houses in Tulsa, Oklahoma, places this theatrical practice within a three-hour drive of Sight & Sound Theatres in Branson, Missouri, and Jill Stevenson's analysis of the Creation Museum in Petersburg, Kentucky, also within a day's drive. In fact, what unites Hell Houses, Sight & Sound Theatres, and other alternate-reality venues like the Creation Museum is placing fantasy within a familiar space, whether that is haunted houses, musical stages, or museums. The Creation Museum uses the familiar setup of a natural history museum to court visitors in an alternate reality where the Earth is only a few thousand years old and dinosaurs coexisted with humans. This setup grants authority to the creationist worldview; even more, it casts evolutionary theory (the Creation Museum's foil) as only *part* of the story and claims that its museumgoers are being gifted a "bible/science blend" superior to secular narratives. By playing off a traditional museum format, "the creationist believer [is] depicted as someone who has assessed the available options logically and chosen biblical 'truth' because it makes more sense."[10] This is no small accomplishment. In an age when more Americans trust museums as sources of truth over newspapers, scholars, or other experts, the Creation Museum crafts a relationship with authority that grants its fantastical narrative legitimacy.[11]

Similarly, Willenbrink's informants suggest that Hell Houses reveal a truth that is scary only because "it has been concealed by other, competing narratives," adding that conversion is fundamentally about "accepting one narrative over another."[12] These religious narratives are often exaggerated realities, if not outright fictions, that require a theatrical veneer to illustrate for the believers a reality unlike the one unbelievers inhabit. The Creation Museum even uses language similar to that of Sight & Sound Theatres to brand their exhibits as bringing "the pages of the Bible to life." The takeaway from all three venues discussed here is that what is singularly true needs coaxing in order to stand out among other competing truths.

Inasmuch as biblical messaging qua Reagan-era politics among Christian fundamentalists today errs on the side of violent overthrow, corrupt authority, and a crude but perhaps necessary escape from mortality in favor of eternal life, Sight & Sound Theatres' shows play into the hands of its major demographic. In fact, theatrical postures among conservative Christian audiences might predict a sympathetic reading of underdogs who violently though righteously save the day. Through narrative, it is a short leap from a corrupted and filigreed Samson, Moses, or Jonah to their redeemed caricatures. Fallen figures litter the landscape of religious mythology, and I wonder if disrepute speaks more to fellow conservative believers in this region who likewise search for narratives that redeem the forgotten and wrongheaded.

Biblically Accurate

The opening song of *Samson* describes him as "Not Your Typical Biblical Hero." That much is true. Samson is a Nazirite—someone set apart from the rest of the world with a vow to abstain from alcohol, steer clear of corpses and graves, and to never cut his hair—and born with a gift of superhuman strength. He kills a lion with his bare hands and massacres an army of Philistine soldiers using only the jawbone of a donkey. His enemies discover through Samson's lover, Delilah, his Achilles' heel—if Samson ever cuts his hair, he will lose his strength. Delilah betrays Samson in exchange for freedom from her debts, allowing a Philistine to cut Samson's hair as he sleeps. Captured by his enemies, imprisoned in their temple, and now depleted of his Herculean strength, Samson prays to God for one last moment of power as he tears down the columns holding up the Philistine temple, killing himself and all the Philistines with him.

I consider myself rather well-versed in biblical mythology, but the last part is all I could remember of the story before sitting down next to Cathy and Carl. Cathy assured me that almost everything I was seeing was part of the four chapters in the Book of Judges that make mention of Samson. That, she reminded me again, was what she appreciated so much about Sight & Sound Theatres. Biblically accurate.

So, while at face value the story doesn't lend itself to overtly evangelical messaging, this production frames the show as a lesson in grace as exemplified by Jesus Christ. The show opens with the narrator (also Samson's father, Manoah) admitting that, of the valiant men in biblical mythology like Abraham, Moses, and Joshua, Samson may not immediately seem to belong among this elite group. Yet, he continues, Samson reveals an important lesson about God's love for his children. At the show's conclusion, the narrator returns to finish the lesson. Audiences are taught that Samson's story underscores the imperfection of all men, which vaults into a familiar evangelical teaching that these wise yet fallen men fail in order to draw attention to Jesus's ultimate triumph over death. I saw the show three times, and this moment in all occasions received the most gratuitous applause and audible reaction from the audience every time. An altar call, designed to bring believers and unbelievers alike to repentance, was announced at the end of the show, and volunteer pastors were made available for counseling. This was the resolution that made the story of Samson a musical; it was also the resolution that made the bloody story meaningful for guests—a reborn life in Jesus after the death of the old self.

As Isaiah told me the next day, you can read the actual story of Samson in a matter of minutes. His point was that musicals have to be more than the story, both in practical terms and because not everyone who needs to hear the story is "a reader." "The fakeness will lead people to realize that these events are very similar to things that have happened, and we tell this story because this is information that needs to be shared," he added. "We have musicals because some people may not be readers."

But I'm thinking back now about Cathy and her insistence that the stage musical was not only accurate but also *biblically* accurate. I wonder what that phrase meant to her and why she found it so meaningful. In order for something to be accurate, doesn't it have to be accurate on its own two feet?

Drawing upon Gilles Fauconnier and Mark Turner's concept of the "counterfactual" to describe blends of reality and fantasy, Bruce McConachie notes that audience members like Cathy and Carl "oscillate between counterfactual blends and perceptions of their actual, material circumstances." "Our ability to engage in make-believe," he continues, "is evolutionarily adaptive, for a hundred reasons, even though it can also impair our ability to see the world clearly."[13] Lottery tickets, for instance, are purchased in counterfactual frames of mind. Gamblers know the odds of winning are outrageously slim, and yet somewhere in their minds they also cannot help fantasize of what they would do with their winnings. Reality and fantasy coexist, sometimes in benign ways and sometimes in hurtful ways. But our ability to manage both the real and the tempered is nonetheless a learned and entrained habit—what can't be imagined in many ways can't be made real, and the real must be reimagined again and again or it loses traction in our lives.

A More Real Real

Musicals can lie in order to make something more real than it would seem otherwise. Sight & Sound Theatres' slogan, "Where the Bible comes to life," clearly captures this sentiment. Musicals are larger than life, make big gestures, and host spectacular lies. It may be that religious communities have to push above the noise and signal most creatively in order to be heard. Isaac Weiner's book *Religion Out Loud* finds the paradox of this position, showing how religious communities in Middle America want to abate secular noisiness while also increasingly being the *cause* of unwanted noise—a true legal dilemma for a nation that prizes both its religious freedom and its civil liberties.[14] One consequence is that we listen differently nowadays, disciplining our bodies and ears to listen past the sonic clutter and attune ourselves to the signal we trust the most. As modernity brings the level of competing truths to a premium, religions likewise may feel the need to carve out space for *sonic signifiance*—Julia Kristeva's term for a kind of loss or absence that liberates "in the space of lack."[15]

Evangelical Christians may find a place for signifiance by using musicals to make the Bible "come alive," but both Christians and musicals come about this practice rather naturally. Musicals, in other words, already enact a form of awakening, extending the power of Jesus and bringing the dead back to life.[16] This speaks to a larger principle of Christian ideology: that absence and presence are mutually reinforcing, if not confusingly so. Christians celebrate the death of God but may cringe when whiffs of a Nietzschean dead God drift too close. Terry Eagleton expresses it well when he says that for Christians "the death of God is not a question of his disappearance. On the contrary, it is one of the places where he is most fully present."[17] Fully present. Brought to life.

For Christians, worshiping involves a substitution of death and life, or recognizing power in absence. An abandoned cross, for instance, conveys a powerful reality of a living God even though the emblem of a God not dead is his executioner's weapon. For Christian audiences, then, the Bible may require theater to make it seem alive again, but that in itself underscores an overarching ideology of religious vicariousness: that absence affirms presence, that death is teeming with life, and that what makes something true may actually be the ease of its falsifiability.

If seeing presence in absence or truth in fiction is a backbone of Christian ideology, then Christians have plenty of practice being good liars. To put it a little less bluntly, Christians are employing creative measures to fill the gaps of their complex narratives. Some of this comes with the territory, as biblical characters are frequently skilled in creative deception: Jacob tricking his father, Isaac, into giving him his brother's birthright and Jesus teaching in circuitous parables, for example, illustrate how deception is sometimes a character flaw and sometimes a measure of divine guidance yet commonly a part of religious practice.[18] Dan Ariely shows that the more creative a person is, "the more we are able to come up with good stories that help us justify our selfish interests," and I suspect the inverse may be just as true.[19] In other words, the more a narrative requires adaptation to fit current needs, the greater demand to look elsewhere for solutions.

Musicals may bring enchantment back to the stories—making the stone *stony* again, as Viktor Shklovsky put it—by bringing them to life without forcing the stories to balance the budgetary demands of reason or be in every way literal.[20] To invoke Philip Salim Francis, music and modern religion are "entangled in a complex substitutionary relationship."[21] That is, musicals can make space for illusion and fantasy in religious expression while also not appearing too illusory and fantastical.[22] Cathy's assurance that Sight & Sound Theatres was showcasing "biblically accurate" stories simultaneously grounds the musical in truth by releasing it into an absence, a specter of fantasy that, like Jesus's universal atonement, substitutes for a real experience.

A larger question that Cathy's sentiment raises is why truth requires untruth. If truth is synonymous here with "accurate," then accuracy can never be enough, or else the story stops; religion requires an evolving and adaptable storyline that could never survive the designation "accurate." Musicals can't be accurate either—trying to make a musical mean truth (as the "history musicals" attempt to do; see chapter 3) is rarely satisfying. We are left to wonder if what is real can ever stand on its own, without the steadying hand of some constant unreality. Such is the crux of resort escapes like Branson, Las Vegas, or Disney theme parks—they work because visitors *want* them to work. I'm reminded of Toni Morrison's admission that she enjoyed Disneyland for its escape from brutal truths, a place "where the deceptions are genuine" and the feeling of contentment welcome despite the obvious machinery that delivers it.[23]

We may ask why religious stories can't do their work without being forced into ahistorical relevancy. We might question what the musical defends against that the Bible can't manage on its own. But truth asks more than whether or not something is real. Mythologies require lived experience in order to convey their relevance and truth. In Christianity this relevance gets channeled through spectacle. Stained-glass windows once did this storytelling work for the illiterate masses; musicals now do similar work for the nonliterate masses. Sight *and* Sound. Not everyone is a reader.

Belonging in Branson

Branson itself is walled off from the outside. Nestled in a valley among the Ozark Mountains, Branson is a bubble in more ways than one. It is a fantasy space, a mythical Brigadoon for conservative evangelical Christians, where visitors fantasize over a Christian worldview that is permissive and predominant, where they can create society bound only by God's laws. Samson himself makes this point clear, singing toward heaven in his eleventh-hour number, "Hold me captive, and I am free."

In a way, Sight & Sound Theatres is held captive, perched atop a rugged mountain face. Driving around the perimeter of the campus—a road appropriately named "Shepherd of the Hills Expressway"—you move up and around the rock walls, a reminder that the stories that believers seek are not of this world. And yet the message is unmistakable: like Joshua in Jericho or Samson at the temple columns, these walled-in beliefs must be torn down to reach the world. What it takes to belong in Branson's alternate world is therefore a willingness to ascend walls in order to topple them. Branson's porousness is a key difference from Las Vegas's permissive unreality—what happens in Branson is not meant to stay in Branson.

Early in the show, Samson is engaged to marry a Philistine woman. This relationship was doomed from the beginning. The Philistines and Israelites had been at war for generations, and in this story the Philistines are shown to be cruel, barbarous, and spiteful toward the Israelites. Nonetheless, Samson and his family travel to her homeland for the wedding, their cultural differences quickly made apparent when the families meet in song. The Philistines sing boisterously of their national pride in a Celtic-inspired "Philistia Brave and Strong." In contrast, Samson leads his family together in singing "the song we Hebrews sing when we work in your fields." What follows is the song "Adonai," a Hebrew name for God that is frequently appropriated in Christian worship. The song concludes with a lovely a cappella, barbershop-style refrain that sounds more at home at an old-fashioned Gaither Homecoming—the gospel music series popular in the 1990s and early 2000s hosted by Christian music impresarios Bill and Gloria Gaither—than an ancient Hebrew world (see example 4.1). In "Adonai," whatever separates ancient Jews and modern Protestants in America collapses and allows a glimpse of a world where such distinctions cease to matter because they simply don't exist. Audiences gleefully stopped the show with their applause here, resonant with the musical messaging clearly directed toward their lived experience.

In both instances, the musical framework helps alleviate more obvious disparities between ancient Hebrew worldviews and modern Protestant ones. The musical illuminates, for instance, the path modern audiences might take to find relevance and meaning in stories that are meant to be understood within much more nuanced contexts. The show violates these principles out of specifics, not vagaries. In one sense, using the structure of a Protestant revival hymn is no big deal; clearly legitimizing it as an authentic Hebrew song, however, does offer a too easy erasure of what makes ancient Jewish culture different from that of today's Middle America. It is the *specificity* of what a Hebrew song presumably sounds like in this instance that seems the more grievous action.

Musicals can so easily and compellingly collapse difference that the violence of that collapse is often disguised. I am reminded here of Moe Meyer's concern that normalizing difference or placing it into the mainstream can lead to erasure. While he speaks specifically to the appropriation of queer culture into heterosexual performance—say, with musicals or reality television—the principal question resonates equally in this case. Normalization is a concern

Example 4.1: Shown here is the closing refrain of "Adonai," performed by Samson's family a cappella. Music and lyrics by Paul D. Mills.

for Meyer mostly because, as a rule, those who have the power to normalize identity, behavior, ideology, or practice are unrepresentative of the difference being placed in turmoil. What may seem a generous impulse of inclusivity can, inadvertently perhaps, result in a situation where what once distinguished a group of people or a set of ideas becomes thrust into the marketplace for use by others less invested in where, what, or who led to that difference being named as, indeed, different. As he argues, difference is erased whenever the paths of difference are "subjected to a dominant interpretation."[24] The pressure to place or name difference leads to an inevitable power struggle over what that difference can mean—if not economize—for others. The question of whether or not difference can ever exist alongside difference haunts almost every cultural endeavor of the late-capitalist experience, musicals included.

What musicals at Sight & Sound Theatres offer their audiences, then, is an accepted path of erasure—Samson pulls at the temple columns to bring down an old way of life and sets an example for modern Christians to do the same. That can mean erasing barriers that stand between the past and the present, between people, or between truth and fiction. In this way, musicals breathe life into the biblical past. They give vitality to a history that retreats further and further into the distance, enabling modern Christians to reclaim a heritage of faith even if reclamation means toppling incomplete facts with convenient fictions.

Infiction, Outfiction

Sight & Sound Theatres' "creative portrayal of a true story" allows audiences to have their cake and eat it too—to have an ancient story relate to current values, avoiding modernity by using a fully modernized genre's storytelling device, and to make that story resonate with current needs, while at the same time convincing audiences that these kinds of departures are not changing the accuracy of the story. The story is still true while the musical is not.

Leaving it at that is probably a disservice to what performers offer and what audiences take away during a performance of this kind. The musical does frame the story as a work of fiction—it can't help but turn the story into a work of fiction—but that may be a *different kind of fiction* than what audiences understand from experiencing the show, a difference David Z. Saltz helpfully illuminates. The entire premise of a musical is a schema trading in what he calls *infiction*, but that is distinguishable from the story or narrative that emerges from the performance itself, which he calls *outfiction*. Even if what comes across as being true first takes shape in a fictional space, the audience may still be confirmed in their appraisal because theater relates stories both inward and outward. "The relationship between narrative and performance runs two ways," Saltz writes, "from narrative to performance (fiction in), and from performance to narrative (fiction out)."[25]

For all the ways *Samson*'s fictions play directly into the hands of its audience, the show surprises us with where it directs some of its fantasy. For instance, in this production Delilah is anything but the one-dimensional seductress the Bible paints; instead she is a widow deeply in debt who begrudgingly accepts a financial offer from angry Philistines looking to capitalize on her intimacy with Samson. Her power ballad "Freedom" reveals this Delilah to be a conflicted though fundamentally good-hearted woman who finally chooses to be free of her debts, rhetorically asking, "What's love ever done for me?" One actor I interviewed referred to Delilah as "a survivor." The show didn't have to cast Delilah in such a sympathetic light; doing so, in fact, almost gives away the game that this biblical musical is a work of fiction.

Casting choices also helped craft a particular mode of outfiction. When I saw the show, Samson was played by a Black actor, as was Samson's mother. Nearly every other person onstage passed as white, including the actor portraying Manoah. In a city mostly catering to white visitors—who, despite the Bible's setting in the Middle East, have been conditioned to think of biblical characters as people who looked like them—Sight & Sound Theatres created a biblical world that in some ways strangely *looked* more accurate than how the Bible has come to be imagined in modern times. For all of its efforts to imagine the story of Samson as relevant today, in this instance Sight & Sound Theatres did not take the predictable route to (at least optically) whitewash their story.

On the other hand, what is accurate often takes a backseat to what is dramatically expedient. For instance, *Samson*'s world includes many characters and scenes not originally in the Bible. Samson's aunt Esther is the most prominent of these additions. Esther is likable and relevant in that she, like her nephew, carries her unshorn past for all to see. She is an unmarried mother, and the show leaves it at that. When I sat down to talk with the woman portraying Esther during my visit, I asked her what it was like to inhabit a character who was invented (infiction) to tell what some described as biblically accurate (outfiction):

> When I first read the script, I was really excited about her. I could connect with her. The reason [the creative team] put her in there is that she is questioning things. Manoah is very straitlaced. Esther is probably more like the normal person who questions things. She is very relatable to our audience. For me, it's nice to know we have a relational journey.[26]

The implication here is that Esther provides audiences with a realistic portrayal of modern values (insecurity, making mistakes, being down-to-earth) against the biblical characters who purportedly are more real than the made-up ones.

But which is fake in this case—the invented, extratextual characters to whom audiences can relate or the biblical characters who in themselves remain outside of reach of our modern world? This seems to be an admission on some level that, on their own, biblical stories are less relevant than they need to be and that musicals give some space where fiction can help augment the frailties of myths being taken literally.

Esther also traffics some of the more virtuosic and deeply felt moments of the show. She is featured prominently during Manoah's funeral, singing what sounds to me like a contemporary praise and worship song—an affective style that Monique M. Ingalls shows can displace the very notion of a church service, "thoroughly pervading evangelical public ritual and the devotional practices of everyday life" (see example 4.2).[27] The repetitive lyrics; focus on grace; and slow, prodding tempo all signify sounds associated with more intimate moments in modern Christian worship—a strong contrast with the "old Hebrew song" Samson's family sings earlier in the show. In musical language, both "Funeral Song" and "Adonai" make audible the generational differences between

Example 4.2: The opening bars of Manoah's "Funeral Song," sung by Esther. The tonic prolongation, repetitive phrasing, and lyrical style are all hallmarks of modern Christian praise and worship music. Music and lyrics by Paul D. Mills.

Manoah and Esther, between tradition and acceptance, between the past and the present. Actors onstage during this scene closed their eyes and extended their arms upward. Some audience members did the same. Clearly this performance rhymed with contemporary evangelical worship styles, and audiences picked up on cues that in this moment they were not watching a musical but instead participating in a praise and worship event.

Here, Esther becomes perhaps an even more relatable character as she seems to step directly outside the ancient Hebrew world and into the lives of modern American Christians. She is a complex but convenient character. Despite her reputation as a "normal person who questions things," Esther is a softball challenger to the Christian ideology: whatever she questions, she doesn't do it loudly. She moves through the show as a harmless, albeit anachronistic, voice of compassion against the foil of stodgier, letter-of-the-law characters culled from the Bible. And yet when she sings at Manoah's funeral, Esther's song *shows* more than it *tells*—that older, less tolerant ways are being buried with Manoah and newer, more relatable ones are already being born. By extending Esther's voice out of the imagined ancient funeral onstage and into the audience's world as an invitation to a modern praise and worship service, Sight & Sound Theatres makes it clear that the Bible has come alive, risen from the tomb of a dead and inaccessible past.

Conclusion

Thomas Merton wrote about theater's wish for happiness while he was living in rural Kentucky, not far at all from where the Creation Museum sits today. Merton was a longtime resident of the Abbey of Our Lady of Gethsemani. He knew the gifts of the Middle just the same as he knew about walls and their affordances. "Brother Matthew locked the gate behind me," he wrote of his entry into the abbey, "and I was enclosed in the four walls of my new freedom."[28] Held captive, and you are free.

I'm returning in my mind to the audiences gathered around the statue of Samson in Sight & Sound Theatres' lobby, held captive by a felled reality. It seemed important for them to document their presence, for the theatergoers to bring home material evidence that they witnessed something magical, ineffable, and that what they experienced felt real to them. Dean Sell spoke with me about "illumination" in theater—that when the stage lights come up on a set-piece, a shower of light catches the audience too. Immersed in light in such a way, audience members are invited to "extend themselves and become part of the character on stage." The Bible tells of awestruck characters who can't keep from witnessing God's love once they have been caught in the light of a divine presence. For Sight & Sound Theatres' audiences, this kind of theatrical experience illuminates their own witness to a reality and puts them in good company of ancient disciples who are eager to share unbelievable stories: I saw this thing—it happened—it made me wish you were happy.

This is the kind of magic Sight & Sound Theatres enables for its audiences, an ability to see and hear themselves in ancient stories even if that involves willing duplicity. *Samson* is a story about walls collapsing; he brings with their collapse the collapse of oppression and injustice. I suspect audiences experience something akin to what Thomas Merton felt—it "nearly tore me to pieces"—and are driven to pose under the statue of Samson's heroic act in order to embody the sensation of being amid one world collapsing and opening up space for a new one to come forth. It's all safe and contained, which is what makes it so fake but also so thrilling. Musicals step in and out of the streams of reality so effortlessly—they erect and distill walls between truth and fiction with such grace and finesse—that it is no wonder the genre has come to be so meaningful for Christians looking to build a world that looks different from our own. Theater can tear us to pieces.

Sight & Sound Theatres teaches that when we are bold enough to make big lies, to trust our unwielded imaginations, the old world crumbles away and a new one comes into sight. Whatever separates us from a new life is thin—a fence, a border. That thin line moves with the currents and tempers the past. Today's wall can be taken down tomorrow. We first have to be willing to believe it.

Walls will fall. We can be torn to pieces. And the wish for a world where we could be happy keeps us rebuilding with our lies again and again and again.

CHAPTER 5

Everything Old Is New Again

People often lie about their age. Call it denial, or maybe a playful swing at immortality. But by now, performing away the years has become an entrenched practice even in polite small talk. Performing small lies, even selfish ones as these may be, is not just something that happens on a stage, of course, but as Erving Goffman and a string of disciples have since shown, the essence of theatricality animates these everyday performances. I'm reminded of a moving exchange between an aging woman and a much younger admirer in Ray Bradbury's *Dandelion Wine*. "It is the privilege of old people to seem to know everything," she admits. "But it's an act and a mask, like every other act and mask. Between ourselves, we old ones wink at each other and smile, saying, How do you like *my* mask, *my* act, *my* certainty? Isn't life a play? Don't I play it well?"[1]

Theater is a convenient and possibly obvious space where people can renegotiate the claims that time has made on their lives. Costumes and stage lights, makeup and whimsy—these are all calculations to preserve some secrecy of the timeless. Theatrical worlds are out of time, out of place; they hold their lies sacred, their beliefs as science. In these spaces, age simply isn't accounted for, because time is largely held unaccountable and at a distance. Like wine cellars and cheese wheels, the stage *embalms* the living. It presents life as if it is to be lived only among the eternally young.

My choice of words here is intentional. The stage musical in America comes to take shape in the late nineteenth century as a container holding this and that—

strands of minstrelsy swirled into operetta, and the rhythm of vaudeville and ethnic theater syncopating the burlesque. Around the same time, the American Civil War necessitated a technology to preserve food traveling toward troops in the battlefield and bodies coming back out of it. Modes of preservation such as canning food, embalming the dead, and, soon after, recording sounds are all techniques developed in response to these crises of nature, as Jonathan Sterne has connected for us.[2]

The musical stage, born of this moment, may also be invested in this kind of preservation ethos, although much more conspicuously. Time and nature hold little sway in theater, the characters and circumstances pumped full of chemical preservatives that allow audiences to return again and again and thus carry home an enduring though disenchanted impression of eternal youth again and again. In her reading of the "time warp" in *The Rocky Horror Picture Show*, Sarah Taylor Ellis explains how this happens in musicals at the song level. "Musical numbers often warp time by speeding it up or slowing it down," she notes, "emphasizing repetition and circularity, dipping into memory, and projecting the future."[3] The future that musicals project might be a hazard: a Philip K. Dickian "time out of joint" nightmare drapes rather loosely over musical theater's fast-and-loose play on temporality.[4] Belief is central to this mode of temporal preservation, though not nearly as conspicuous as examples in the previous chapters have highlighted. To insist on a world where aging is irrelevant and even nonexistent is as much a process of theatrical imposture as that which fibs about the past in order to make the religious present more real. Inasmuch as I have argued in this book how musical theater often enables a shift from chaos to order and that the permission to imagine worlds that can and do change for the better may be enough to push us into a better world ourselves, I spend time here considering how much the musical stage erases in its rush toward resolution. Among those pressed into form onstage and moved to the margins of the real world are the aged and aging.

For three years I served as musical director and arranger for a musical revue known as the Oklahoma Senior Follies. The performers ranged in age from fifty-five to eighty-six. As part of the much larger Senior Follies movement, the Oklahoma Senior Follies makes a place on the musical stage for aging musical theater performers. During my time with the group, I experienced up close the remarkable local talent represented by the cast members and likewise witnessed the importance of having a platform to express one's voice in all stages of life.

Yet the ageist conditions that necessitate a theater like the Senior Follies call for a complicated response. Inasmuch as the Oklahoma Senior Follies attempts to reframe aging as positive, performers frequently resort to the same ageist stereotypes they hoped to frustrate. They lie onstage—they lie about lying. I see this complicated response to conventional narratives of aging arising from a conflict between the musical format of the Follies and constraints effected by the local theater industry. In this chapter I give explicit attention to how seniors have attempted to resist marginalization through performance and push themselves closer to center stage. This pushback invests a great deal of make-believe into a style of music that is already well saturated with unreality. In this way, lying can redirect narratives about aging in the real world by drawing attention to the musical as a process for embalming. Here, geography meets temporality. Performers in the Oklahoma Senior Follies demonstrate how you couldn't be more in the Middle and yet teeter so very close to the edge.

The Authority of Death

Stories are about the end of time, not the absence of time. They require an ending, whether that is captured in the story itself or rendered in the mind of its listener. The storyteller, as Walter Benjamin evocatively puts it, "has borrowed his authority from death."[5]

Musicals nonetheless operate mostly as if time holds little sway over the bodies and spirits of its characters. They tell stories of redemption or of overcoming seemingly impossible odds, and the genre's treatment of age seems, at least in notable cases, to fit within this narrative of suspending time's inevitable work. Stephen Sondheim's *Follies*, for instance, moralizes the theme of second chances and buoys an indefatigable refrain in Carlotta Campion's torch song "I'm Still Here." In the real world, fans allow space for doyennes like Elaine Stritch and Bea Arthur to work into old age under the allowances of divahood.[6] Until a few years ago, Ted Neeley continued to spellbind audiences as the title character in *Jesus Christ Superstar*—never mind that his aging body and voice betrayed any resemblance to the thirty-three-year-old biblical martyr.[7]

Yet these are exceptions that prove the rule. Despite the prominence of well-known and senescent characters like Mother Superior in *The Sound of Music* and Henry Higgins in *My Fair Lady*, most aging performers today find their careers curtailed. Musical theater performers have little room to evolve over the course of their careers because the industry favors the young; even lateral moves are limited. Particularly in popular dance musicals like *West Side Story*, *Guys and Dolls*, *Grease*, and *42nd Street*, where almost all performers have to dance at some point, lead characters must of necessity be around the same young age. And in the most demanding platforms, the grueling schedule of eight shows a week certainly makes a career on Broadway hazardous and largely unsuitable even for the most disciplined minds and bodies.

Musical theater's tendency to look past aging performers reflects mainstream societal values that also marginalize those growing older. Raymond Knapp has argued along these lines regarding other marginalized populations, writing that "commercial calculation, standards of believability, and the dynamics of assimilation" have all "reinforced the dominance of the mainstream in musicals."[8] This realization comes despite the genre's reputation for problematizing cultural and societal norms. Musical theater stands distinct as a sometimes progressive space where depictions of the elderly onstage nonetheless reaffirm stubborn mainstream sensibilities.

These beliefs affirm a particularly distorted image of aging. Like other forms of popular culture, the Broadway musical contributes to a presumed connection between aging and deterioration, what cultural critic Margaret Morganroth Gullette, in her book *Aged by Culture*, describes as the "master narrative of decline."[9] This decline narrative is apparent in musical theater's penchant for younger characters, exaggerated and unfair categorizations of senility or decrepitude, instances of older characters being portrayed by younger actors, and fewer meaningful roles onstage for the aging population.

Consider these few examples: In the musical *Grey Gardens*, the old woman and her daughter, both named Edith ("Big Edie" and "Little Edie"), are played by young actresses who alternate roles midway through the show. Madame Armfeldt, mother to Desiree in Sondheim's *A Little Night Music*, remains haughty and pitifully archaic in her wheelchair; she even falls asleep before she can finish singing her featured number, "Liaisons"—her choked voice perhaps musical theater's most damning signifier of social insignificance. In *Pippin*, Pippin's grandmother urges him to take advantage of life while he has the chance, "'cause spring will turn to fall in just no time at all."

In these and many other instances, decline is implied in musical theater as an absolute condition of aging. We know that seeing ourselves performed back to us plays significantly on our own self-perception, and this is no less true for aging audiences absorbing the narrative of decline.[10] Theater is an influential space for not just play-acting but for real-world imaginings too. As Augusto Boal puts it, "Theatre is born when the human being discovers that it can observe itself; when it discovers that, in this act of seeing, it can see itself—see itself in situ: see itself seeing."[11] If this is the case on the musical stage, where stage magic and convention resolve even the most implausible of dilemmas, then musical theater may be one of the cruelest spaces for the aging population to in effect "see themselves seeing."

Yet from that cruel feature of musical theater has surfaced a form of entertainment designed to make room for older audiences and performers. In 1988 the first production of what would be known as the Anderson Senior Follies took place in Anderson, South Carolina. Decades later this annual musical production continues to entertain audiences throughout the region, providing, in the words of director Annette Martin, "a shot in the arm" for the local aging communities.[12] The Senior Follies has since become a veritable movement, with productions opening and closing over the years in communities as diverse as Palm Springs, California; Dallas, Texas; Rockford, Illinois; and, more recently, Oklahoma City, Oklahoma. While each rendition of the Senior Follies is distinctly local, all feature aging performers who put on a musical variety show. The movement's reach is remarkable: From 1990 to 2014, the Fabulous Palm Springs Follies played for audiences totaling over four million. In 1997 the group was even the subject of a documentary appropriately titled *Still Kicking: The Fabulous Palm Springs Follies.*[13]

The Senior Follies cuts across the traditions of musical theater to create a vaudevillian escapade that uses farce and mockery to complicate this narrative of decline. Bobbie Burbridge Lane, founder of the Oklahoma Senior Follies, still understands the movement as making a statement about hope and individual worth. She described the Senior Follies as "a movement to make seniors' lives very valuable and not to be thrown away, to sit in a chair and watch TV, be depressed, be worthless"; it is "something to make it the best [period] of their life."[14] The purpose of the Senior Follies is not only to engage this "master narrative of decline" but also to repurpose the conventions of musical theater that for so long have coupled aging with disability or, more commonly, with *invisibility*. "You've got to feel like you still have value," said one Senior Follies cast member, "and that's what this does."[15]

Lying about Your Age

In *Staging Ageing: Theatre, Performance, and the Narrative of Decline,* Michael Mangan offers the following description of the master narrative of decline: "Broadly speaking, the master narrative of decline is that invisible but dominant cultural 'message' which encourages men and women to experience and articulate growing older essentially in terms of loss, isolation, and diminished physical mental and material resources."[16] The narrative permeates so deeply into popular culture that its presence often goes undetected.

Nonetheless, the negative effects of a decline narrative are becoming more apparent. According to one watch group, "In 2005, the number of people age 65 and older had risen to 12.7 percent of the American population," though "elders were represented in less than 2 percent of programs on prime-time television." "Nothing could convey the low status of elders in our society better than their invisibility," the study concludes.[17] Even in films that highlight life within the aging population, such as *The Best Exotic Marigold Hotel* and *Quartet*, the fresh look into elderly life disguises the means by which those depictions are made. "Of course, there's a lovely wrinkle implied in pop-culture examples of the elderly," writes Lisa Kennedy. "Although growing older themselves, the actors are gainfully employed, still doing what they presumably love. How enviable. In doing the work of acting they defy the very thing they may also be representing: decline."[18]

Recent scholarship attempts to turn this persistent and harmful narrative on its head by situating the decline narrative as a cultural assumption that bears little resemblance to the biological aging processes. Advocating what she terms "aging-in-culture," Gullette argues, "We are aged more by culture than by chromosomes."[19] She also acknowledges the pernicious staying power of the decline narrative, writing that it is "as hard to contain as dye. Once it has tinged our expectations of the future (sensations, rewards, status, power, voice) with peril, it tends to stain our experiences, our views of others, our explanatory systems, and then our retrospective judgments."[20] Although the decline narrative is often concealed, its presence in popular culture challenges normative aging processes and exaggerates aging to seem grossly debilitating. "At the level of ideology," adds Mangan, "our experience of aging is also determined by the ways in which our culture constructs the very concept of old age: by the kinds of spoken and unspoken assumptions and messages that circulate about what old age 'is', and, most importantly, by the ways in which we internalize such messages."[21] All of this together means that the social construction of age and the ideology surrounding the aging process make the prospect of aging *positively* all the more troublesome.

Gullette and Mangan both suggest the power of resistance that lies within the aging population. Speaking of the challenges inherent in a society that believes there to be an association between age and enfeeblement, Gullette writes, "There is a way out if one recognizes that decline is an ideology, learns more about its techniques, and invents resistances."[22] Mangan likewise points out that "resistance and transgressiveness are most easily and frequently associated with adolescence and young adulthood," which are life stages notably categorized by Victor Turner as occupying a liminal space relative to society.[23] Yet Mangan troubles these categorical norms, wondering how such liminality could also be "reappropriated for the in-between-ness"—the *Middle*-ness—"of old age."[24]

Empowering the aging requires a repertoire of resistance, and opportunities for enacting that resistance are manifest in various social performances. These performances often are built from a platform of ageism (instances of injustice erupting explicitly from conditions of aging). Varied attempts to reconcile these stereotypes are indicative of ageism's reach; in attempting to correct ageist mind-sets, often these performances of resistance likewise fail to escape ageist tendencies.

This is a potential hazard in almost every fight of marginalized populations. At a certain point, the necessary scaffolding erected to topple towers of injustice threatens to become a stronghold of ridicule itself. As with the well-known honorific "the greatest generation," popularized in the late 1990s by senior NBC newscaster Tom Brokaw, the Senior Follies movement has at times overreached ageism correction in promoting old age at the expense of those in other age brackets. It has proven difficult to validate the aging population without essentializing old age as superior to other life stages. In speaking about her Anderson Senior Follies, for example, director Annette Martin calls attention to the eminence of child-rearing practices of previous generations as contributing grit to the senior population: "The great part about working with seniors is they'll give everything a try. They're going to give it their best shot because they were raised that way. They were raised to not give any excuses—just do it." All Senior Follies productions also limit participants based on age, inviting only those fifty-five or older to join rank. Using the kind of dramatized rhetoric Martin employed above and discriminating participation based solely on age are obvious examples of ageism that, under other circumstances, might appear more pronounced and insidious. Efforts of the marginalized to regain voice can be messy affairs, and in this regard the Senior Follies is no exception.

Almost all of the performers I worked with had found their age a deterrent in getting cast in local productions and were happy to find a venue to perform in and an appreciative audience to entertain. Of the few who were still active performers onstage, the quality and type of parts available to them had dwindled to what many considered unmeaningful roles. The majority of the cast saw the Oklahoma Senior Follies as a playful opportunity to put positive aspects of growing older on display and, for some, a chance to reclaim the role of musical theater performer. However, this eagerness to put age on display, coupled with the slapstick format of the show that I describe below, often resulted in ageist stereotypes being aggressively displayed for laughs. The political message the Senior Follies intended for its audiences therefore had to be filtered through a revue format that promised laughs and spectacle but not necessarily serious contemplation.

The Oklahoma Senior Follies, as with the other Follies shows, is modeled after the famed *Follies* created by Florenz Ziegfeld Jr. Essentially a musical revue, the Ziegfeld *Follies* featured a variety of musical numbers, dance routines, and some of the most beautiful women to ever appear onstage, all exotically and erotically (un)dressed. Often plumed in flowing, sequined gowns and elaborate headdresses, these Ziegfeld Girls came to establish the showgirl as an American stage icon. Ziegfeld's productions were a lot of things—frivolous and seedy entertainment but also topical and sophisticated critiques of current events or figures—and, as Jonas Westover shows in his book *The Shuberts and Their Passing Shows: The Untold Tale of Ziegfeld's Rivals*, the revue format that was dominant at the time was a fiercely competitive enterprise that allowed a great deal of flexibility and innovation because of (and despite) its low mark in artistic ambition.[25] Choreography and musical numbers could change on a whim, and often did, in order to meet the last-minute demands of the production's exacting impresarios. The musical material needed to be as flexible and interchangeable as the delicate fabrics draped over the bodies on display.

The occasional, provocative, and jesting nature of the musical revue makes for a complex medium to display the vitality and presence of an aging population. On the one hand, the musical revue format celebrates frivolity and immediacy, which are easy to brush off. On the other hand, musical revues defy codification. Portions of the show can simply be transplanted or completely restructured from year to year, city to city, even show to show. For the Senior Follies, this loose-fitting format allows for local concerns and societal habits to infuse readily into an evening billed as harmless middlebrow entertainment. The very medium through which the decline narrative is combated on these stages allows for the message to carry beyond the auditorium. Still, audiences are expected to decipher the important message—if they even are searching for one—amid the codes of an entertainment format that inherently resists the solemn or austere.

The adaptation of the musical revue's sexual provocations is a case in point. Most, if not all, of the Senior Follies productions devote significant time to displaying aging Ziegfeld Girls—or "Beauties" as the Oklahoma Senior Follies called them—through an elaborate and spectacular pageant of aging women dressed in outlandish outfits. In the Oklahoma Senior Follies, the Beauties were a major selling point. All of the print and digital publicity art features a close-up image of a smiling, attractive woman bespangled in a huge feathered headdress and glittering gown. The colorful leotard is cut low in the back and high around the thigh. Beads, brocades, and mesh hosiery all signify the iconic showgirl of yesteryear. At first glance, one might never have guessed the model was a great-grandmother who had survived two husbands.

The tight-fitting clothes and heavy stage makeup are part of a calculated and witty plot twist in the standard story of growing old that nonetheless has an unclear message. Are audiences supposed to flatten these Beauties into sexual provocations, as they were meant in Ziegfeld's productions, or are the Beauties meant to be understood as cultural enactments that challenge objectifying stereotypes about beauty and old age? Implying elegance and beauty in old age is one thing, but the Ziegfeld context asks audiences to see these women as sex objects, sending mixed signals about where value in the maturing body ought to be placed.

The Senior Follies movement may attempt to disassociate aging from decline, but the musical and dramatic structure of the revue format forces performers to make claims about aging through slapstick comedy, often at their own expense. I remember one production in bad taste in which older tap dancers who were otherwise abled performed a routine in wheelchairs while wearing adult diapers. Another year, two local comedians danced a striptease-gone-wrong to a bossa nova–inspired rendition of "Tea for Two." As the routine went on and the paper cutouts that covered the women's tops and bottoms increasingly got smaller and flimsier, the audience was treated to a rather frank reveal, only to be relieved by a perfectly cued blackout at the end. In that same show, six men and women performed a version of "Friendship"—made popular in the 1962 revival of Cole Porter's *Anything Goes*—that included a refrain mimed without any teeth. Sprinklings of similarly spirited jokes about impotence, incontinence, and menopause broke up more sanguine moments about the condition of empty-nesting or longing sentiment for times past.

The revue format is largely why the Senior Follies has found momentum; it provides an effective platform in part because people don't expect to take it seriously. Annette Martin told me "the three Fs" that make up her litmus test for material in her shows: "Fast, Funny, Familiar—everything in the show must have at least one of these characteristics," adding that seniors are willing to be laughed at, whereas people in other generations "would just die."[26] It was clear from my experience with the Oklahoma Senior Follies that for most of the cast, getting laughs was a highlight of the entire show. After all, the Follies cast was only *pretending* to be decrepit. The performers were still able-bodied and socially active. Everyone knew they were simply donning a character type that brings attention to matters of interest to the aging population while getting easy laughs at the expense of those some sociologists have called the "old-old."

The performers' willingness to engage in often demeaning or self-defacing antics through the musical stage makes the Senior Follies as much a form of minstrelsy as a means for challenging ageist assumptions. This is perhaps a weakness of the revue model since the format encourages audiences to respond with laughter rather than contemplation, though this is precisely where the revue's theatrical predecessors held their power—Peter Mondelli, for example, suggests that the buffoonish quality of nineteenth-century operetta made European musical stages "an ideal medium for critique."[27] Still, the opportunity to take ownership of inevitable bodily deterioration or personal loss and spin it positively as just one aspect of an otherwise viable and potentially blissful phase of life likewise positions the Senior Follies as one of the few places where matters of aging become refocused as things that do indeed matter—where audiences can learn to recognize the decline narrative as a farcical, rather than purely essentializing, part of modern society.

This strategy mirrors the way in which recent approaches to disability favor acceptance over unrealistic overcoming narratives, recognizing that with acceptance can come the capacity to celebrate that acceptance, thereby creating a space where other possibilities can be imagined. In fact, it is helpful to see the work of the Senior Follies as contributing to a dialogue on disability. The decline narrative already suggests a certain framework of bodily and cognitive disability not lost on the Follies personnel (the stage director for the Oklahoma Senior Follies was legally blind, for instance).

But the case goes deeper than that. Various incarnations of ageism have pushed aging employees out of work (or, in the case of musical theater, off the stage, as will be discussed below) and stoked dystopic fears about a growing population of inept and dependent elders feeding off the efforts of younger, employed populations. Through systematic ousting from employment or exile to retirement centers and nursing homes, the aging have been removed from neoliberally defined "meaningful" positions, disabled from prioritized interactions, and withheld from conversations of value.

The Glory Days

A glance toward Oklahoma City's local theater scene shows how aging performers there came to be devalued in and displaced from the musical stage. Since 1963 Lyric Theatre of Oklahoma has been the state's "leading professional theatre" and a prized gem in Oklahoma City's crown.[28] The peculiar politics of the state and the simmering rivalry between the two largest cities—Oklahoma City and Tulsa—play out on even the slightest of battlefields, musical theater included. In the arena of professional theater, however, Oklahoma City hit its stride first. It would be another twenty years before Tulsa's Gilbert and Sullivan Society would come to form, an organization that would later evolve into

Light Opera of Oklahoma (LOOK) and, as of 2012, LOOK Musical Theatre. Lyric Theatre of Oklahoma aspires to "enrich the quality of life for the people of Oklahoma" and has even garnered some national accolades in its history. According to Lyric Theatre's website, in 2005 *USA Today* even named the theater one of the "10 great places to see the lights way off Broadway."[29]

Lyric Theatre has had to evolve along the way to meet such success. The two largest adaptations occurred within recent memory. The first was the 2002 move from the vintage, but dated, Kirkpatrick Theater on the uptown campus of Oklahoma City University to the newly restored Civic Center Music Hall near downtown. The Civic Center renovation was part of a larger capital improvement campaign known as MAPS (Metropolitan Area Projects), which, following the devastation of the bombing of the Alfred P. Murrah Federal Building in 1995, provided the necessary funds for the city to rebuild and rebrand itself. Moving Lyric Theatre's productions into the Civic Center was not just about showcasing a newer and bigger space. The Civic Center also became an emblem of Oklahoma City's cultural renaissance, a determination to move past its dusty stockyard image in the light of this unexpected national attention. Displaying talent on that stage every summer linked Oklahoma City's commitment to the arts with a commitment to its identity as a city coming into its own.

For its first three decades, Lyric Theatre functioned more or less as a professionalized community operation. "Lyric was a glorified community theater," one former cast member told me, "but professional in that we got paid. It was kind of like our summer camp."[30] Local performers cut their teeth on the Kirkpatrick stage. Leading roles in the summer musicals mostly went to local actors, and the ensemble was almost entirely made up of local college students. Like many regional theaters at the time, Lyric Theatre was not affiliated with any actor or stage manager unions and thereby kept expenses down. Its reputation as a non-Equity theater likewise made for an abundance of opportunities for local performers and audiences to connect without the mediation of mega-corporate sponsorship or prohibitively high ticket prices. As one Senior Follies cast member remembered, "We didn't have to have corporate sponsors. It was just done."[31]

This all changed in the mid-1990s when Lyric Theatre became an Equity theater and began "farming out all the principal roles" to members of Actors' Equity.[32] It takes a great deal of theatrical exposure and experience in the right kind of roles and in the right kind of theaters for an actor to get their Equity card; this is just one reason why most Equity members live not in the tree-lined suburbs of Oklahoma City but among the bustling boroughs of New York City. The effect, of course, is that fewer roles are now available for those once-active

Oklahoma City performers. Instead, audiences have become trained to recognize great talent by its accompanying New York pedigree. Out-of-town performers book three-to-four-week gigs with small companies like Lyric Theatre before moving on to the next opportunity. This puts pressure on local theaters to bring in experienced stage directors, musical directors, set designers, lighting designers, sound designers, and choreographers from New York and other large urban theatrical centers to further entice Broadway talent to come to these smaller communities. Costs go up. It is still customary to stock the ensemble with local college or high school students who are willing to work for cheap, but in almost every other way regional theaters like Lyric Theatre have adapted their way out of local theater and instead have become the primary mediator between Broadway talent and regional audiences.[33]

Theatrical spaces have long been a site of negotiations among classes, races, and politicized bodies, as Lawrence Levine convincingly argued in his often-consulted book *Highbrow/Lowbrow*.[34] Significantly, these negotiations were handled by a mixture of both lay and professional actors. Pageantry, perhaps the most pronounced and prominent of these local theatrical traditions, offered locals the opportunity to enact the history of their particular place and people—to help "explain the city to itself," as David Glassberg put it—even though those dramatizations were organized and directed by professional pageant masters from New York or Boston.[35] Particularly in the years between the American Civil War and World War I, pageantry and other community theater traditions provided Americans a dramatic platform for issues of local importance; even productions by professional touring troupes were subject to regional fluctuations in ideologies or political commitments. In her book *Local Acts*, Jan Cohen-Cruz fleshes out the rich and complex history of nonprofessional theater in the United States: "The basic unit of [community-based performances] is the people who contribute to it through their stories or their co-creation as performers, people who are intimately connected to the theme of a given production via lived experience, which is facilitated but not replaced by professionals. Community-based performance will always offer a first-voice account of a situation that most professional art does not."[36] Thus, the interplay between professional and amateur performers has traditionally been in the service of local needs. Community theater provided a means of giving voice both to performers seeking validation through the stage and to the audience that came to the theater seeking assurance that there was a place where their lives and treasured ideals still held value.

The actuality of regional musical theater today, however, does not always resemble that ideal. Large tax-funded spaces like Oklahoma City's Civic Center provide a place for the community to gather, yes, but they also favor large productions of homogenized or generic road shows and national tours. Smaller, local productions can hardly compete with these larger attractions with larger budgets. By moving to the much larger facility, Lyric Theatre of Oklahoma created a financial scenario that pushed out local performers with the expectation that such a policy would entice more bodies to fill the increase in seats. In doing so, the company has become subject to the whims of corporate giving. Courting corporate sponsors, not consummate artistic ability, has become the necessary skill and a primary job of these theaters' artistic staff.

For the Senior Follies cast members I worked with, this kind of change came at a high cost. Privileging Equity holders silenced the voices of not only local but also aging performers. As one performer sadly recounted, "Between 1972 and 1992 I did twenty-five roles—mostly leading roles—at Lyric Theatre. Then all of the sudden they didn't need me anymore. Lyric was like a family and now it's all very impersonal."[37] Even though many of the Oklahoma Senior Follies cast were not yet "seniors" when Lyric Theatre began casting younger Equity actors, the act of estrangement "aged" the performers out of business and thereby removed an important means by which local performers communicated local matters to local audiences. Unfortunately, Gullette's words find easy application here: "At no age would anyone be able to say, of being aged by culture, 'Not my issue.' Of no identity could anyone say a priori, 'Aging-in-culture has nothing to do with this.'"[38]

In no small way, the voice of locality and of the aging in Oklahoma City lost the means by which it could be valued in the wake of Lyric Theatre's restructuring. The consequences for this loss of voice are significant. The impulse for narrating and voicing one's life issues and perspectives is so embedded in human experience, as sociologist Nick Couldry has articulated, that "to deny value to another's capacity for narrative—to deny her potential for voice—is to deny a basic dimension of human life."[39] To lose one's voice is to become not only inaudible but also invisible. I was reminded of the former invisibility of my cast members each night during the show. As conductor, I was made privy to intermission banter among audience members sitting near the orchestra pit, who regularly made a comment along the lines of "I didn't realize there were that many really talented old people in our community"—as if glimpsing aging bodies onstage made it suddenly clear how little their absence until then was felt.

I have already suggested how musical theater makes little room at the table for aging performers. Combined with the loss of local performing outlets, those aging performers who depended on the musical stage for supplemental income, camaraderie, and opportunities for self-expression found themselves doubly unvoiced.

This is the atmosphere out of which the Senior Follies emerged. "For ten years I didn't perform at all," said one cast member. "[Senior] Follies came along at a really good time for me because there weren't roles for people like me."[40] The Oklahoma Senior Follies took a chance on the aging performer population—"people like me"—the way few had been willing or able to do. Those who had worked in Lyric Theatre's "glory days" were reunited onstage, and audiences who adored them once came out in droves to hear and cheer them again. Even the choice of venue—Oklahoma City University's beloved Kirkpatrick Theater—seemed designed to redeem older, forgotten qualities of musical theater culture in Oklahoma City: "It was like going home."

Through the Senior Follies time stood still, reversed its course, and Peter Allen's lyric was made magically real: everything old *was* being made new again.

Mashup

The Oklahoma Senior Follies was in its third year when I began as musical director. While the Ziegfeld model complicated an easy response to what exactly the aging performers onstage were attempting, the musical structure and arrangements made the point clearer. The basic ingredients for the Follies were straightforward: there had to be the right mix of dance numbers, featured soloists, and group songs. Cheeky skits and one-liners were easy to fit in wherever and whenever we needed them. Since the show is built anew each year to meet the needs of changing personnel (in this kind of theater, death is the most dependable of all considerations) and to keep the show fresh and buoyant, the creative team had a difficult task of building cohesion into the otherwise scattershot revue format. Particularly in the farcical context of the Ziegfeld structure, the challenge was to select stylistically appropriate music that also reinforced the implicit message that aging ought to be celebrated rather than feared, ridiculed, or bemoaned.

The solution to that challenge was to make explicit the piecing together of unlike songs and genres through a system of mashups. Mashups became a sonic emblem of what Claude Lévi-Strauss called "bricolage," helping frame the Oklahoma Senior Follies as a space where old means are reused to achieve new ends.[41] Our use of mashups made the Oklahoma Senior Follies a bit like the inverse of the television series *Glee*, where youth is celebrated and the sexual tension of adolescence is underscored with a musical theater–inspired sound track. In *Glee* musical theater songs that would normally be prescribed by body type, gender, or race are disassociated from their original context and "mashed" together with pop songs to create a unique narrative device for the show. One pluvial episode, for example, featured a clever overlaying, or "mashup," of Arthur Freed and Nacio Herb Brown's iconic song "Singin' in the Rain" with Rhianna's "Umbrella." The result is nothing like Gene Kelly or Rhianna but instead a new creation of its own fashion.

The same possibilities arose in the Senior Follies. We frequently found opportunities to mash together unrelated songs from disparate genres or time periods—finding commonality among them sometimes only in a single phrase—and create something original. The musical mashup consequently served as an emblem of the aging population's metamorphosis into something neither old nor young but completely new, bold, and wildly interesting.

The world-making potential of the mashup also expands into the religious. Although this wasn't made explicit in the Oklahoma Senior Follies and certainly remains unstated in *Glee*, tucked behind the impulse of mashup is a particular form of piety. Theology has responded to this fractured postmodern age by embracing the rhetoric of what I'll call a *combinatory culture*—the press toward reconciling and arranging the world's many, many things. John McClure even goes so far as to say that "lived religion resembles a mashup."[42] He implores theologians to engage the concept of the mashup as a means for accomplishing "theological invention." In other words, he sees the mashup as a helpful model for rethinking and practicing a relevant theology that celebrates, rather than demonizes, the modern penchant for plurality.

Framing the mashup in religious terms elevates popular culture to the role of priestly intermediary, and McClure's conceptions provide a useful framework for reconsidering the power of popular culture:

> Instead of language and culture becoming more and more atomized and fragmented . . . theologians find themselves in a mashup situation in which they stand the great opportunity of beginning to treat language and culture as more contingent, fluid, malleable *things* alongside them in the world, things that can be stylistically morphed in the communication of theological meaning and truth. This, in itself, constitutes a certain exiting of tradition, language, and culture—paradoxically at precisely the moment in which ideas of tradition, language, and culture have become the most popular, powerful, and divisive terms in our midst.[43]

McClure identifies theological invention as grounded in text but simultaneously outside the confines of the linguistic. Similarly, we may begin to understand the mashup as an expression of this linguistic paradox. As the example from *Glee* illustrates, the mashup is built around an original text—organized around and in fact in existence because of the text—but it also signals a new way of thinking outside the bounds of language. Mashups point to a world where the purposeful conflation of language aggrandizes it precisely at its moment of confounding. Curiously, the mashup functions like a religious text, though it isn't a text at all. It is an *anti*-text—part of a larger combinatory worldview that eradicates singularity in favor of purposeful juxtaposition, all the while framed by a musical structure designed solely to gloss discrepancies between musical syntaxes of each piece.

The mashup becomes an implicit argument against fundamentalism, which is a betrayal of the lived and multifarious expression of the past (see chapter 3). Like Bakhtin's dialogism, the mashup affirms the everyday promise of complexity by finding unity among competing discourses. Andrew Robinson's exegesis of dialogism helps position the mashup within a broader dialogue of competing voices and unity in popular culture: "Because many standpoints exist, truth requires many incommensurable voices. Hence, it involves a world which is fundamentally irreducible to unity. There is no single meaning to be found in the world, but a vast multitude of contested meanings. Truth is established by addressivity, engagement and commitment in a particular context."[44]

A plentitude of voices disguises the sublime in an effort to reach it. Paradoxically, this rumbling murmur clogs the auditory channels of modern society, making silence or reflection a discomfiting rarity. I once overheard a Unitarian Universalist put it this way: "I don't need a reason to speak. I need a reason *not* to speak." That sentiment reminded me of the political foray into mass media during the first decades of the twentieth century. As Republicans and Democrats threw more and more money into radio airtime featuring orations from presidential hopefuls, in 1952 Democratic presidential nominee Adlai Stevenson took out a newspaper editorial suggesting someone buy a half hour of silence after the debates so that listeners could ponder and meditate on what they had just heard.[45] For Stevenson, even then the power to switch off the radio, to silence the voices for a respite from information, felt out of his hands. The desire for authority to sanction silence—to give a reason not to speak—lies at the heart of the modern predicament.

Thus the impulse behind combinatory culture is one of conflicting desires. On the one hand, a mashup reveals a desire to discover meaning amid seemingly random or unconnected concepts. On the other hand, a mashup injects yet another voice into the welcoming abyss of air and radio waves. It admits the loquacity of God yet seeks to hush the noise by speaking over the babbling crowd.

What we have then is a modern-day Babel, a clamoring for clarity and reason when so many competing voices speak past one another. The mashup seems a pious attempt to reengage with humanity. Reflecting the pluralistic penchant of contemporary society, the mashup takes disparate ideas, bits and pieces of the found world, and suggests an individualized yet comprehensive plan behind the chaos—perhaps even an intelligent ordering unheard by and invisible to mortals. This is why the structure of *Glee*'s mashups is significant and why the form resonated with the goals of the Oklahoma Senior Follies. By allowing each song to resonate on its own before working mashup magic, the show's creators make deliberate the found quality of each piece. The implication seems to be that these songs were found lying around in a heap of other detritus and, almost miraculously, they work together. In the process of combination, they create something new, something beyond language yet rooted in it, something, perhaps, that helps to make sense of the maddening effluence of voices and eases the anxieties inherent in a life framed by compulsory freedom.

To Make New

Although they functioned as a metaphor for malleability and value, mashups were used selectively in the Oklahoma Senior Follies, making room for conventional, stand-alone songs to be played against onstage high jinks. And, as with most revues, the music was sourced from a variety of styles and periods that bowed to the genteel tastes of our cast and audience. Musical theater standards were common but used inventively. Gershwin's "Let's Call the Whole Thing Off" was once reimagined as the sound track accompanying an awkward first date of an old-acting-young couple. One year there were three men with particularly resonant, classically trained voices who sang an arrangement of Leonard Bernstein's sailor crooner "Lonely Town" from the musical *On the Town* that reportedly held the ladies in the audience in rapture. Patriotic and religious songs likewise kept these Bible Belt theatergoers entranced. And in the state of Oklahoma, no other piece of music holds more religious fervency than the state's official song, Rodgers and Hammerstein's title number from *Oklahoma!* When Oklahomans of a certain age hear that ascending bass line introduction, they jump to their feet, the women wave handkerchiefs high in the air, and the room bellows with state pride. The tune is broadcast every weekday at 5:00 p.m. on local radio stations, the University of Oklahoma's Pride of Oklahoma Marching Band interpolating—mashing up—the school's "Boomer Sooner" anthem into the fabric of the song (see example 5.1)—a telling musical signifier of age, actually, in this era of "boomer" dismissiveness by the young and politically

Example 5.1: The final bars of "Oklahoma" with "Boomer Sooner" interpolation, as played by the University of Oklahoma Pride of Oklahoma Marching Band. "Oklahoma," music by Richard Rodgers. "Boomer Sooner," lyrics by Arthur M. Alden, music taken from Yale University's "Boola Boola" and attributed to Allan M. Hirsch. Courtesy of Brian Britt.

vibrant. Everyone at the Senior Follies knows the song by heart, and we ended every show just like that.

One year we mashed together the song "Tiny Bubbles" with Lerner and Loewe's "The Night They Invented Champagne" from *Gigi*. With a nod toward Hawaiian performer Don Ho's original version, "Tiny Bubbles" was performed as a solo accompanied by ukulele, soft-shoe dancing, and a bubble machine—all reinforcing the connection between "tiny bubbles in the wine" and the sparkling froth of champagne. Aside from the more obvious textual connection the two songs share, the mashup was crafted to make a clever statement regarding aging stereotypes. The film-turned-musical *Gigi* is mostly known for the humorous song "I Remember It Well," which entails an older couple reminiscing about their early courtship, yet neither one can quite remember well enough to get the facts straightened out. Instead, we chose "The Night They Invented Champagne" as a companion to "Tiny Bubbles" in order to frustrate that assumption of decline and pump more bubbly energy into the beginning of the show.

A more poignant moment later in the evening was a mashup of "It Was a Very Good Year," famous for Frank Sinatra's 1965 melancholic performance, with "Let the Sunshine In" from the musical *Hair*.[46] The combination of the two seemed opportune. "Let the Sunshine In" is already known as a mashup of sorts. Its attachment to the song "Aquarius" from *Hair*, by the 5th Dimension, made it to the top of Billboard's listing of pop singles in 1969 and has led more than a few listeners to hear "Let the Sunshine In" as the ending to the preceding song rather than a separate number altogether. Likewise, the song's six bars of interminable oscillation between major and minor conjures feelings of melancholy or bittersweet, its resisting of easy modal description a comfortable likeness to the Senior Follies penchant for defying convention, for easing into the Middle. I restructured the Sinatra-associated tune to allow time for several of the more prominent cast members to sing their respective ages and harmonized it to better fit the upbeat sixties groove. "It Was a Very Good Year" originally makes a case for happiness at the ages of seventeen, twenty-one, and thirty-five. Our cast sang a canon of more mature age admissions during the mashup, starting with "when I was seventeen, twenty-one, thirty-five" and so on, and ending with a resounding and applauded "eighty-six"—the age of our oldest cast member.

Finally, we slightly tweaked the last verse to better fit the ideology of the Senior Follies. Originally, Sinatra croons about the shortened days of old age—"the autumn of my years"—and looks backward as vindication of a life well lived, singing that, *back then*, "it was a very good year." In our version, the cast pulled out miniature glow sticks, identical to those distributed to the audience upon admission, and pronounced "it *is* a very good year." The singers overlaid the final bars of the first tune with hums to a slow groove of "Let the Sunshine In." The lights in the house dimmed to almost nothing. Hands clutching neon sticks slowly waved back and forth as the tune got louder and then faster, ceasing only upon the interruption of that familiar ascending bass line that got everyone not already standing to their feet in a hurry.

You're doing fine, Oklahoma.

The Oklahoma audience sang their beloved state song for the thousandth time but now with plastic glow sticks jostling together with handkerchiefs in the air just above their bodies—traces of their proud belonging making lazy circles in the sky.

Take Me Back

While rehearsing one Sunday afternoon, a cast member jumped out of his seat, scooted me off the piano, and searched with his long fingers for the chords to an old song. As he played and sang the lyrics to "Take Me Back to Oklahoma City," eyes lit up around the room and bodies pressed closer. It was clear this was a tune with a history for many of these performers. First introduced in 1967 at the Petroleum Club of Oklahoma City—a place billed as "the club above all clubs"—the song held a great attraction to the locals. It was penned by an Oklahoman, first of all—the one condition that only somewhat deflates the glory of Rodgers and Hammerstein's beloved song. Second, many of the performers in the cast were present when it premiered. The Senior Follies cast immediately began making room in the lineup for the newly resurrected song, and "Take Me Back to Oklahoma City" became that show's anthem for a time and place that no longer existed but everyone loved to remember well.

Oklahoma City's tenuous political and economic history illuminates why "Take Me Back to Oklahoma City" was so significant to these performers. On April 22, 1889, land unassigned to any tribe in the center of Indian Territory went from unpopulated to a city of ten thousand literally overnight, in the first of what would eventually be seven land runs. In 1928 oil was discovered beneath Oklahoma City, beginning a relationship with petroleum companies that has determined the ups and downs of the city over the years. Prosperous periods meant the construction of stately mansions and a growing downtown sector. However, by the time "Take Me Back to Oklahoma City" was first performed, in 1967, oil prices had plummeted and the city was in a long period of decline. City officials hired Chinese architect I. M. Pei to restructure the city's layout, hedging bets that the redevelopment would anchor downtown as a desirable place to both live and work despite the mass migration of white and middle-class families to the growing suburbs.

The decision seemed well reasoned—any major city that just appears overnight is bound to have infrastructural issues. Known as the "Pei Plan," the initiative called for the demolition of hundreds of old buildings to make room for more parking structures, office space, and retail development. To become a modern city, Oklahoma City was asked to prune its edges, to make everything old new again. The timing and implementation of Pei's vision proved disastrous, however. The pool of money dried up before the proposed new structures could be built, leaving large patches of vacant lots scattered over Oklahoma City's landscape. The city looked worse than it did before the redevelopment, and Oklahoma City spent the next several decades in economic stagnation, a shell of its onetime glory.

Example 5.2: "Take Me Back to Oklahoma City," words and music by John Curry.

It seems clear why "Take Me Back to Oklahoma City" emerged out of this ruinous situation—like any good theatrical number, the song lies. The song clings to the kind of sentimentality that helps gloss over the present reality and focus on a hopeful version of the past. For the Senior Follies production, the cast rewrote the lyrics to capture the changes in Oklahoma City's character since 1967. A lot had happened in those intervening decades. Horizontal drilling (also known as fracking) within previously unattainable or passed-over deposits of natural gas brought an enormous influx of interest and money to Oklahoma City's natural gas companies and thereby to the city itself. The city's MAPS program, responsible for the Civic Center's facelift, also began to dress up downtown Oklahoma City as a place worth living. Amenities like a new NBA team, unique Olympic water training facilities, and a low cost of living have made the city one of the hottest places for entrepreneurs to set up shop.

The Senior Follies cast members lived through all these periods of Oklahoma City's development, and the reuse of the song seemed apropos for a city and a group of its people in the midst of reinvention. The song opens with an admission of far-flung travels:

I have seen the lights
Of old Manhattan nights
I have been alone and blue.
San Francisco's fame
Adds attraction to her name;
I have seen that lovely view.

This opening establishes validity for the speaker's opinion, of course. To have gone to New York City and yet remained faithful in one's heart to Oklahoma City is the kind of valor people in this region adore. Even more, though, this opening verse positions the local performers favorably in an otherwise merciless preference for New York performers that the local Lyric Theatre had maintained for so many years. In the context of the Senior Follies, these performers suggest a scenario in which New York City does not match up to the opportunities of Middle America.

At the refrain, the thrust of the song becomes apparent: loneliness is the prime condition of life in the big city, while friendly community keeps Oklahoma City close to the heart.

> Take me back to Oklahoma City
> Where I'll see again
> All the folks in Oklahoma City,
> That's where they knew me when.

The song continues for a few more verses, but I show this much to illustrate how and why the number became so emblematic for the Oklahoma Senior Follies. "Take Me Back to Oklahoma City" remains a viable anthem for these local performers because, like the city finally experiencing the renaissance it planned long ago, the Senior Follies performers enact through their singing their own form of determination and resiliency.

This performance of "Take Me Back to Oklahoma City" put a fine point on the seniors' resistance of conventional notions of aging and decline. The sentimental song—written when Oklahoma City was in a downturn but about the time when it wasn't—was refashioned in the Senior Follies to celebrate not just a fading memory of the city's past but the actuality of a bright future as well. The cast rediscovered in the Senior Follies the promise of a voice formerly denied them. The very resonance of their aging voices suggests that the future is not written in stone but lies in wait for those willing to believe there is something of value still left in it for them.

Conclusion

To return to Walter Benjamin once more, the storyteller trades in time. We are at a deficit to time, Benjamin writes: "Less and less frequently do we encounter people with the ability to tell a tale properly. More and more often there is embarrassment all around when the wish to hear a story is expressed. It is as if something that seemed inalienable to us, the securest among our possessions, were taken from us: the ability to exchange experiences."[47] Information, which Benjamin lays bare as the virus killing modern storytelling, "does not survive the moment in which it was new. It lives only at that moment; it has to surrender to it completely and explain itself to it without losing any time."[48] Information arrives preserved like a can of vegetables, its nutritional value already depleted. We have to consume more and more of it in order to feel satiated—it gives the illusion of value while offering actually very little in substance.

A story, on the other hand, is released slowly, burning brighter as it ages. Stories are organic in this way, going in and out of the earth like humus feeding the living through the richness of all that came before.

The theater aspires to be a space where illusion can be tempered by what is real, to become, in Jill Dolan's words, "utopian performatives" that "make palpable an affective vision of how the world might be better."[49] That promise must be effectively measured to all kinds of people, however, and not just the lovely and the young. The thing about utopias, in fact, is that they are not real and so they easily slip into presenting the real world in less realistic ways. If the utopia of a musical stage—or any kind of stage, for that matter—is to be pure fantasy and holds no limits on what can be imagined, then musical theater has traded the real deal for a malnourished one. For if it can't be imagined on a stage, how can it possibly be enacted in our own world?

Although the Oklahoma Senior Follies was about challenging the narrative of decline, the effect is more about a renewal of community than a political statement. This renewal happened on two levels: not only did the Senior Follies mash up a group of aging and displaced performers, but it also reinvigorated a belief in true community theater in Oklahoma City. Other Senior Follies groups likewise sense the performances themselves as a statement about community. "It can never be about one person or one talent," says Annette Martin. "It has to be about a community of talent. It has to be a lot of people doing a lot of different things and become basically a microcosm of what the world needs to be."[50] Idealistic sentiment is not out of place here. The Senior Follies confirms that the aged and aging *can* have a place on the musical theater stage, that local talent needs a voice of value, and that audiences who "knew them when" need to feel they can know them again, and likewise.

For the Oklahoma Senior Follies, this idyllic spirit of community succeeds in part because of the particular conditions the local theater culture has constructed. The restructuring of Lyric Theatre of Oklahoma into an Equity house served as a watershed in the history of Oklahoma City musical theater. For those local performers who worked with Lyric Theatre prior to its restructuring, the Senior Follies has been a means of reuniting old friends and providing a musical-theatrical space where aging is performed as an asset rather than a liability. If the Senior Follies continues and eventually becomes populated by performers who have never experienced the non-Equity days of Lyric Theatre, that sense of community may lessen or at least be changed. For now, though, the Oklahoma Senior Follies is succeeding as both a remedy to an industry that is unresponsive to the conditions of aging performers and as a framework on which local performers have been able to reclaim their voice and, in certain ways, their identity.

Even more, the impermanence that this style of theater upholds—that people change, that what and which kind of people a community values can change—points to the very spaces this community inhabits. If musical theater holds as firm to a static and unchanging Middle America as it does to a singular and youthful version of life, then the Oklahoma Senior Follies disrupts on both fronts. The middle of the country "is geared to permanence," Richard C. Longworth writes, though demographic and industrial shifts due to globalization wobble the Middle's presumed stability. To be fair, Longworth adds, "It isn't handling this transformation very well."[51]

The Oklahoma Senior Follies therefore has found a way for aging performers to redeem value in the marketplace of worth both in musical theater and in a region undergoing remarkable change, a strategy that problematizes the conveniently drawn line between productivity and old age, between biological fate and cultural determinism, and between fact and fantasy. By putting the needs and lives of the aging center stage, these performances demonstrate the make-believe of aging and the graceful way some have chosen to amplify the power of local voices.

Aging bodies and voices may still look in vain for validation today, but the rise of the Senior Follies in the Middle suggests that an entirely new way of being can be possible and that it starts by big imaginings, big stories, and larger-than-life lies. It takes this kind of deception—it can only work with this kind of deception—to truly make everything old seem new again.

Mezza Voce

The voice is at the center of musical theater. Musicals employ the voice to demonstrate belonging, convey emotion, and establish the worlds of fantasy that are so readily associable with the stage. People knowingly approve of this kind of vocal theatricality precisely because it so clearly defines musicals. Raymond Knapp writes that even the first notes of underscoring, a hint at the impending singing, are "like a set of arched eyebrows serving as quotation marks around whatever is ostensibly being expressed, whether musically or dramatically."[1] These sonic eyebrows rise even in the most inane of situations, yet nothing seems lost in the dramatic message. The opening bass line of "Summer Nights" clearly situates *Grease* as a musical, for example, but makes defiant working-class teen Danny Zuko no less of a tough guy for vocalizing over that bass, no mere singing dandy.

To the contrary, musicals use voice to legitimize belonging. Zuko's gang of T-Birds (originally known as the slightly less brawny Burger Palace Boys) is made palpable and even believable precisely because it takes part in the musical's song-and-dance routines. Members of their rival gang, the Flaming Dukes, on the other hand, aren't given a voice in the musical. They don't—or even more provocatively, *can't*—sing, which reinforces for audiences whose story this really is. Andrea Most points to a similar scenario in the musical *West Side Story*. The Jets are the dancing and singing gang; the Sharks either lack the ability or aren't afforded much of an opportunity. Under musical theater's conventions, the Jets become "privileged" in that, unlike their rivals, they "are a group of well-developed characters with songs, dances, and psychological motivations for their actions. Both groups are eager to tussle over complex issues, but the structure of the musical ensures that the audience's sympathy lies with the Jets."[2] Another way to put it is that singing or not singing makes it clear to the audience which characters are authentic, or believable, and which are not. Even (and perhaps especially) in depictions of working-class life, musicals create a space where theatricality and self-consciousness are prized for their own sake. Voice allows the musical to lie because it lies in the Middle.

This centered quality of the voice belies its complex significance, both in musicals and elsewhere. Being in the Middle is a form of resistance, a pushback against classification. The voice speaks to so many possibilities, and many presumptions of value come attached to the sounds people make—and even the sounds people *don't* make. People who love musicals love the feeling of singing strongly and of watching people—particularly women—sing with power. As I show later, research has even suggested that audiences, performers, and teachers alike believe that such robust singing is one of the most honest sounds a woman can make.

When women belt in this way, audiences respond in kind with cheers. No matter the context, no matter the words uttered or where they fall in the musical phrase, ovations pierce the belt as if skewering the truth before it slips away into the wild. It's a condition of the musical that the sound of a woman belting has come to represent the sound of truth. Friedrich Kittler, for one, was wary of the way women characters in popular culture took so easily to metaphors of empowerment, associating their staged personas even with machinery and mechanics. "Women who have been subjected to phonographs and typewriters are souls no longer," he writes, adding, "they can only end up in musicals."[3] (Machines and musical theater voices are not wholly incompatible ways of thinking, as I explain later.)

This line of thinking resonates with broader observations about sound and partisan echo chambers today—that listeners predictably are eager to celebrate the sounds they have been conditioned to hear as true while, conversely, hearing all other sounds with suspicion. The #MeToo and #BelieveSurvivors campaigns express the dangers of such a pernicious listening habit, asking pointed questions of our selective deafness to victims of sexual assault:

- Under what conditions can what a victim says be heard and believed?
- Would listeners accustomed to hear truth only in terms of muscle be completely unable to detect sounds that come softly?

- In what ways does the perception of *how truth sounds* discipline our ears to perceive those sounds as truth?

The world of musical theater is more understanding than that of political theater. Women in musicals belt and are heard. And when she is heard, more often than not she is believed. Cheered not jeered, her shouted truth resonates with listeners who have been primed to hear her sound and believe it. For those who have witnessed what I'm describing, those sounds can come like a religious conversion, an acceptance of one sonic narrative over almost all others.

Musicals may represent (to some) a better version of our world, but in themselves they are fake, notoriously unreal in their song-and-dance routines. Women who aren't playing a role onstage shout into a void. They are mocked for even mouthing the words. In the fake world of musicals, the sound of the belt predicts honesty. By now we know that in this world, the sound of a woman speaking—of her body, her issues, her assault—elicits disbelief or angry shouts intent on silencing her. The real world has no blunt tool like a belt to frame when and how women can be heard and trusted. Here, women grow mute. Society grows deaf. Rape culture is real. Musicals are not.

A character in a fake world sings with strength only because a woman in the real world learns how and decides she likes the feeling of being heard and trusted. Yet giving voice to her truth is only half of the equation. Performers on-stage make sounds believable because listeners in the audience have come to the theater prepared to believe. The ultimate conviction of such moments relies not just on the sounds the woman *makes* but also on the way the listener *hears*. Anne Carson notes, "It is in large part according to the sounds people make that we judge them sane or insane, male or female, good, evil, trustworthy, depressive, marriageable, moribund, likely or unlikely to make war on us, little better than animals, inspired by God."[4] If Carson is correct that the voice is central to our perceptions about character and identity—that, following scholars like Nina Eidsheim and Roshanak Kheshti, the listener "authors" the sounds we hear from others—then voice is also caught in the middle of our misunderstandings, our mishearings, and our injustice.[5] "Voices exist most characteristically in the interstices of encounters," adds Martha Feldman in her Lacanian reading of the vocal break, "the spaces of transition, the space in between: between voice users and voice listeners, or 'voice apprehenders,' imaginary and real."[6]

He who hath ears, let him hear.

This chapter cross-examines the centeredness of voice in demarcating the imaginary from the real. The voice here functions as something in-between, what I theorize as a *mezza voce*—a voice in the Middle. Because the voice earns such high marks within musical theater, I turn to the source of that vocal economy to better understand the work voice does. I investigate how differing pressures on the musical theater industry can manifest as vocal sameness and explore how collegiate and professional training programs in Middle America have manifested these needs through their training of the voice. Vocal training in such programs ensures a sonic conformity—a middle-ness—that presumably improves the marketability of the performer in an industry demanding predictable sounds, but it may also help imagine a more just political future. Furthermore, the growth of the Broadway musical as a tourist attraction, the homogeneity of Times Square, the rise of the so-called megamusical, and the formation of this voice are all interrelated phenomena, enabled by a new corporatizing ideology in musical theater that has disciplined the body of the Broadway performer for decades and continues to shape the industry's sound elsewhere.

This practice of deception can be useful in theaters of far more significance. In musicals the voice traffics the real world into the imagined one. We must better understand the voice, then, for its deceptive power, its concentrated potential for mobilizing new worlds of our own making.

Branded Sounds

"Without much fanfare," boasts the *New York Post*, "Broadway has become an economic cornerstone of New York City, as big a tourist magnet as the Empire State Building and Katz's Deli."[7]

In conjunction with the revitalization of Times Square during the 1980s and '90s, the Broadway musical during this period became a commodified and heavily mediated tourist experience. Mega-corporations like Disney, Warner Bros., and Viacom International were interested in buying real estate as "a marketing opportunity made possible by a Times Square address," as Lynne B. Sagalyn has documented in *Times Square Roulette*. "The place," she notes, "was a branded address."[8]

The branding potential of a Times Square address soon rebranded Times Square itself as the family-friendly corner of New York with something for everyone. One of the leading architects of the revitalization project put it like this: "Everybody in New York thought it was . . . so we said it was the center of the world, but was it really? Well, it really is . . . at least for a New York tourist."[9]

Along with the revitalization of Times Square and the repurposing of Broadway as a dependable tourist industry, the vocal sound of Broadway musicals has also been redesigned. The voices behind musical theater have narrowed over the decades into a singular, focused sound—a vocal ideal and process that I call the *Broadway voice*. Broadway performers today are experiencing certain vocal pressures that have influenced the sonic development of the Broadway musical. These pressures—including the increasing use of belting, stylized (some say overdone) diction, and the unique challenges of using compact microphones in modestly sized theaters—are also met by an audience expectation that they hear the type of voice or performance familiarized on the cast recording. The result is that, for all the widely varying musical styles erupting onto Broadway over the past several decades—from pop, to rock, to hip-hop, blues, and country—at the center of that apparent variety lies a singular specific quality of vocal sound so ubiquitous that it gets paid little attention.

Musical theater composer and lyricist Dave Malloy has been paying a good deal of attention. He notes that Broadway training has only enhanced performers' dependence on this narrow style of singing. He laments that during a time of "embrac[ing] idiosyncrasies" and "champion[ing] subtlety" in other genres of music, musical theater "remains chained to an orthodoxy of diction, projection, and extroversion."[10] Malloy feels that the "problem" with musical theater today is that singers "adhere to a very learned, imitative, uniform style that has evolved over years of fusing classic Broadway singing with jazz, rock, and pop. It's a style that is usually the result of years of training in over-articulating, over-enunciating, and over-emoting, presumably to ensure that the words are heard and understood."[11]

Malloy's grievance seems well placed. The tension between textual clarity and an expressive vocal resonance has come to characterize even the economic viability of Broadway musicals. A genre like opera is part of an economic model that emphasizes new productions and castings. Musical theater, on the other hand, measures long, uninterrupted runs with expectations of seeing and hearing the same show as performed by the initial staging and original cast. While Broadway superstars like Idina Menzel enrapture fans with seemingly "individualized," "exceptional," and "distinctive" voices, the pressures on singers to keep up with such vocal models can function as a strong suggestive force for both singers and teachers.[12]

One frequent experience I have had working as an audition pianist for regional theaters in the Middle is that most performers, no matter how unique they imagined their performance of a particular song to be, almost invariably sound exactly like the person in the room who last sang that tune. Part of this has to do with similar—if not identical—audition songs. There is a limited and trusted musical theater audition repertoire in circulation, and only rarely does something unexpected emerge in auditions. In those rare instances when a group of performers happens to bring in a new or trendy song that I have not played before, however, the performances are still so much the same—down to the finest of stylistic or interpretive choices—that in those moments I feel like I know what the cast recording sounds like without ever having heard the original. These auditionees often are musicians of a very high caliber, who certainly have the ability to learn a song without parroting a recording. Their sameness seems likely a response to a paradoxical pressure to use their distinct voice to sound the same as everyone else.

This patented sound smacks as disingenuous. The musical theater community prides itself for its artistic and social individuality and ingenuity, its *realness*. A number of young performers find their way out of rural communities and into these Middle training centers with the promise of the musical's fantasies, a life in New York purchased with a degree in musical theater. Many of them queer, and most others out of place, their path toward acceptance cuts straight through the deceits of musicals.

Since much of life in and of the Middle is built upon a willful imagination, musicals may seem a natural means for envisioning a way out of it. Lauren Zuniga captures the heights of rural deceit in her poem about the small town of Poteau, Oklahoma, titled after Poteau's position near the so-called World's Tallest Hill. All the young characters in her story are caught in the gravity of a hill country boastful of its *almost* status—almost a mountain, as close as you can get to being a mountain, never quite enough. Some work in strip clubs or build meth labs for money; others are terrified of religious backlash; the queer ones may not survive if they can't get out. She writes of Daniel—a "brutal wink of a boy"—working and saving money to "get the hell out of here." And of Liz, who came to prom in a tux and left with a bloody face. "This is how we build pride," Zuniga says satirically, "one foot shy of a mountain."[13]

I see these characters in so many of the young performers of my orbit. Empowered by the big sounds they can make. Desperate to belong. Seized by a chance to be heard and feel recognized. Believing the rich utopia of musicals can trickle down into their own lives. Believing that singing means belonging.

But the voice lies.

Musical theater has moved away from the iconic in favor of the fabricated—the voices are not real; they're really the same. As Malvina Reynolds might say, this Broadway voice is all made out of ticky-tacky. It all sounds just the same.

The ticky-tacky is made particularly obvious in the Broadway "supercuts" videos popular on YouTube, where a well-known musical theater song—"Defying Gravity" from the musical *Wicked*, for example—is presented as a montage of various performers from the worlds of Broadway, pop, and even the television show *Glee*. Tucked behind the idiosyncratic vocal mannerisms of the different performers is what amounts to the common voice for "Defying Gravity"; having the performers aurally lined up side by side actually makes this point quite evident. The purpose for creating these "supercuts" is not to highlight the prevalence of a Broadway sound but rather to allow an aural comparison for fans to determine the "best" performer in that role. ("Who is your favorite Elphaba? Let us know in the comments section below!") The effect, funny enough, is that these montages *model* artistic individuality yet *mirror* the uniformity of voice underlying that artistry.[14]

On the one hand, it seems probable that, to a degree, a performer like Idina Menzel set a vocal standard for "Defying Gravity" that all subsequent Elphabas in *Wicked* feel the need to emulate. The supercut, in fact, begins and ends with Menzel singing the song as Elphaba and returns to her five more times throughout the piece, making clear that the point of comparison is not random but strategically focused on how closely the original is replicated. My experience hearing auditionees closely model a performance from a show's original cast album points to this same phenomenon. Yet, on the other hand, the industrial calculations motivating the creation of a megamusical like *Wicked* indicate that these voices aren't just similar but are actually "cloned"—each iteration of Elphaba heard on Broadway since Menzel originated the character is merely a vocal "franchise" of a larger corporate operation. As Jonathan Burston observes, with the advent of the megamusical came "the attainment of a level of standardization in production regimes previously unknown in the field of live theatre," and "most megamusicals' sonic texts reflect an increasing homogenization of both music and acoustics within the world of the stage musical."[15]

The rise of the megamusical coincides neatly with increased corporate interest in Broadway theater. Initially associated with European-imported musicals in the 1980s and '90s such as *Les Misérables, Cats, The Phantom of the Opera*, and *Chess*, the megamusical genre consists of epic plots, often sung-through music, large sets, and spectacular scenic design. They are also known for their intense international marketing or branding schemes, their ability to translate and transport cross-culturally, and, significantly, often featuring a strict division between audience adoration and puzzled critical response. As Jessica Sternfeld points out, "The new advertising style generated so much interest in a show that poor reviews, and a lack of pithy positive quotes attached to a show's ad campaign, went unnoticed. And audiences kept coming, long after the initial hype had subsided."[16]

Although many of these musicals continue in perpetuity on Broadway, the 1980s version of the megamusical is largely outmoded. Still, aspects of the megamusical survive in new shows, not only in convention and scope but also in ideology. Sternfeld notes that, to a degree, all new musicals today have been influenced by the megamusical, arguing, for example, that "without *The Phantom of the Opera*, *Wicked* would not be the same show."[17] And, as Burston contends, the megamusical's "rationalizing, industrial logic" introduced musical theater to a new level of quality control, one that could "replicate technical and artistic production details with such rigour as to delimit the interpretative agency of performers to a significantly new degree."[18]

Yet the curtailing of individuality by the musical theater industry begins not among the busy streets of New York but within musical theater training programs of more modest location. By 2002 there were over two hundred undergraduate programs in the United States offering degrees in musical theater, with more joining ranks every year. While some of the more popular programs, as might be expected, are geographically centered near New York City (upstate Ithaca College and Syracuse University, for example) or are in the city itself (as with Pace University or New York University's Tisch and Steinhardt Schools), the densest block of coveted programs in the nation is in the Middle. The expanse of country stretching as far north as Ann Arbor, Michigan, east to Pittsburgh, Pennsylvania, south to Tallahassee, Florida, and west to Oklahoma City, Oklahoma, not only harbors a high number of musical theater programs but also, surprisingly, boasts of being home to some of the most successful and celebrated ones in the world, including those at the University of Michigan, Northwestern University, University of Cincinnati College-Conservatory of Music, Roosevelt University (Chicago), Webster University in St. Louis, and Oklahoma City University. I admittedly draw the boundaries of the Middle rather liberally here and throughout this book, but I do so in part to demonstrate the perplexity of what is largely understood to be an urban American musical genre that is greatly dependent on what James Shortridge calls "the most American part of America" for the bodies (and voices) that occupy its stages.[19]

Not only does the Middle supply many of the voices for Broadway, but, even more broadly, musical theater bristles from a fascination with the region—a preoccupation Cara Leanne Wood has dubbed "domestic exoticism."[20] As the site of negotiation between the city it occupies and the fertile farmland that supplies its top performers (and audiences, as I discuss later), Broadway likewise manages to construct a voice that is at once able to merge urban exoticizations of the Middle with the necessary commodification that tourism demands.

It is a voice from the Middle, America's mezza voce.

Training Center

But this is not exactly how the performers hear things. Commodification and homogeneity are not at all how people discuss musical theater vocal training. On the contrary, vocal coaches and voice instructors teach that the most beautiful-sounding voice is one that is unique to that person, and they consequently train students to "find their voice" rather than sing through imitation. This individuated voice becomes a fetish object in itself, often described in terms of its truthfulness or authenticity. As vocal practitioner Karen Morrow puts it, "I think any voice that's unencumbered and comes from a person freely, is basically the truth. And I think the truth is always attractive in performing."[21] Mary Saunders adds that she teaches "correct belting"—a particular kind of vocalizing discussed later—as being "more along the lines of what I consider authentic or truthful. Because beauty is a dramatic sense, in terms of how truthful it is."[22]

It is also true that these programs are designed to meet industry standards and audience expectations and must prepare students to be proficient in a wide variety of styles within four years. For many of the top musical theater training programs, such as the University of Cincinnati College-Conservatory of Music (CCM)—the oldest musical theater program in the country, founded in 1968 and thus coming into development around the same time as the musical was undergoing the significant cultural and structural changes noted above—training involves a careful balance between teaching students to navigate the unique vocal pressures of the genre in an individualized manner while also preparing them to maintain a relationship with the standardized vocal sounds currently on Broadway.

Students are placed in a demanding position. The idealization of a performer able to "do it all" is so entrenched within the pedagogical infrastructure of musical theater training that CCM dedicates a thorough explanation on their website to what they call "The 'Triple Threat' Philosophy," for which the preference for young performers equally accomplished in singing, dancing, and acting is couched within a curious mixture of what may best be described as intimidation, tough love, and industry hazing.

At CCM we are in the business of turning out "Triple Threats." . . .

We have a demanding and difficult course of training with intensive classwork and little time for relaxation. However, we provide our graduates with the wherewithal to survive in a highly competitive field.

Please remember that the training at CCM is rigorous. We are preparing young people for an inordinately difficult and heart-breaking profession. It is not the school for everyone and not everyone is the kind of student for us.[23]

CCM is not alone in its strident pedagogical approach; this tough-love rheto-ric and assembly-line attitude ("At CCM we are in the business of turning out 'Triple Threats'") is indicative of a careerist mentality that is prevalent in many top training programs. As the oldest and one of the most competitive programs in the country, CCM takes an unapologetic stance on this issue, stating that they "see no inconsistency in our dual roles of career builders and educators." For all the talk of focusing on "individual ingenuity" and "examin[ing] the nature of artistic communication," CCM's philosophy turns a strange corner when, at the bottom of the document, we learn that "training in musical theatre is *not about being famous or becoming a star*. It is about learning to work in ways that contrib-ute positively to the art of musical theatre, about the unique interaction among the many and varied aspects that make up the musical stage."[24] Contrary to the rhetoric of freedom, truthfulness, and authenticity surrounding vocal training, CCM's philosophical statement reads like a devotional to musical theater—a simulacrum of a totalitarian regime where ceaseless, tiring work is valued for its means to an individualized "artistic communication" but where uniformity is actually strictly enforced. So which philosophy should be followed? To seek truthfulness and individuality of voice, or to format the body to fit narrow con-scriptions as but a member of a larger and more important body?

At the crux of this paradox lies the vocal coach. While the student may be molded to fit uniformly within an industry that "demands a high level of com-mitment from the student," fostering an individual voice is still prioritized. Alumni and faculty insist that CCM helps students "find their inner voice" and that they don't value a "cookie-cutter approach."[25] For many years I heard simi-lar expressions while working as a musical theater vocal coach and musical director in the Middle. It is not unusual to hear those in top programs claim that students from rival programs sound too similar, all while explaining away similar accusations of vocal sameness leveled against their own training.

It's a classic bait and switch. A young performer steps inside one end of the Broadway machine expecting to discover their unique voice only to come out the other side a carbon copy, often none the wiser. The delusion is tempting. Industries skewed toward the young and idealistic often preach a gospel of individuality even if in practice they reward conformity. No one likes to think of themselves as simply cogs in a machine, especially if that's in fact what they are.

The work of a vocal coach is to somehow broker a deal between the pressures of an industry and the ideology of vocal training. Thanks to the work of voice scholars like Nina Eidsheim and Jennifer Stoever, we can understand better the political favors that voices afford listeners.[26] Voices, for instance, can seem black or queer, male or aged, depending less on the quality of the voice per se and at least to a degree on the aural logics employed by listeners. Individualized voices are largely imagined—what we hear with each voice may more honestly and fruitfully be described as a *sonic bibliography*. With every instance of voice, listeners are invited to hear the pedagogy inscribed in the making and hearing of that sound. The sound and its disciplining come out together.

In other words, the voice is always already manufactured. The vocal coach exists in this sphere, therefore, as an arbiter of our vocal fantasies—maintaining on the one hand the belief that training a particular way will enable a more honest and unique vocal sound while on the other hand disciplining the sound to fit a mold and model. Performers have been led to believe they are truly being honest and sing with an authentic, unique voice—their training *centers* the voice in truth telling.

The whole setup is a wishful lie. Mouths agape passionately pour out their sameness, audiences mishear the meeting of their expectations as something real, and the vocal coach haunts backstage as the master puppeteer pulling our heartstrings with the same show over and over and over again.

Covering Up the Middle

But this vocal trickery is not as simple as it sounds. What distinguishes one vocal sound from another primarily has to do with two somewhat opposing concepts: articulation and resonance. The articulators are the lips, tongue, teeth, jaw, and palette. Diction, elocution, and enunciation are all tools of articulation. Resonance, on the other hand, is often closely associated with an individual's "true" sound, or vocal identity, and is both an aural and physiological sensation. More particular to musical theater vocal pedagogy, the concept of resonance encompasses an idealized way the vocal mechanism can be manipulated (or "released") to achieve the purest or most "honest" sound; consequently, a fully resonant sound has more overtones and is better able to fill a large theater than a less resonant one. Articulation and resonance sometimes do get in the way of each other, however, and when this conflict surfaces in musical theater, the demands of articulation almost always tip the scale.

This tension between articulation and resonance is what frames the paradoxical musical theater vocal training in the Middle. Perhaps more than anything else, the musical theater "belt" sound presses this conflict most forcefully. The belt is a sound accomplished with Middle-ness—a negotiation (or "mix") between lower and upper resonances. Once described as a "brassy, sassy, sort of twangy sound," the belt has increasingly become a fixed aesthetic in musical theater over the past few decades.[27] More than an aesthetic, it's also an identity. The more passionate vocal sounds of Barbra Streisand, Idina Menzel, and Ethel Merman, for instance, are not just the sound of the belt but also qualify these women to join the elite ranks of *belters*.

A true emblem of modernity, the belt cuts across time and context and positions itself as a natural voice for all that is true and ordains those who sing with it as priestly intermediaries of truth. Regardless of musical style or the physical type of the singer, the successful Broadway performer almost invariably must have or be able to mimic this particular sound. One study found that in comparing ads on a musical theater job posting website between October 2012 and April 2013, only 5 percent of employers sought performers who could sing "legitimately," a thinly veiled and often pejorative description of the seeming inauthentic sound of continuous vibrato in "classical" singing.[28] Clearly there is a market preference for the belted voice. Vocal pedagogue Karen Hall suggests that the appeal to this abrasive sound lies within its sounding dangerous or edgy. She writes:

> Unlike the classical voice, belting has been considered emotionally edgy and verging on the brink of sounding out of control. It is this unique quality that so many singers have attempted to emulate in the past sixty years. There is no denying that the belt voice has established itself as a vocal quality that is desired and hired in the professional arena and as such demands attention to healthy production.[29]

Truth itself is messy, out of control, and on the brink of destruction. In times of doubt, truth sounds edgy. Dangerous. In musical theater, almost everyone onstage belts the truth. Which is maybe a circuitous way of admitting that no one onstage tells the truth. Or knows the difference.

Musical theater is believed nonetheless. It speaks truth to power with a voice culled from the Middle, a mezza voce of its own creation. The sounds musical theater has come to trust as the most honest and direct are also made out of negotiations with the Middle. Although I started this chapter showing how women are the more frequent belters in musicals, men make these sounds too. I want to point to the evolution of the voice of Curly in Rodgers and Hammerstein's *Oklahoma!* as a helpful reference point in following the development of this voice and how it is managed. I'll compare the voice of Alfred Drake—Broadway's original Curly in 1943—to subsequent performances by Gordon MacRae in the 1955 film version, Laurence Guittard in the 1979 Broadway revival, Hugh Jackman's London interpretation in 1998, and Damon Daunno in the most recent Broadway revival, in 2019. Each performer has to cross a middle portion of the voice, a vulnerable set of pitches in a singer's range. How each manages that middle space is indicative of an evolving and narrowing vocal aesthetic, one that is derived in more than one way from the imagination.

Oklahoma! is already a story about a Middle space—the middle of the country, the middle of a feud between ranchers and farmers, performed for America in the middle of a world war. Here we also contend with the middle-ness of the musical theater voice. The *voix mixte*, or "mixed voice," is a blending mechanism between head voice and chest voice, but it also emblematizes some of the imagined work the voice does in musicals. Every singer possesses a middle space in their voice—an imaginary zone that is used to negotiate between high and low registers. This middle passage (so named from the Italian *passaggio*) is actually no space at all. It's nonexistent. At least, you can't find a resonant middle voice on any map of the body. It is instead felt, largely imagined. As the passageway to what audiences and performers have come to believe to be honest sounds, it might as well be real.

The trick is to disguise the middle space, to make its absence noticed, to cover the entire range of the voice. For honesty to be heard, the singer has to give the impression that honest sounds come naturally and effortlessly. That's easier said than done.

In the opening number, "Oh, What a Beautiful Mornin'," Drake sings with a consistent and even vibrato indicative of classical training and a dominant vocal aesthetic of the time, lending his voice to modern ears an "operatic" quality. Overall, his voice is full with lots of pharyngeal resonance. He manages the few challenging pitches between his lower register and upper register by negotiating this middle space. This allows the voice to resonate more fully and grants the illusion of consistency between vocal registers without his having to shift completely into a thinner and less convincing sound up top. Because Drake uses his full resonance, the transition through the mixed spaces makes rounder vowel shapes—what might be heard as a swallowed sound farther back in the throat. Had the voice been farther forward to begin with, the vowels would narrow and brighten and the middle space become more exposed.

Inasmuch as Drake's more swallowed navigation of the middle is emblematic of vocal aesthetics of the 1940s musical stage—and the kind of voice *Oklahoma!*'s creators probably had in mind—each subsequent voicing of Curly represents a shifting value of this middle voice. Gordon MacRae's singing of the show's opening number seems mostly in line with what Drake created, though we might note overall the brighter, flatter vowels in places that make the cowhand sound less contemplative and more conversational. By the time we hear Laurence Guittard's bright, ringing, and nasal sound when singing about corn growing

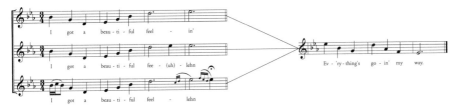

Example 6.1: "Oh, What a Beautiful Mornin'," music by Richard Rodgers and words by Oscar Hammerstein II. Top: Alfred Drake manages the middle of his voice using a covered, swallowed sound. The tricky shift from D to E-flat is made less apparent, though the vowel on the highest note is noticeably farther back in the throat. Middle: Hugh Jackman switches to a brighter, more forward position in the middle of the word "feelin'," adding an extra vowel syllable to cover the middle space. Bottom: Damon Daunno manages the middle range by disguising a shift into a belt sound. The small added notes come across as a yodel and affective style choice for the singing cowboy. These added notes also give Daunno cover to brighten his vowels on "feelin'." The result is an "eh" shaped and belted sound.

as high "as an elephant's eye," it is clear that a shift in vocal aesthetics has occurred. Guittard's performance places Curly within a clear evolution toward a new vocal sound, one that is concerned less with rounded, full resonance and more with textual clarity and dramatic believability.

This evolution is all the more apparent in the most recent versions of Curly. Hugh Jackman's "Oh, What a Beautiful Mornin'," compared to Drake's, involves far less singing and much more speaking; we might say Jackman *approximates* the pitches rather than allows the voice to resonate on each one. Perhaps the most prominent deviation of Jackman's version from that of Drake's is Jackman's use of a belt sound, rather than a *voix mixte*, on those highest notes of the phrase. While singing the first syllable of "feelin'," Jackman leaps out of the high D and into the E-flat by adding a shadowed "uh" and modifying the very next vowel from "in" to "ehn." Turning the word into "fee-uh-lehn'" allows Jackman the vocal space to shift the highest note into a brighter pocket, giving the final vowel more of an [ɛ] color (like the sound in "wed") than the [ɪ] timbre of Drake's covered version, which is a more closed vowel sound (as in "win"). Damon Daunno's Curly, finally, makes a similar (though much more discreet) path into the belt, disguising the vocal shift in a yodel-like crack between the two pitches. Yodeling brings Daunno's Curly closer to the singing cowboys Gene Autry and Jimmie Rodgers than to the rich baritone of Alfred Drake. But the yodeling also helps with the singing, making space for a brighter vowel at the top. The melismatic additions cover his tracks across the gaping middle of the voice.

This close listening reveals changing beliefs about the voice. The contemporary sound of the Broadway voice has become a singular tool to manage that imagined, though nonetheless very real, middle space. It seems likely that the pragmatics of the belt eventually created a new standard for how musicals should sound, an adaptation that essentially aestheticized a diminished vocal resonance and invited audiences to hear the middle, to hear the machinery at work, as evidence of truth telling. According to those in the musical theater industry, that abrasive and brassy ring in the voice allows the text to clearly be heard. In fact, the primacy of the text over the sound itself may define the aesthetics of modern musical theater.

And yet clarity of text comes at a cost. Selling a song through belting involves a quashing of vocal resonance, pushing the resonating sensation farther into the front of the face and, often, closing off the vocal mechanism itself with hard muscularity in order to project as loud and as piercing a sound as possible. Belting requires a great deal of force since, perhaps counterintuitively, the performer must use greater volume to compensate for overtones lost in the practice of diminishing resonance. The likely deleterious effect of belting has occupied vocal pedagogical literature for decades; both the American Academy of Teachers of Singing and the Voice Foundation have cautioned students and teachers about the dangers of belting.[30] Caution has done little to mute its appeal.

Belting is an audible renegotiation of the Middle, a disappearing of it and in more ways than one. The wider the vocal range and broader the middle space to negotiate, the greater the chances of injury. The more a belt is in demand, the savvier the recruitment of performers in the Middle to escape into the fantasy of a sound unique to them and a world of their belonging. The price of the belt is high—climbing clear up to the sky. One foot shy of a mountain.

Paying for the Voice

According to a report by the Broadway League, "In the 2018–2019 season, Broadway shows welcomed 14.8 million admissions, an all-time high," with tourists comprising sixty-five percent of those admissions.[31] The most likely Broadway theatergoer for that season was white, middle-aged, and, on average, had an annual household income of $261,000. The relative wealth of today's Broadway audience brings to relief the soaring costs of producing musicals, which helps explain a dramatic increase in ticket prices. Not everyone is so pleased with this economic shift in musical theater nor the reasoning given for such prohibitive costs. Broadway veteran and notorious provocateur Patti LuPone once quipped that exorbitant ticket prices "[have] more to do with greed than . . . with anything else."[32] Regardless of the explanation, money is rolling in. In 2011 Michael Riedel wrote that ticket prices for hit shows were more than three times the cost of what they were in the early 2000s. "As a result," he writes, "weekly grosses for hit musicals run to $1.5 million."[33] Broadway has hit a stride with its new audience and doesn't mind catering to its tastes. A *Time* magazine article from January 2013 pointed to tourists as the reason for the near disappearance of dark theaters, adding that tourists are "more and more, influencing what kinds of shows make it to Broadway."[34] As more tourists pour into its theaters and, increasingly, movie studios try to reproduce Disney's early success in the theater market, all the rabid interest in the area makes it undeniable that, in Riedel's words, "Broadway's the hottest ticket in town."[35]

Demographic reports like this are a reminder that a great deal of money is exchanged in the musical theater industry. Many of those dollars are spent in less obvious ways, however, and often in places far removed from the streets near Times Square. Unknowable figures from years of dance lessons, voice lessons, acting workshops, musical theater camps, and, of course, trips to Broadway itself, all fill the lines of checkbook expense ledgers of families in the Middle who are eager to assuage their budding performers' ambitions—and all this before going to college. It takes a lot of resources and relative financial privilege to prepare to become the kind of performer who places like CCM call for—and therefore presumably to succeed on Broadway—just as it takes a similarly privileged position to travel to New York City to experience a Broadway show as an audience member.

But what exactly are audiences and students paying for? At one level they are both paying for an authentic voice—the means of entertaining and of being entertained. Yet, of course, the actuality of such an authentic voice on Broadway today has already been problematized. For all the money and labor that goes into highly individualized musical theater training, as well as the financial means of paying for a ticket to a show, the musical theater industry makes demands on the performer to find or replicate a fixed voice that is able to be exchanged and interchanged with that of any number of other Broadway constituents. The resources required to "find your voice," to get on Broadway, are rendered invisible and, with few exceptions, any instance of an individuated voice made suspect.

Uniformity can be measured in nonvocal ways too—an outcome of the grueling schedule a life in the theater demands. In virtually every way, being in a show determines a performer's everyday lifestyle. A Broadway performer typically performs eight shows over a six-day work week; Sunday nights and Mondays are usually their only time off. There is considerable pressure to stay fit and maintain consistent eating habits; even the slightest fluctuation in weight could require a costume refitting, an expense sometimes more considerable than finding a replacement who fits the costume. Given the uniform size and physique of many performers, interchanging ousted performers with near-identical replacements is an easy way to cut costs. Therefore, workouts and meal plans occupy the attention of performers even on off days. Cast members report early to the theater for fittings, fight calls, and last-minute rehearsals and often leave theaters late at night after completing necessary tasks like costume changing or mingling with fans backstage. While not all of these intrusions directly affect the voice, such a lifestyle certainly contributes to inevitable vocal fatigue and exhaustion.

Technology often makes up for losses accrued from such demands. Microphones can act as a crutch for a faltering voice, and amplification helps make a demanding Broadway schedule tenable, if not merely provisionally so.[36] Even more, the same conditions and expectations for standardization in voice are often at work in sound design. Burston writes provocatively that the use of sound on Broadway reduces the "singing body" to "the status of cipher" and notes the voracious appetite for loudness that is characteristic of Broadway producers. Others have taken note as well. After observing a sound engineer set the decibel level for the orchestra in *Beauty and the Beast* to a startlingly high 110 decibels, celebrated voice teacher Jeannette LoVetri asks, "Why are producers requiring this?" and answers her own question: "Because they don't know much, don't know singing, don't know acting, don't understand the voice, and don't know what else to evaluate except volume. If it's loud, it's great! No, it's pathetic."[37]

Louder sounds and amplification processes again contribute to the everpresent conflict of demanding articulation over the body's natural ability to resonate. But with less resonance and thus fewer overtones present in the belted voice, artificial amplification is often the only recourse for actually hearing the voices onstage. Such a process leads to what can be an unsettling sensation of hearing an *acousmatic* sound—a phenomenon where the source of a voice seems displaced from its visual signifier onstage. This corresponds with Patti LuPone's admission of feeling "disenfranchised from [her] experience" as a theater audience member because of the ambiguity of the voice's origin: "I don't know where the voice is coming from. It's not coming from the stage any more [*sic*]. My eyes are looking at the stage, and my ears are searching for the sound that the mouth is producing."[38]

The labor of the voice as siphoned through amplification remains hidden and obscured, no longer a part of the body onstage, leaving behind "a filtered, synthetic trace."[39] Despite the loudness and overwhelming presence of the vocal sound in the space, the performer's voice is disembodied, rendered invisible, erased. It is as if Broadway is using loudness to compensate for the choked-out voices even as the sinews and tissues themselves rattle with the intensity of a belt. "The productions are just too loud," says LuPone. "You can't have an intimate experience in the theater anymore. And that's what it's about. It's really about the unification of an audience, having a collective audience, individually, and listening. And we're not allowed to listen anymore because the sound level is too loud."[40] To put it another way, articulation is killing resonance; the system is sonically burying the performers whose voices keep it running. Meanwhile the audience has stopped listening, delightedly deafened by the roar of a voice-eating machine.

Conclusion

"Close your eyes and listen as [Broadway performers'] larynxes stretch and vibrate with the pain of being an underdog and the joy of being really loud," writes Ben Brantley of the *New York Times*. "Bet you can't tell them apart."[41] From the training centers in the middle of America to the bright lights of Broadway, the business of musical theater can best be summarized by the old Holiday Inn tag line "the best surprise is no surprise" at all. While the rhetoric fetishizes vocal uniqueness, the voices prepared for Broadway are actually sounding conformity. Critics are conflicted with this scenario, since some ideal of conformity is obviously bringing audiences to the theaters, or at least not inhibiting them. Brantley bristles at the idea of Broadway with "eminently replaceable" cast members yet acknowledges that it is probably good for business: "Sui generis stars are not necessarily advantages for investors hoping for long, sold-out runs. . . . So it would seem to make good commercial sense to create musicals that put the emphasis less on individual performance than on overall concept."[42] Although the rhetoric of a distinctive, individualized voice remains a part of Broadway's mythology of the Middle, the building of the Broadway voice plainly illustrates how an economic model can drive a certain type of vocal economy. Musicals are lying about the voice—what a surprise.

Musical theater has built a network of sonic byways that connect labor sources in the Middle to its major commercial centers. Clearly this aids the industry in selling the same vocal and theatrical products again and again, as I've gone to some pains to outline here. And perhaps the industry fares all the better for sourcing these vocal materials from a region that is characteristically everyday and American in order to continue the branded image of New York's elite theater making as somehow accessible or relevant elsewhere. Beyond Broadway's dallying with voices for industry purposes, however, the mark of the voice as a fantasy of individuality within a manifest reality of sameness puts the voice in the center of a much larger concern.

The fantasy of an individual, unique voice is a leftover from Romantic notions of subjectivity—that a person's voice is messily entangled with a soul or selfhood. Nina Eidsheim places this vocal assumption alongside technological developments. The invention of the stethoscope in the nineteenth century, she shows, corresponds neatly with Freud's psychoanalytic hypothesis that the essence of malady or discontent within the human body or psyche can be discerned by listening to the sounds deep within it.[43] Doctors and therapists, in other words, learned to listen acutely to the body's insides to determine something true about sickness and, it turns out, about interiority itself. While almost everything about medicine and psychology have since changed, most people have never thought to question this prevailing assumption about the voice.

In the political arena, the voice represents this same individuality and selfhood. The metaphoric language surrounding democracy employs the voice as if by now its truest essence is self-evident. *Voicing* opinions, letting your *voice be heard*, and electing a *voice for the people* become democratic linchpins, pinching together an increasingly fragile ideal of individuality. James Q. Davies holds that there is some slippage in these metaphors today. A declining faith in our political elections, or of fair and equal treatment under the law, corresponds with a lackluster discrimination against the ineffable. As Davies writes:

> What does seem clear is that the old Romantic-modern model of "making your (unique) voice heard" is eroding, probably in the wake of eroding faith in the politics of representation. It may be that the once-useful trust in vocal freedom has become politically destructive, in the same way that the old identity politics has become politically destructive. It is difficult, after all, to sustain belief in liberalism when such nonhuman things as the biosphere, corporations, or money also demand political voices. Would it not be illiberal to deny a voice to each? And, furthermore, what is the point in having your own voice when you get the same government over and over again no matter whom you vote for?[44]

It is clarifying to ask what the semblance of a unique voice costs us politically.

Musicals fall prey to this kind of logic but in other ways challenge it. Our current political moment sees young voters jousting for political change while deeply uncertain that change is ever possible. It is not nothing to see young people in loud, defiant ways proclaiming on a musical stage that their voice is unique and that it matters. Many of the voices in musical theater are manufactured—in some ways fake—and problematically so. But audiences largely don't know that. They believe the voices, not for what they *say* but for what they are assumed *to be*: markers of inclusivity, our truest selves, and referents of what the musical offers as a better world. Having a space outside of a voting booth where the voice is hailed as individual and real can be a productively prosocial lie in the face of despotic rule and a disenchanted votership. Clearly these are works of deception, but deceit has a higher exchange rate than truth. If the voice is always apprehended as an in-between, then the voice is all that stands between us and a world more vibrantly resonant, because each voice actually matters. The fantasy of a unique voice may be exactly that, but does the truth warrant any better outcome?

In this respect, musicals are not that different from America itself. To belong in this community, you sound the same. We make sure the sounds are the same. We are all excellent vocal coaches.

Measuring our voices against some metric of belonging often means changing our tune, pretending, becoming a franchised American with every sigh, gasp, laugh, cry; in every "oh say can you see" and recitation of all fifty states and capitals; in the inhalation before speaking to the police; and within every thought and prayer and ringing ears after one roaring gunshot fades into another and another and another. America is retuning your world. America is disciplining your sound. America is transposition, harmony, blend, and silence.

America is a voice lesson we learn from the Middle. Always one foot shy.

CHAPTER 7

The Afterlives of Truth and Musicals

This story began out of place. Place has been our *un*-territory, that vagrant fantasia, our mischievous specimen that resists being pinned and plotted. Musical theater's utopias are always just out of grasp. Utopia means "no place," after all. Yet musicals and their fantasies need to be *re*-placed to do the work we need of them—and that will involve zooming out to get a closer look at the landscape.

You may not have realized it at the time, but as I was writing and as you were reading, we were together charting a map of America, the same way Michel de Certeau's city streetwalkers unknowingly write urban "texts" during their strolls, illegible even to them.[1] If we are all liars, then we are also all mapmakers. By now we have drawn lines to and from Broadway. It's a messy map, I know, but look closely and you'll see where we've been—see the small wires snaking through the Middle, the thick and thin borders here and there, the improvised and mashed-up byways, and the farmlands growing with urgency their seasonal crop of unique voices. This isn't a book of spells. Our new map shows us where we have been the whole time, but it does not tell us where we might be going. It is descriptive and incomplete but not useless. We have to begin someplace and wander about a bit—be pleased in our lostness and charmed by the incompleteness of our fold-out map—before we can orient ourselves to the next place.

I've been thinking a lot about how musicals might retreat from the landscape itself. Clearly this book suggests that musicals exist out of place already, so what they might look like literally out of *place* is a question haunting my thinking.

Musicals and other forms of theater exist these days in virtual spaces—podcasts, livestreams, videos, and recordings. In some ways this virtual space is nothing new for theater, always "a space of illusory immediacy," as Matthew Causey puts it.[2] And Laurence Maslon is right to point out in his exuberance that "the music of Broadway no longer has any geographic boundaries. It has burst far beyond the Theater District and is as boundless as the soaring breadth and inspiration of its most enchanting creations."[3] The power that musicals hold over us partly comes from their unboundedness: disconnected from reality, from place, and from the truth about who we really are.

This can all be true, though I still wonder if musicals are destined for actual replacement. Musicals, like maps, divide reality from representation; that's what they are good for, their inaccuracy. The kind of nonchalance that musicals carry about fantasy worlds is of greatest power when we ourselves lack the ability to imagine other ways of being.

But we won't need musicals if the worlds they build look like our own. Musicals stop their work if we engineer our own utopias. What happens if we take seriously the playful ideas I entertain in this book—that deception of the brand that musicals perpetuate will need to be a common language in order to shock us out of the malaise of post-truth? What if what we have come to understand and believe about musicals becomes outmoded? If musicals begin telling the truth—that is, if we come to believe that musicals are no longer *representative* of new worlds but actually *reflective* of our own—then we no longer have a map but a kingdom. Fantasy and deception stand in parallel with a post-truth era but look obtuse whenever truth is made to pay its bills again. No, if we do this right, musicals disappear.

In this final chapter, I consider how musicals and truth have come, will come, or are already coming to an end, a dead end. I invoke the concept of an afterlife for all of its meanings. Musicals and belief are central to the idea of America building and rebuilding in the imagination again and again. What happens when musicals and the truth they disguise have fulfilled their purpose? What awaits them? What becomes of us?

I sketch three scenes depicting these afterlives, each concentrating on an end wrought from this scenario: the end of lying, the end of human, and the end of truth. These three scenes point to a different relationship with and about musical theater and its deceptions and correspond with the themes I develop in these pages. While most of this book has been concerned with the work musicals perform in offbeat locations, this chapter steps back considerably to observe how the network of musical theater measures against a future ecology of deception.

Scene One: The End of Lying

It is late 2016, and at curtain call for Broadway's *Hamilton*—the hit musical Barack Obama only five months earlier had called "a civics lesson our kids can't get enough of." Vice President-elect Mike Pence and his wife are in attendance this evening, and the cast takes an opportunity to lecture the audience on the values of America's history. A diverse America is the true America, they say, and everyone deserves to belong and be protected *here*:

Here—the musical stage.

Here—the American stage.

The implication of the curtain call speech and the show itself is that America's immigrant past should be celebrated, if not on the merits and values of immigrants as humans, then at least because our map, through Alexander Hamilton, shows that immigrants are foundational to America's storied past—X marks the spot, as they say.

Trouble is, the singing and dancing Hamilton is not quite the same as the actual ten-dollar-bill Hamilton. The musical takes liberties, invents, erases, and builds; the musical lies a little, or a lot. Positioned during the curtain call between the real world of the audience in front of them and the fake world of the theater just behind, the cast lectures about a false story to correct a narrative in real life. The power of the moment, it seems, is not that what is said is necessarily true but that it is spoken from the Middle. The audience is still willing to imagine and the cast is still able to parlay the magic of make-believe. From that fragile Middle space a new world is able to come into existence.

Musicals are bad at telling the truth, and I'm not one for forcing them to change their habits. I appreciate what the fantasy of musicals clarifies about our actual world. I much prefer the empathetic Alexander Hamilton of Miranda's imagination to the real one, whose position toward immigrants was, by today's standards, less, um, palatable. I like to fantasize about a simple reality as much as the next person. That's one of musical theater's greatest affordances, actually: its ability to represent lives much grander than those we struggle with every day. It is a map.

There are many stories about maps, but the one by Jorge Luis Borges is my favorite.[4] A kingdom needs mapping. The royal cartographers devise a map so perfect it ceases to represent anything but itself. This map with a ratio of 1:1 captures every blade of grass, every nuance of incline, every breath of breeze in such perfection that it simply becomes the kingdom. These mapmakers never get in on the joke Borges has cast at their expense. Readers well know that maps are meant to represent—they're useful *because* they are imperfect, imprecise, topographical pretend. Maps lie. It's ridiculous to even consider a map trying to be honest.

I find that maps and theater have a lot in common in this regard. The word "representation" is having a bit of a moment in the musical theater community. I sense a great deal of uncertainty among students and professionals about what work that word is doing. Representation is, of course, the business of show business; actors are always pretending to be someone else. But these days, musical theater, like other corners of popular culture in the post-truth era, is increasingly self-aware of its political platform. As primarily a young people's line of work, and with a reputation as a safe haven for LGBTQ+ people, musicals manifest much of that awareness as progressive dogma. There are more and more musicals being written by and for people of color, for instance, or women, or immigrants, or transgender persons, and a host of characters and dramatic situations that are at times brazenly at odds with what for so long passed as typical Broadway fodder. The pace is debatable, but on this issue Broadway is leaps ahead of Hollywood's #OscarsSoWhite missteps. Their progressivism is extroverted: the musical theater community is falling in love with itself before our very eyes.

Such self-awareness and fresh narratives have started a chain reaction within the musical theater world. As a corrective to pernicious blackface, yellowface, brownface, or queer minstrelsy, the musical theater industry has committed to casting actors who at least *look* like the characters they are playing, or, as in *Hamilton*'s color-conscious casting, who purposely antagonize what American power looks and sounds like.[5] Theater's map scale expanded, though only slightly. Broadway in some ways remains shackled to a traditional mode of representation because, again, that's what theater is.

And yet the cartographers continue to work. Fueled by a raucous and polemic political diet, the musical theater community today seems less content with its imperfect map of representation and more interested in something much closer to reality.

Not long ago, I was the audition pianist for a summer stock theater whose season included Lin-Manuel Miranda's Tony Award–winning musical *In the Heights*. The show follows Nina, a college-age New Yorker ("the Heights" meaning Washington Heights) of Puerto Rican descent whose story in many ways dictates that she be portrayed by someone who can represent that heritage. In a stage show, heritage almost always rhymes with optics—meaning Nina should be played by a performer of color.

During these auditions, a young woman came into the room to sing Nina's featured act 1 song "Breathe," but not before offering the disclaimer that despite her light skin and blond hair she was right for the part ("I'm Puerto Rican, I swear"; she inherited the lighter hair and complexion of her father, she explained).

For me in that moment, the creases in musical theater's mapmaking blurred the way forward. Was she truly right for the part? Yes, this woman could lay claim to Nina's story as her own, if representing heritage accurately was the director's goal.

But also, no.

Musical theater today is committed to portraying identity optically. Visual truth telling remains, for musicals, the primary metric of inclusivity; there are fewer voices insisting that actual Mormons be cast in *Book of Mormon* or that only Jewish performers appear in *Fiddler on the Roof,* for instance. She couldn't really *be* Nina if it appeared she was only *pretending to be* Nina. She didn't get the part.

This scenario has resonance even outside of theater. With genetic testing kits like 23andMe, theatergoers and everyday people alike might struggle knowing how to identify with a heritage they may not optically signal (and vice versa). Performance underscores the problem—that is, which identity we choose to inhabit may be at odds with what we look like. At the moment optics is just easier in theater, though that's not to dismiss their importance. Directors and audiences may not need to bother with the complexities of heritage as long as the performers look the part, a knowing concession along theater's path toward righting the racial wrongs of the past and present. On the other hand, if audiences expect an actor to *be* the role, not *act* the part, then musicals become something other than representational. They stop lying. They become fully enwrapped by a grand map of their own likeness. They become, perversely, *true.*

Oscar Wilde noticed a similar "surrender of an imaginative form" in English melodramas of his day. Wilde bemoans characters who speak onstage the same as they might speak in real life. Their goals and dreams are ho-hum and everyday, hardly the stuff of imaginative storytelling. "And yet how wearisome the plays are!" he writes. "They do not succeed in producing even that impression of reality at which they aim, and which is their only reason for existing. As a method, realism is a complete failure."[6]

Wilde hammers the point that when art fails to do its imaginative work, then art cedes its power. It ends. This is similar to Arthur C. Danto's observation that art transformed from imitation to philosophy in the 1960s with the work of Andy Warhol; we may call subsequent pieces "art," but the job of Art has come to an end.[7] One hundred years after Wilde, Francis Fukuyama similarly argued that history ended when any challenge to Western liberalism's reach collapsed in 1989 with the Berlin Wall. It now looks like theater's cartographers have drafted a map that foretells the end of representation. The drafting predicts increasingly a world without pretense, which is also a world absent of analogy, metaphor, and perhaps imagination—a world where actors are not acting, neo-Nazis are not in disguise, politicians no longer pretend to have your interests at heart, and every living being is a representation of nothing more than the identity it claims. The end of representation means the end of lying.

That's the grind in America. Theater and, let's not forget, democracy are first and foremost about representation; actors and politicians are always pretending to be or act on behalf of someone or something they are not. Clearly that's not enough. Being cast in the role you seem right for is no substitute for doing the job and doing it well. There is important work to do in reframing how power looks in America, and theater is and should be active in doing so. It is life that imitates art, Wilde insists, and not the other way around.

As an immediate rebuttal to the viperous post-truth era, I see the appeal. Theater and maps aren't just about representation; they tell people what they need to know to navigate what might be unfamiliar terrain. But what do you do with an unwieldy map that can only tell the truth? Even glancing at it seems like a surrender of uncertainty; there is, after all, a real value to being lost.

Scene Two: The End of Human

As the horrific close of the second world war drew near, James Agee's pen drew justification for a prosocial fantasy of America "merely petulant and flattered" as the world around it spins into chaos: "Incurable through pity, love, guilt, fear; / A dying grandmother, babbling of a ball: / Take her just so, Death; let her enjoy it all."[8]

Agee's poem sees the humanity in deception, especially at its end. Humans have survived catastrophes of their own making by outsmarting the threat. We now face challenges that are seemingly insurmountable: pandemics, climate change, stubborn resistance to social equity, and, maybe worst of all, a refusal to even imagine ways of meeting these challenges. In the event no matter of smarts can thwart our ending, we may be left to face an end to humanity by spinning falsehoods, not truth.[9]

Here are two examples of how film and television use musicals to foretell the end of human. By "end of" and "human," I mean two things: literally, the end of human life on Earth and, figuratively, as in the end of what makes us human. Caught in the middle of these visions is the fantasia of musical theater. Musicals give license to lie and deceive, but if held down and questioned under a bright light, they may also tell a haunting truth of human fate.

1. We begin in the middle of nowhere. "Out there" is how the 2008 animated Pixar film *WALL-E* puts it. Shots of stars and empty space give a sense of placelessness to Michael Crawford's voice singing Jerry Herman's opening lines to *Hello, Dolly!*'s chipper "Put on Your Sunday Clothes"—"out there, there's a world outside of Yonkers, way out there beyond this hick town, Barnaby." The camera moves in on what appears to be a ball of filth—a planet that looks like maybe it used to be Earth—while Crawford, unawares, sings of a place *out there*, "full of shine and full of sparkle." Our viewpoint cascades into Earth's polluted atmosphere and space junk until we slow our descent into an absolutely abysmal vision of New York City. "Hick town" pretty well sums it up.

Out of place. A ruinous and abandoned Earth is inhabited by only the hardiest of creatures. Humans are parked in a distant spaceship waiting out the half-life of their pollution, having left the dirty work of cleaning up the planet to their automatons. We meet WALL-E, a trash collector tasked with collecting and organizing the heaps upon heaps of garbage left behind by humans. Amid the detritus, and left largely to his own devices, WALL-E brings home interesting objects he finds lying around, piecing together what is left and learning about his home's previous tenants.

One of his most treasured finds is a VHS recording of the musical *Hello, Dolly!* (a show actually from the Middle—it held tryouts in Detroit, Michigan, before landing in New York). WALL-E has learned about human emotion, the highs and lows of love and community, by watching a musical. Wired into the middle of his body is a tape deck, which he uses to record and continuously play the music he finds. Two numbers from the show, "Put on Your Sunday Clothes" and "It Only Takes a Moment," figure into WALL-E's relationship with himself and the mysterious new robot, EVE, who has come to Earth in search for any signs of life.

The show is in many ways a nonmusical musical—that is, the threadbare setup of low-class worker falls for high-brow debutante plays out between WALL-E and EVE. But it's also a posthuman musical that second-guesses if musicals continue to matter once humans aren't around to be lied to.

Even in a world devoid of humans, musicals continue to showcase what is (or was) most human about us. WALL-E moves through the abandoned New York streets playing the showtunes as an eerie echo of what once was. At one point he discovers a single living plant, something he has never seen before. He carefully collects the plant inside his body, just below the tape deck.

I mention this at length because the future world that *WALL-E* brings to life is a touching foretelling of how musicals might also figure into the afterlives of humans and life as we now know it. Humans in this film grow ever more cartoonish the longer they are away from Earth—which is seven hundred years by the time our story begins. The robots living on Earth, on the other hand, have adapted to human waste and refuse. Earth's trappings pull them closer to the human. At least a few of them engage empathetically with one another and with other living things.

WALL-E adopts and cares for a lone cockroach, for instance, and sees value and beauty in the small plant he finds growing—miraculously—inside an abandoned refrigerator. WALL-E hosts the organic life inside his body, the same body that emanates the sounds of musical theater outward—*out there*—toward the humans who are millions of miles and as many heartbeats away from what they once were. Organic life, then, becomes held within WALL-E and protected just the same as the touching love songs of *Hello Dolly!* also are held dear.

Various adventures ensue, and WALL-E ends up in space, caught in the orbit of the giant ship holding all of humanity. Once aboard the ship, WALL-E's antics start turning the humans away from their distraction and toward one another, and, so it goes, a low-class robot who has learned to understand human emotion through musical theater slowly starts to teach humans how to become human again. He bridges the gap between life and death. He shows them the essential value of the Middle in being human.

Even in *WALL-E*'s fantasy of human doom, whatever promise musicals offer us delivers from the nightmare and awakens humans into a better world, even if that world may come at the end of our own.

2. The first sound we hear is a film reel spinning—*Real spinning—Unreal spinning*—then, an unfamiliarly familiar sound. Singer Jeanette Olsson quietly, breathily, sings the Rodgers and Hammerstein anthem "Edelweiss" from *The Sound of Music*.

The song was already a faux folk song that the duo penned, though like any folk song worth its salt "Edelweiss" has enjoyed a rambling and unmoored afterlife. The Captain von Trapp of Rodgers and Hammerstein's imagination once led an audience of patriots in this nationalist tune. Now, in this context, it is only a nightmarish shadow of what it once was—a "lullaby that is soothing precisely because it insists, against all odds, on staying awake," Megan Garber of the *Atlantic* writes.[10] Olsson's voice is thin, hesitant, grasping at words that one feels she is at pains to sound. The accompanying acoustic guitar gestures emptily toward its captain's former caress. So much about this seems forced, insincere, occupied.

The accompanying images crumble beneath the strains of "Edelweiss." Cinematic shots of wartime America appear out of place. Shadows of paratroopers descending from the air look like falling tears upon the granite carvings of Mount Rushmore's George Washington and Thomas Jefferson. Smoke from a smoldering plane billows in the face of the Statue of Liberty. Futuristic warplanes project into America's national parks. The trailing tears sound like a weeping guitar, Lady Liberty's smoky cough becomes Olsson's hissing sibilants. We see a map of the United States covered in unfamiliar markings—"Japanese Pacific States" covers the West Coast and east to the Rocky Mountains; "Greater Nazi Reich" extends east of the Rockies and to the Atlantic Ocean. America's map is torn. The broken record is made sound.

So spin the opening credits of the Amazon Original Series *The Man in the High Castle*. Loosely based on Philip K. Dick's 1962 novel of the same name, *The Man in the High Castle* is an alternate history of World War II. The story begins in this world's version of 1962. The allied forces have been felled by a nuclear warhead covertly developed by the Third Reich. The resulting fallout has split the American continent between the remaining world powers, Germany and Japan. The middle space between the two powers is dubbed "the neutral zone" and is populated by the rugged, fugitive, and lawless, including someone known only as "the Man in the High Castle"—a cinephile hideout in Wyoming distributing contraband reel-to-reel tapes, the contents of which threaten to topple the narrative nightmare many find themselves living within.

Life in this new America is terrifying, violent, and uncertain. Mysterious persons risk their lives trafficking these reels of films from the neutral zone outward. The world depicted in the films is actually our own world—*our* world is *their* alternate reality—but it is unfamiliar and unrecognizable to those living in this one. These reels reveal what is real. Its fantasy is nonetheless a threat to the social order; powers from both empires work tirelessly to snuff it out.

While *The Man in the High Castle* isn't really about musical theater, the whimsical reputation of musicals frames the fantasy effectively through these opening credits. Humans in this world are overrun with terror. Fascism threatens to disappear hundreds of thousands of people from the face of the earth. Characters are worn down here. They follow their worst instincts, becoming the most inhumane versions of themselves. It's a dystopian fantasy made all the more terrifying because their *could have been* so closely resembles our *what could become*.

"Edelweiss" sets up this alternate reality as both an upside-down version of what we know to be true and an explanation for the power of play, fantasy, and narrative in disrupting that sense of truth. What was originally an anthem covertly disrupting Nazi forces (and spinning a fantasy of Austrian innocence along the way) is now an unsettlingly calm statement of a fascist presence in the world. Viewers are asked to confront the terrors of this reality but also to name the unacknowledged terrors of our actual world.

Figure 7.1: Map of a divided America, cut through the middle by a "neutral zone," from the opening credits of the Amazon Original Series *The Man in the High Castle*.

Example 7.1: Musical description of "Edelweiss" as sung in the original film (top line) and as performed by Jeanette Olsson in the opening credits of *The Man in the High Castle* (bottom). The missing phrases in the bottom version are a sonic representation of the missing Middle America as imagined in the television series. Music by Richard Rodgers and words by Oscar Hammerstein II.

I'm returning in my mind to the map of this fractured America. The unclaimed space in the middle of the map can be heard in the song; Olsson omits the third and fourth phrases of the opening line, crafting a sonic neutral zone of its own. What we hear, then, and see vividly in example 7.1, is a familiar musical phrase beginning an arc that never lands on the other side. Much like this reimagined and bifurcated land, the song is made unfamiliar, strange, and unstable by the missing Middle. It is shot full of holes, incomplete. An antecedent with no consequent. An America with no heart. Without the Middle the center cannot hold, and things—nations, musical phrases, people—fall apart.

The lovable innocence of *WALL-E* disguises its dystopia, but there are good reasons to be terrified of both of these imagined futures. For all their association with *happy* endings, musicals can just as easily be imagined as the soundscape for *human* endings. A planet without humans still resounds with the fantasy of human deception. A fantastical world thinly tied to a false narrative can be imagined most easily with a musical theater prologue. Both concoct a map of the future where musicals still exist but other things that make us human do not.

The revolutions of a sick planet. A spinning tape reels. The babbling of a ball—all turning and turning in the widening gyre.

Scene Three: The End of Truth

Thomas Frank may have seen this coming years ago. "What divides Americans is *authenticity*, not something hard and ugly like economics," he writes in *What's the Matter with Kansas?*

> While liberals commit endless acts of hubris, sucking down lattes, driving os-tentatious European cars, and trying to reform the world, the humble people of the red states go about their unpretentious business, eating down-home foods, vacationing in the Ozarks, whistling while they work, feeling comfortable about who they are, and knowing they are secure under the watch of George W. Bush, a man they love as one of their own.[11]

Frank's concern here is that Americans in the Middle frequently find purchase with senseless political leaders, ones who hold little if any actual interest in their Ozark Mountains vacations or what food they eat. They were duped—caught in some fantasy world where Disney's Snow White is the foreperson clanging the work bell and handing out meal tickets for those who whistle the loudest while working the hardest to line somebody else's pockets with cash.

It is fiction, and fiction is destroying America.

Musicals, as Frank probably inadvertently invokes here, are reliably spin-ning yarns about this kind of community. He was right to point out the ease of fantasy, but he was wrong about its borders. Fantasy is nonpartisan, and I don't think it's just in Kansas anymore, Toto. Americans prefer to live *in*authentically, if that's the word Frank wants to use. *Epistemic difference* is perhaps more on the nose—a disagreement about the ways we know what we know. Frank's inac-curate aim has been typical of journalistic sharpshooters trying to pick off an answer for why "flyover states" consistently vote against their best interests and buy into hastily built falsehoods. The easiest answer may be to condemn those in the Middle as gullible, naïve, or the products of stubborn anti-intellectualism. The correct answer is that deception has become a trading language in America, and those in the Middle speak it well.

Fast-forward from Thomas Frank's gaze at the Middle and consider where this inattention to truth has landed America today. Musicals, predictably, are at the center of it.

Before answering Donald Trump's call to pull the stopper on Washington, D.C.'s swamp, his personal attorney and henchman Rudy Giuliani took a bow for draining another city's swamp, New York's Times Square. Not that long ago a gritty, peep-show-filled pocket of Manhattan, Times Square now houses Disney and an Applebee's, thanks in part to former New York City mayor Giuliani's redevelopment efforts. Musicals may owe him a lot. Shortly after 9/11, Giuliani propped up his city's economy by propping up the Broadway industry. "If you really want to help New York City," he said, "come to New York. Go to a play. Spend money in New York City."[12]

Giuliani is an unsuspecting impresario, but then again so is his boss—a character who might as well have stepped right out of Meredith Wilson's Rock Island express train ("you can talk all you wanna but it's different than it was"). Americans may have put a reality star in the Oval Office in 2016, but the ballot seems to have been cast for fantasy, not reality. Giuliani, Trump, and musicals are all prominent exports of New York and share a fantastical relationship with the truth. The alignment of all three suggests that lies are more precious than reality and that visions for newer worlds are just beginning to unravel the fabric of the actual.

"Truth isn't truth," Giuliani told NBC reporter Chuck Todd in 2018, defending a man whose statements PolitiFact rated as more than 70 percent "mostly false, false, or pants on fire."[13] Giuliani later took to Twitter—that enclave of 280-characters-or-less stories out of place—to clarify: "My statement was not meant as a pontification on moral theology but one referring to the situation where two people make precisely contradictory statements, the classic 'he said, she said' puzzle. Sometimes further inquiry can reveal the truth[;] other times it doesn't." Giuliani's defense of dishonesty boots political deception out of the moralistic universe where lying is frowned upon. This is not about morality, he is claiming, but about reality. Spoken like a true Times Square visionary—ya gotta know the territory.

I don't need to explain here the tremendous uncertainty and confusion that Giuliani's truth-isn't-truth statement creates. Nor am I crafting a defense or explanation for such political maneuvering. This is simply to say that if truth cannot be summoned for its day in court—cannot be brought out in broad daylight and described in a newsletter, will not be easily distinguished from its neighbors—then truth has stopped holding power in our lives. That is not to say that truth disappears. Truth *ends*. It stops being a metric of our world. We stop believing in it. Increasingly, evangelizing for that reality will be a losing battle. People finally tire of truth's tirades and slipperiness, its inconvenience and shame. Lies and deception may come with a price but only in the kind of economy where truth has a bounty.

What comes after truth appears hazy but is not too hard to imagine—that glossy-eyed look we get when existing in the here-and-now but dreaming of the then-and-there, a new world that is not like this one. It sounds ideal, the kind of yarn longtime host of *A Prairie Home Companion* Garrison Keillor might spin about the charmingly fictional town Lake Wobegon (as in "woe-be-gone"), where "all the women are strong, all the men are good looking, and all the children above average." People want the best stories to be true, Keillor once told reporters. It doesn't matter that what's true about Lake Wobegon isn't where it lies on a map (it's somewhere in central Minnesota, for the record—the middle of the Middle). The metric of its realness is the passive invitation it gives audiences to actively imagine a better real. "All I do is say the words: cornfield and Mother and algebra and Chevy pickup and cold beer and Sunday morning and rhubarb and loneliness, and other people put pictures to them."[14] Keillor is performing modesty here, but this kind of imagination takes real work. If you listen closely enough, maybe you can hear what Frank did—the faint but persistent chorus of America whistling as it works to build its unreality.

This theatrical permissiveness is at the core of musical theater's charm. Like the political wordsmithing of modern times, musicals are also patently unreal. Broadway traffics in fact when it means fiction, makes up endings to better fit the narrative, and makes fistfuls of cash doing it. If musicals held press briefings or spoke through personal attorneys, we might be more flummoxed with their deceit.

They are what they are, some would shrug.

Would you believe? others might scoff.

I like that they tell it like it is, loudly, from the back corner.

And so we could say—as so many have said—of the major actors in this nativist and populist theater. There are sections of this country that would prefer the pleasant world of musicals over the unfair one we have, and there are people who prefer to believe simple falsehoods from podiums and iPhones over the complex and brutal truths of our time. These are not the same people yet they are the same people.

Perhaps there are degrees of difference between lies of imagined rural Minnesota and lies of an imagined American past told by rogue political leaders. Fair enough. But what separates truth from fiction in all of these contexts is a willingness to play along. That's the connection, the thin small wire Anne Sexton says is enough, that is all we need. More to the point, it may be *all we have*. Whatever binds together our political theater and musical theater is bipartisan—a love for making convenient fictions out of inconvenient truth. Our musicals and our Lake Wobegons entice with otherworldliness for precisely the same reasons our political leaders succeed in permitting American's otherworldliness. They are completely true to their untrue selves.

After the End

Sew these scenes together, crease them tri-fold. Tuck it in your back pocket.

Let's call it a map.

Which is handy, since plotting out where and how truth makes its home will require a new cartography. These crisp maps fold out into a landscape imagined anew because they come out of a quest for a fresh reality about space, time, and belief in what is real. Musicals have given us an opportunity for experiencing other worlds in part because musical stages invite embodiment. We live the truth or we live the lie ourselves, in our own bodies and of our own minds. David Whyte knows this about honesty: "Where we cannot go in our mind, our memory, or our body is where we cannot be straight with another, with the world, or with our self."[15] Truth is a kind of geography—imagined or real makes little difference.

With the ends of humans, of truth, and of lying, we can expect a beginning of something more real, something to believe in that is here. Now. A belief anyone can feel as real because everyone has been invited to come and touch it.

Ever the satirist, Mark Twain offers a surprising moment of lucidity in calling for a renewed effort to deceive for the greater good and to do so with firm conviction that imagining new worlds is nothing to be ashamed about. It may be our only hope. "Lying is universal," he writes. "We *all* do it."

> Therefore, the wise thing is for us diligently to train ourselves to lie thoughtfully, judiciously, to lie with a good object, and not an evil one; to lie for others' advantage, and not our own; to lie healingly, charitably, humanely, not cruelly, hurtfully, maliciously; to lie gracefully and graciously, not awkwardly and clumsily; to lie firmly, frankly, squarely, with head erect, not haltingly, tortuously, with pusillanimous mien, as being ashamed of our high calling. Then shall we be rid of the rank and pestilent truth that is rotting the land; then shall we be great and good and beautiful, and worthy dwellers in a world where even benign Nature habitually lies.[16]

Whatever distance between fact and fantasy there might have been in Mark Twain's America, it seems unlikely to match that of our own. And of the future? It's hard to say where the ends meet.

But the charge to "lie healingly, charitably, humanely" feels *real* to me. Brutal truth has proven no match for us; we need an art of humane deception now more than ever. The consequences of casting the burden on truth alone to deliver us from our own devices will prove disastrous. We need to adjust our spatial awareness of reality first, to:

- Learn to lie, and lie well.
- Craft better worlds than the one we have.
- Dwell stubbornly and fiercely in the Middle.
- Devise something unbelievable out of big, bold dreams.
- Line our pockets with threads of untruth and fill them with the misshapen curiosities we stoop to pick up along our paths.

Until our musicals stop being musicals, we can look to them as guides for our storytelling. And until we stop being human, we can live up to our highest calling as liars. But a future without musicals means we eventually must do the work of building new worlds on our own—wherever we are, in whatever Middle place we find ourselves. Maybe that's Branson, Missouri, or Colorado City, Arizona, or Oklahoma City, or Cincinnati. But we could also be in Salina, Kansas. Duluth, Minnesota. Kearney, Nebraska. Dalhart, Texas. Miles City, Montana. Normal, Illinois. A spaceship hovering in outer orbit. Broadway's Richard Rodgers Theatre. The places where musicals deceive us are everywhere. Anyplace will do, and we are never out of places.

It is not too late to seek a newer world, Ulysses. Our next show calls for something new and exciting, a story no one has thought to think before. An audience is gathering to the Middle, restless and eager to believe. Even now, there comes a voice calling for places.

Places, everyone.

Thank you, places.

Notes

Chapter 1. Stories Out of Place

1. Stacy Wolf, *Beyond Broadway: The Pleasure and Promise of Musical Theatre across America* (New York: Oxford University Press, 2019).

2. See Ian Bradley, *You've Got to Have a Dream: The Message of the Musical* (Louisville, KY: Westminster John Knox Press, 2004), 73.

3. Mircea Eliade, *Shamanism: Archaic Techniques of Ecstasy* (Princeton, NJ: Princeton University Press, 1951), 511.

4. Lyrics from Friedrich Holländer, "Münchhausen," in *Modernism and Music: An Anthology of Sources*, ed. and with commentary by Daniel Albright (Chicago: University of Chicago Press, 2004), 349.

5. Johan Huizinga, *Homo Ludens: A Study of the Play-Element in Culture* (New York: Routledge, 1980).

6. Jill Dolan, *Utopia in Performance: Finding Hope at the Theater* (Ann Arbor: University of Michigan Press, 2005), 6.

7. Oscar Wilde, "The Decay of Lying: An Observation," in *Intentions* (Auckland: Floating Press, 2009), 28.

8. Dan Ariely, *The (Honest) Truth about Dishonesty: How We Lie to Everyone—Especially Ourselves* (New York: HarperCollins, 2012), 165.

9. Mark Twain, *On the Decay of the Art of Lying* (Portland, OR: Floating Press, 2008), 11.

10. Ariely, *The (Honest) Truth*, 187–88.

11. See Emma E. Levine and Maurice E. Schweitzer, "Prosocial Lies: When Deception Breeds Trust," *Organizational Behavior and Human Decision Processes* 126 (2015):

88–106; Sanjiv Erat and Uri Gneezy, "White Lies," *Management Science* 58, no. 4 (2012): 723–33.

12. Levine and Schweitzer, "Prosocial Lies," 95.

13. Mary Douglas, *Purity and Danger: An Analysis of Concepts of Pollution and Taboo* (New York: Routledge, 1966).

14. See, for example, Immanuel Kant, *Groundwork of the Metaphysics of Morals*, trans. and ed. by Mary Gregor and Jens Timmermann, with an introduction by Christine M. Korsgaard (New York: Cambridge University Press, 1998).

15. Mary Douglas, *Natural Symbols: Explorations in Cosmology* (London: Cresset Press, 1970). Douglas's work on the Grid-Group model expanded under the work of Michael Thompson, Richard Ellis, and Aaron Wildavsky to include not only the evolution of religious expression from primitive communities to modern ones, which was Douglas's original design, but also political and economic models directly applicable to modern communities. See Thompson, Ellis, and Wildavsky, *Cultural Theory* (Boulder, CO: Westview Press, 1990).

16. For a discussion of Jud's perceived blackness and outsider status, see Andrea Most's chapter, "'We Know We Belong to the Land': The Theatricality of Assimilation in *Oklahoma!*," in *Making Americans: Jews and the Broadway Musical* (Cambridge, MA: Harvard University Press, 2005), 117. Marian Wilson Kimber places the women of *The Music Man* within a broader history of elocution and arts advocacy in her chapter, "Grecian Urns in Iowa Towns: Delsarte and *The Music Man*," in *The Elocutionists: Women, Music, and the Spoken Word* (Urbana: University of Illinois Press, 2017).

17. René Girard, *Violence and the Sacred* (Baltimore: Johns Hopkins University Press, 1979).

18. See Max Weber, *Economy and Society* (New York: Bedminster Press, 1968).

19. Raymond Knapp and Mitchell Morris, "Tin Pan Alley Songs on Stage and Screen before World War II," in *The Oxford Handbook of the American Musical*, ed. Raymond Knapp, Mitchell Morris, and Stacy Wolf (New York: Oxford University Press, 2011), 83.

20. Alex Preston, "Author Will Ashon: 'There's a Real Value to Being Lost,'" *The Guardian*, March 26, 2017. For his comparison of historiography to jigsaw puzzles, see Will Ashon, *Chamber Music: Wu-Tang and America (in 36 Pieces)* (New York: Faber & Faber Social, 2019), 25.

21. Phil Ford, "Disciplinarity (Or, Musicology Is Anything You Can Get Away With)," *Dial M for Musicology*, June 28, 2015; emphasis mine. https://dialmformusicology.wordpress.com/2015/06/28/disciplinarity/.

22. Randall Collins, *The Sociology of Philosophies: A Global Theory of Intellectual Change* (Cambridge, MA: Harvard University Press, 1998), 32.

Chapter 2. Re-Placing the American Musical

1. From Teasdale's poem "Places" in Teasdale, *Flame and Shadow* (New York: Macmillan, 1920), 15.

2. Lately, scholars of musical theater and popular music studies more broadly have been engaged in conversations surrounding how authenticity and shame factor into musical theater's place within the field. See Jake Johnson et al., "Divided by a Common Language: Musical Theater and Popular Music Studies," *Journal of Popular Music Studies* 31, no. 4 (2019): 32–50.

3. Chief among those margins you'll find the gay communities, who gathered around musicals as a subversive and safe space while the advent of youth culture stole away much of the popular and familiar energy surrounding musicals. See, for instance, John Clum, *Something for the Boys: Musical Theater and Gay Culture* (New York: Palgrave Macmillan, 2001). For examples of gender fluidity on American stages in the nineteenth century, see Gillian Rodger, *Just One of the Boys: Female-to-Male Cross-Dressing on the American Variety Stage* (Urbana: University of Illinois Press, 2018).

4. Cara Wood, "Representing the Midwest in American Stage and Film Musicals, 1943–1962" (PhD diss., Princeton University, 2010), 15.

5. Allen Ginsburg, "Wichita Vortex Sutra," in Ginsburg, *Collected Poems, 1947–1997* (New York: HarperCollins, 2010), 402.

6. Thomas Frank, *What's the Matter with Kansas? How Conservatives Won the Heart of America* (New York: Metropolitan Books, 2004), 36.

7. Richard C. Longworth, *Caught in the Middle: America's Heartland in the Age of Globalism* (New York: Bloomsbury, 2008), 103.

8. Clayton M. Christensen, *Competing against Luck: The Story of Innovation and Customer Choice* (New York: Harper Business, 2016).

9. See what J. J. Gibson calls the "affordance" of objects in *The Senses Considered as Perceptual Systems* (Boston: Houghton Mifflin, 1966); the political language of "artifacts" in Langdon Winner's "Do Artifacts Have Politics?," *Daedalus* 109, no. 1 (1980): 121–36; and Bruno Latour's discussion of nondeterminative and determinative uses of objects as "technologism" in "Where Are the Missing Masses? A Sociology of a Few Mundane Artefacts," in *Shaping Technology/Building Society: Studies in Sociotechnical Change*, ed. W. E. Bijker and K. Law (Cambridge: MIT Press, 1991): 151–80.

10. Alexander Nemerov, "Interventions: The Boy in Bed: The Scene of Reading in N. C. Wyeth's *Wreck of the 'Covenant*,'" *Art Bulletin* 88, no. 1 (2006): 67.

11. Recent cross-examined studies of the musical outside of Broadway include monographs such as Wolf, *Beyond Broadway*; Andrea Most, *Theatrical Liberalism: Jews and Popular Entertainment in America* (New York: New York University Press, 2013); and my own *Mormons, Musical Theater, and Belonging in America* (Urbana: University of Illinois Press, 2019). Judah M. Cohen and I coedited a special issue of the journal *Studies in Musical Theatre* (March 2020) devoted to decentering the musical through ethnographic work; see also ethnographic studies of Broadway and off-Broadway musical theater by Elizabeth L. Wollman, *The Theater Will Rock: A History of the Rock Musical, From* Hair *to* Hedwig (Ann Arbor: University of Michigan Press, 2006), and Wollman, *Hard Times: The Adult Musical in 1970s New York City* (New York: Oxford University Press, 2013). Finally, the mediatized musical experience through television

and film likewise dislodges the musical from its Broadway stronghold; see Kelly Kessler, *Broadway in the Box: Television's Lasting Love Affair with the Musical* (New York: Oxford University Press, 2020), Todd Decker, *Music Makes Me: Fred Astaire and Jazz* (Berkeley: University of California Press, 2011), and Laurence Maslon, *Broadway to Main Street: How Show Tunes Enchanted America* (New York: Oxford University Press, 2018).

12. Pierre Bourdieu, *Masculine Domination*, trans. Richard Nice (Stanford, CA: Stanford University Press, 2001), 82.

13. Ian Hodder, *Entangled: An Archaeology of the Relationships between Humans and Things* (Hoboken, NJ: Wiley-Blackwell, 2012).

14. Alexander Saxton, "Blackface Minstrelsy and Jacksonian Ideology," *American Quarterly* 27, no. 1 (1975): 3–28.

15. Raymond Knapp, "Popular Music contra German Idealism: Anglo-American Rebellions from Minstrelsy to Camp," in *Making Light: Haydn, Musical Camp, and the Long Shadow of German Idealism* (Durham, NC: Duke University Press, 2018), 137–220.

16. Katherine Preston, *Opera for the People: English-Language Opera and Women Managers in Late 19th-Century America*. AMS Studies in Music. (New York: Oxford University Press, 2017), 3.

17. Michael V. Pisani, *Music for the Melodramatic Theatre in Nineteenth-Century London and New York* (Iowa City: University of Iowa Press, 2014), xii.

18. David Glassberg, *American Historical Pageantry: The Uses of Tradition in the Early Twentieth Century* (Chapel Hill: University of North Carolina Press, 1990), 161–62.

19. Raymond Knapp, *The American Musical and the Performance of Personal Identity* (Princeton, NJ: Princeton University Press, 2006), 67.

20. David Z. Saltz, "Infiction and Outfiction: The Role of Theatrical Fiction in Theatrical Performance," in *Staging Philosophy: Intersections of Theater, Performance, and Philosophy*, ed. David Krasner and David Z. Saltz (Ann Arbor: University of Michigan Press, 2006), 203.

21. Maslon, *Broadway to Main Street*, xv.

22. Steve Young and Sport Murphy, *Everything's Coming Up Profits: The Golden Age of Industrial Musicals* (New York: Blast Books, 2013), 8. The delightful 2018 documentary film *Bathtubs over Broadway* was based on Young's book.

23. See, for instance, John Strausbaugh, *Black Like You: Blackface, Whiteface, Insult, and Imitation in American Popular Culture* (New York: Tarcher, 2006), and Most, *Theatrical Liberalism*. Mormons, too, took up blackface for similar reasons, though they were largely doing so in faraway Utah rather than within any New York City borough. See Jake Johnson, *"Promised Valley*, Integration, and the Singing Voice," in *Mormons, Musical Theater, and Belonging in America*, 55–82.

24. John Koegel, *Music in German Immigrant Theater: New York City, 1840–1940* (Rochester, NY: University of Rochester Press, 2009); Sabine Haenni, *The Immigrant Scene: Ethnic Amusements in New York, 1880–1920* (Minneapolis: University of Minnesota Press,

2008), 9. Other noteworthy studies of ethnic theater in the United States include Peter Graff, "Music, Entertainment, and the Negotiation of Ethnic Identity in Cleveland's Neighborhood Theaters, 1914–1924" (PhD diss., Case Western Reserve University, 2018); Edna Nahshon, ed., *New York's Yiddish Theater: From the Bowery to Broadway* (New York: Columbia University Press, 2016); Maxine Seller, ed., *Ethnic Theatre in the United States* (New York: Greenwood Press, 1984); Mark Slobin, *Tenement Songs: The Popular Music of the Jewish Immigrants* (Urbana: University of Illinois Press, 1982); Janet Sturman, *Zarzuela: Spanish Operetta, American Stage* (Urbana: University of Illinois Press, 1990); Joshua S. Walden, "The 'Yidishe Paganini': Sholem Aleichem's Stempenyu, the Music of Yiddish Theatre, and the Character of the Shtetl Fillder," *Journal of the Royal Music Association* 139, no. 1 (2014): 89–136.

25. See Karen Ahlquist, "Musical Assimilation and 'the German Element' at the Cincinnati Sängerfest, 1879," *Musical Quarterly* 94, no. 3 (2011): 381–416, and Lei Ouyang Bryant, "Performing Race and Place in Asian America: Korean American Adoptees, Musical Theatre, and the Land of 10,000 Lakes," *Asian Music* 40, no. 1 (2009): 4–30.

26. Nicolás Kanellos, *A History of Hispanic Theatre in the United States: Origins to 1940* (Austin: University of Texas Press, 1990), xiii.

27. Ibid., xiv–xv. See also Steven Loza, *Barrio Rhythm: Mexican American Music in Los Angeles* (Urbana: University of Illinois Press, 1993).

28. John Koegel, "Mexican Musical Theater and Movie Palaces in Downtown Los Angeles before 1950," in *The Tide Was Always High: The Music of Latin America in Los Angeles*, ed. Josh Kun (Berkeley: University of California Press, 2017), 53. Koegel adds that "Mexican *revistas* were often scrappy, catchy, and risqué; they presented a humorous, sardonic take on the news of the day that was of immediate interest to audiences."

29. Thomas shows that, although originating in Spain, this Spanish-language genre of musical theater flourished in Havana as an important space for negotiating gender roles in early twentieth century Cuba. See Susan Thomas, *Cuban Zarzuela: Performing Race and Gender on Havana's Lyric Stage* (Urbana: University of Illinois Press, 2009), 27.

30. The villancico was a genre of song and poetry popular throughout Spain and Latin America. See Andrew A. Cashner, "Playing Cards at the Eucharistic Table: Music, Theology, and Society in a Corpus Christi Villancico from Colonial Mexico, 1628," *Journal of Early Modern History* 18 (2014): 383–419; Cashner, *Hearing Faith: Music as Theology in the Spanish Empire* (Leiden: Brill, 2020).

31. Nancy Yunhwa Rao, *Chinatown Opera Theater in North America* (Urbana: University of Illinois Press, 2017), 7.

32. See, for instance, Laura McDonald's study on American musicals in China in "The Sound of Musicals: Japan and Korea Have Embraced and Nurtured Western-Style Musicals: Can China Be Far Behind?" *American Theatre* (May/June 2017): 28–31, 58; and Jiyoon Jung, "The Right to See and Not to Be Seen: South Korean Musicals and Young Feminist Activism," *Studies in Musical Theatre* 14, no. 1 (2020): 37–50. See also

David Savran, "Broadway as Global Brand," *Journal of Contemporary Drama in English* 5, no. 1 (2017): 24–37.

33. Rao, *Chinatown Opera Theater*, 8.

34. This religiosity cast upon musicals often takes the form of racial tokenism, specifically in granting space to a marginal character (usually a woman of color) to moralize the show with a racialized musical language, such as gospel or soul. See, for instance, Dan Dinero, "A Big Black Lady Stops the Show: Black Women, Performances of Excess and the Power of Saying No," *Studies in Musical Theatre* 6, no. 1 (2012): 29–41.

35. Friedrich Kittler, *Gramophone, Film, Typewriter*, trans. Geoffrey Winthrop-Young and Michael Wutz (Stanford, CA: Stanford University Press, 1999), 96–97.

36. Leigh Eric Schmidt, *Hearing Things: Religion, Illusion, and the American Enlightenment* (Cambridge, MA: Harvard University Press, 2000).

37. John Hollander, *The Untuning of the Sky: Ideas of Music in English Poetry, 1500–1700* (Hamden, CT: Archon Books, 1993).

38. This portion of my argument builds upon previous work on religiosity and popular music. Some of the biggest influences on my thinking include Bradley, *You've Got to Have a Dream*, Robin Sylvan, *Traces of the Spirit: The Religious Dimensions of Popular Music* (New York: New York University Press, 2002), and Mitchell Morris, "Kansas and the Prophetic Tone," *American Music* 18, no. 1 (2000): 1–38.

Chapter 3. Fundamentalism, Produced

1. Maslon, *Broadway to Main Street*, 67.

2. Textual poaching often takes the form of fan fiction. See Henry Jenkins, *Textual Poachers: Television Fans and Participatory Culture* (New York: Routledge, 1992). A more theoretical analysis of poaching and combinatory culture, including musical mashups, arguably begins with Mikhail Bakhtin's concept of heteroglossia, as developed in *The Dialogic Imagination* (Austin: University of Texas Press, 1983).

3. Lawrence Levine, *Highbrow/Lowbrow: The Emergence of Cultural Hierarchy in America* (Cambridge, MA: Harvard University Press, 1990).

4. Tara Westover, *Educated: A Memoir* (New York: Random House, 2018), 86.

5. Carolyn Jessop, *Escape* (New York: Broadway Books, 2007), 210–11.

6. Patrick Q. Mason, *The Mormon Menace: Violence and Anti-Mormonism in the Postbellum South* (New York: Oxford University Press, 2011).

7. "'His Little Widows' an Amusing Show," *New York Times*, May 1, 1917.

8. See Danielle Ward-Griffin, "As Seen on TV: Putting the NBC Opera on Stage," *Journal of the American Musicological Society* 71, no. 3 (2018): 595–694, for a history of the NBC Opera Company and an accompanying list of productions mounted between 1949 and 1964.

9. Daymon Smith, "LDS Anthropologist Daymon Smith on Post-Manifesto Polygamy, Correlation, the Corporate LDS Church, and Mammon," *Mormon Stories* podcast, May

13, 2010, https://www.mormonstories.org/podcast/daymon-smith-on-correlation
-the-corporate-lds-church-and-mammon/.

10. See Martha Sonntag Bradley, *Kidnapped from That Land: The Government Raids on the Short Creek Polygamists* (Salt Lake City: University of Utah Press, 1993).

11. Brett D. Dowdle writes, "Although acknowledging that the war would come at a tremendous cost to the nation, Brigham Young believed that America had contracted a substantial debt through its persecution of the Saints and that any result other than the 'overthrow' of the nation 'would rob justice of its claims.'" See Dowdle, "'What Means This Carnage?': The Civil War in Mormon Thought," in *Civil War Saints*, ed. Kenneth L. Alford (Provo, UT: Religious Studies Center, 2012), 107–125.

12. Bruce R. McConkie, *Mormon Doctrine* (Salt Lake City: Bookcraft, 1958; 2nd ed., 1966), 578. Polygamy also continues in principle through Mormon temple ceremonies. See Peggy Fletcher Stack, "Polygamy Lives on in LDS Temples, Spurring Agony, Angst, and a Key Question: Who Will Be Married to Whom in Heaven?," *Salt Lake Tribune*, November 24, 2019.

13. While this is an ideological point, the FLDS are forced into some of these arrangements. Randi Kaye of CNN writes, "Polygamists have multiple wives and dozens of children but the state [of Utah] only recognizes one marriage. That leaves the rest of the wives to claim themselves as single moms with armies of children to support. Doing that means they can apply for welfare, which they do. And it's all legal." "How Polygamy Affects Your Wallet," CNN, May 11, 2006, https://www.cnn.com/CNN/Programs/anderson.cooper.360/blog/2006/05/how-polygamy-affects-your-wallet.html.

14. Stephen Singular, *When Men Become Gods: Mormon Polygamist Warren Jeffs, His Cult of Fear, and the Women Who Fought Back* (New York: St. Martin's Press, 2008), 29.

15. Brent W. Jeffs, *Lost Boy: The True Story of One Man's Exile from a Polygamist Cult and His Brave Journey to Reclaim His Life* (New York: Broadway Books, 2010), 9.

16. Johnson, *Mormons, Musical Theater, and Belonging*, 57–58.

17. Philip Salim Francis, *When Art Disrupts Religion: Aesthetic Experience and the Evangelical Mind* (New York: Oxford University Press, 2017), 9.

18. David Barry, Ralph Bathurst, and Lloyd Williams, "Cadences at Waco: A Critique of 'Timing and Music,'" *Academy of Management Review* 28, no. 3 (2003): 367–68.

19. "Cult's Founder Turned from Music to UFOs," *The Vindicator*, March 28, 1997, https://news.google.com/newspapers?id=WfZJAAAAIBAJ&sjid=EIUMAAAAIBAJ&pg=3096,8762810.

20. See John Lynch, "Charles Manson's Brief and Strange Relationship with the Beach Boys," *BusinessInsider*, November 20, 2017, https://www.businessinsider.com/charles-mansons-relationship-with-the-beach-boys-explained-2017-11.

21. Quoted in Schmidt, *Hearing Things*, 32.

22. Terry Eagleton, *Culture and the Death of God* (New Haven, CT: Yale University Press, 2014), 198.

23. Quoted in ibid., 62.

24. Anne Sexton, "Small Wire," in *The Awful Rowing toward God* (Boston: Houghton Mifflin, 1975), 78.

25. Raymond Knapp, "Saving Mr. [Blank]: Rescuing the Father through Song in Children's and Family Musicals," in *Children, Childhood, and Musical Theater*, ed. Donelle Ruwe and James Leve (New York: Routledge, 2020), 59–79.

26. Showcasing Max's Jewishness may not be as problematic for fundamentalists as one might imagine. Mormon theology has long held that Mormons are of the House of Israel and therefore call themselves Jews. See Johnson, *Mormons, Musical Theater, and Belonging*.

27. Jessop, *Escape*, 211.

28. Raymond Knapp, "History, 'The Sound of Music,' and Us," *American Music* 22, no. 1 (2004): 136.

29. See Ben McPherson's discussion on the virtual and vocal hyperreality of bio-musicals in McPherson, "Baudrillard on Broadway: Bio-Musicals, the Hyperreal, and the Cultural Politics of *Simuloquism*," *Journal of Interdisciplinary Voice Studies* 5, no. 1 (2020): 43–57.

30. See Knapp's discussion in "History, 'The Sound of Music,' and Us."

31. Elissa Harbert, "Unlikely Subjects: The Critical Reception of History Musicals," in *The Routledge Companion to the Contemporary Musical*, ed. Elizabeth L. Wollman and Jessica Sternfeld (New York: Routledge, 2019), 316.

32. See Levine and Schweitzer, "Prosocial Lies." See also Emma E. Levine and Maurice E. Schweitzer, "Are Liars Ethical? On the Tension between Benevolence and Honesty," *Journal of Experimental Social Psychology* 53 (2014): 107–117.

33. Lionel Trilling, *Sincerity and Authenticity* (Cambridge, MA: Harvard University Press, 1973).

34. Jason Frank and Isaac Kramnick, "What 'Hamilton' Forgets about Hamilton," *New York Times*, June 10, 2016.

35. Freddie Rokem, *Performing History* (Iowa City: University of Iowa Press, 2000), 102.

36. Scott Magelssen, "Making History in the Second Person: Post-Touristic Considerations for Living Historical Interpretation," *Theatre Journal* 58, no. 2 (2006), 305.

37. Kirsten Walsh and Adrian Currie, "Caricatures, Myths, and White Lies," *Metaphilosophy* 46, no. 3 (2015): 422.

38. There appears to be more than just momentum. The State of Utah decriminalized polygamy in 2020.

39. Janet Bennion, *Polygamy in Primetime: Media, Gender, and Politics in Mormon Fundamentalism* (Boston: Brandeis University Press, 2012), 7.

40. Nate Carlisle, "Think Mormon Offshoots Have the Most Polygamists in U.S.? Think Again," *Salt Lake Tribune*, April 15, 2016.

41. Bennion, *Polygamy in Primetime*, 16.

42. Francis Fukuyama, *The End of History and the Last Man* (New York: Free Press, 1992).

43. Eagleton, *Culture and the Death of God*, 155.

44. Ben Lerner, *The Topeka School* (New York: Farrar, Straus and Giroux, 2019), 273.

Chapter 4. Biblically Accurate

1. Thomas Merton, *The Seven Storey Mountain*, 50th anniversary ed. (1948; New York: Harcourt, 1998), 380.

2. Quoted in Bradley, *You've Got to Have a Dream*, 72. See Jake Johnson, "Post-Secular Musicals in a Post-Truth World," in *The Routledge Companion to the Contemporary Musical*, ed. Elizabeth L. Wollman and Jessica Sternfeld (New York: Routledge, 2019), 265–72.

3. C. S. Lewis, *Mere Christianity* (New York: Harper Collins, 2009), 196.

4. Dean Sell, phone interview with the author, October 16, 2019.

5. Quoted in Sissela Bok, *Lying: Moral Choice in Public and Private Life* (New York: Vintage, 1999), 47.

6. Interview with the author, September 29, 2018.

7. Denise Von Glahn, *The Sounds of Place: Music and the American Cultural Landscape* (Boston: Northeastern University Press, 2003), 8.

8. Elliot Lanes, "Theatre Review: 'Samson' at Sight and Sound Theatre in Lancaster County, PA," March 21, 2016, *MD Theatre Guide*, https://mdtheatreguide.com/2016/03/theatre-review-samson-at-sight-and-sound-theatre-in-lancaster-county-pa/.

9. Ann Pellegrini, "'Signaling through the Flames': Hell House Performance and Structures of Religious Feeling," *American Quarterly* 59, no. 3 (2007): 912. For more on Hell Houses in America, see Hank Willenbrink, "The Act of Being Saved: Hell House and the Salvific Performative," *Theatre Journal* 66, no. 1 (2014): 73–92.

10. Jill Stevenson, "Embodying Sacred History: Performing Creationism for Believers," *TDR* 56, no. 1 (2012), 100.

11. Roy Rosenzweig and David Thelen, *The Presence of the Past: Popular Uses of History in American Life* (New York: Columbia University Press, 2000), 105.

12. Willenbrink, "Act of Being Saved," 80, 83.

13. Bruce McConachie, "Falsifiable Theories for Theatre and Performance Studies," *Theatre Journal* 59, no. 4 (2007), 568. See also Gilles Fauconnier and Mark Turner, *The Way We Think: Conceptual Blending and the Mind's Hidden Complexities* (New York: Basic Books, 2002).

14. Isaac Weiner, *Religion Out Loud: Religious Sound, Public Space, and American Pluralism* (New York: New York University Press, 2013).

15. See Roshanak Kheshti's reading of "sonic signifiance" in *Modernity's Ear: Listening to Race and Gender in World Music* (New York: New York University Press, 2015), 70–73.

16. In my previous work, I discuss how musicals use reprises as a form of reincarnation. See "'I've Heard That Voice Before': Reprising the Voice in Sacred Time," in *Mormons, Musical Theater, and Belonging*, 113–41.

17. Eagleton, *Culture and the Death of God*, 160.

18. Andrea Most positions Jacob's theatrics as part of the ambivalence Jews have felt toward theater and their eventual acceptance of film and musicals as spaces to display American fantasies of liberalism. See Most, *Theatrical Liberalism.*

19. Ariely, *The (Honest) Truth,* 172.

20. Viktor Shklovsky, "Art as Technique," in *Russia Formalist Criticism: Four Essays,* trans. and with an introduction by Lee T. Lemon and Marion J. Reis (Lincoln: University of Nebraska Press, 1965), 12.

21. Francis, *When Art Disrupts Religion,* 14.

22. Seth Brodsky has made similar observations about modernism's reliance on musical fantasy to represent a negation or absence. See Brodsky, *From 1989; or, European Music and Modernist Unconscious* (Berkeley: University of California Press, 2017).

23. Toni Morrison, "On to Disneyland and the Real Unreality," *New York Times,* October 20, 1973.

24. Moe Meyer, "Reclaiming the Discourse of Camp," in *The Politics and Poetics of Camp,* ed. Moe Meyer (New York: Routledge, 1994), 5.

25. Saltz, "Infiction and Outfiction," 215.

26. Interview with the author, September 29, 2018.

27. Monique M. Ingalls, *Singing the Congregation: How Contemporary Worship Music Forms Evangelical Community* (New York: Oxford University Press, 2018), 2.

28. Merton, *Seven Storey Mountain,* 410.

Chapter 5. Everything Old Is New Again

1. Ray Bradbury, *Dandelion Wine* (New York: Bantam Books, 1957), 142.

2. Jonathan Sterne, "A Resonant Tomb," in *The Audible Past: Cultural Origins of Sound Reproduction* (Durham, NC: Duke University Press, 2003), 287–333.

3. Sarah Taylor Ellis, "Let's Do the Time Warp Again: Performing Time, Genre, and Spectatorship," in *The Routledge Companion to the Contemporary Musical,* ed. Elizabeth L. Wollman and Jessica Sternfeld (London: Routledge, 2019), 273.

4. Philip K. Dick's 1959 dystopian novel, *Time Out of Joint,* dramatizes how everyday reality may be circumspect and how time may be created for us with particular ends in mind.

5. Walter Benjamin, "The Storyteller: Reflections on the Works of Nikolai Leskov," in *Illuminations: Essays and Reflections,* ed. Hannah Arendt (New York: Schocken Books, 2007), 94.

6. While beyond the scope of this chapter, a larger study of aging in musical theater should take into account the particular and gendered space carved out by aging female performers. Mitchell Morris writes of the diva that she is "a woman who struggles to overcome ineradicable marks of a stigmatized identity. . . . To become a goddess, she must first appear as a victim." See Morris, *The Persistence of Sentiment: Display and Feeling in Popular Music of the 1970s* (Berkeley: University of California Press, 2013), 170. Aging may be one of those stigmas the diva displays; age is almost always a condition

of the diva, marking not only her tenure onstage but also her persistence in spite of increasing years. The role of the diva is thus a calculated performance in itself, often contrived to play into the pathos of hard-won success.

7. Ted Neeley starred as Jesus in the 1973 film version of *Jesus Christ Superstar* and subsequently performed that role over a thousand times. In 2010 he returned to the stage as Jesus at the Fox Theater in Riverside, California. See Jasmine Regala and Pamela Hogan, "A Conversation with Ted Neeley," *Fox Riverside Theater Foundation*, April 9, 2010.

8. Raymond Knapp, "'Waitin' for the Light to Shine': Musicals and Disability," in *The Oxford Handbook of Music and Disability Studies*, ed. Blake Howe, Stephanie Jensen-Moulton, Neil Lerner, and Joseph Straus (New York: Oxford University Press, 2015), 815.

9. Margaret Morganroth Gullette, *Aged by Culture* (Chicago: University of Chicago Press, 2004).

10. Gullette illustrates how watching depictions of the decline narrative in television shows, films, and onstage makes audiences feel older, to feel the decline, adding to her argument that aging is a cultural phenomenon, not simply biological fate.

11. Augusto Boal, *The Rainbow of Desire: The Boal Method of Theatre and Therapy* (London: Routledge, 1995), 13.

12. Annette Martin, phone interview with author, June 16, 2015.

13. *Still Kicking: The Fabulous Palm Springs Follies*, dir. Mel Damski (Little Apple Film Productions, 1997). This thirty-nine-minute documentary was presented at the Palm Springs International Short Film Festival and was nominated for an Academy Award for Best Documentary Short Subject.

14. Bobbie Burbridge Lane, email correspondence with author, June 16, 2015.

15. Jim Henline, phone interview with author, June 17, 2015.

16. Michael Mangan, *Staging Ageing: Theatre, Performance, and the Narrative of Decline* (Chicago: University of Chicago Press, 2013), 8.

17. Jessica Walker, "Elder Stereotypes in Media and Popular Culture," www.aging watch.com. October 30, 2010.

18. Lisa Kennedy, "Movies and TV: Popular Culture Is Giving Old-Age a Fresh Look," *Denver Post*, February 1, 2013.

19. Gullette, *Aged by Culture*, 101.

20. Ibid., 11.

21. Mangan, *Staging Ageing*, 21.

22. Gullette, *Aged by Culture*, 135.

23. See, for example, Victor Turner, "Liminality and Communitas," in *The Ritual Process: Structure and Anti-Structure* (New Brunswick, NJ: Aldine Transaction Press, 2008).

24. Mangan, *Staging Ageing*, 73.

25. Jonas Westover, *The Shuberts and Their Passing Shows: The Untold Tale of Ziegfeld's Rivals* (New York: Oxford University Press, 2016). Westover argues that the revue's

noted satirical punches were not wholly new; instead, they inherited a topical awareness and penchant for mocking its source material from the burlesque (see 182–83).

26. Annette Martin, interview.

27. Peter Mondelli, "Offenbach's *Bouffonnerie*, Wagner's *Rêverie*: The Materiality and Politics of the Ineffable in Second Empire Paris," *Opera Quarterly* 32, nos. 2–3 (2016): 138.

28. "History," Lyric Theatre of Oklahoma, https://lyrictheatreokc.com/about-lyric/our-history/.

29. Ibid.

30. Christy Carson, phone interview with the author, June 17, 2015.

31. Jim Henline, interview.

32. Christy Carson, interview.

33. For more on the economic and artistic negotiations common among regional theaters today, see Jeffrey Ullom, "Musicals in the Regional Theater," in Wollman and Sternfeld, *Routledge Companion to the Contemporary Musical*, 408–417.

34. See L. Levine, *Highbrow/Lowbrow*.

35. For his extended analysis of this phenomenon, see David Glassberg's chapter, "To Explain the City to Itself," in *American Historical Pageantry: The Uses of Tradition in the Early Twentieth Century*, 157–200.

36. Jan Cohen-Cruz, *Local Acts: Community-Based Performance in the United States* (New Brunswick, NJ: Rutgers University Press, 2005), 26.

37. Jim Henline, interview.

38. Gullette, *Aged by Culture*, 38.

39. Nick Couldry, *Why Voice Matters: Culture and Politics after Neoliberalism* (London: Sage Publications, 2010), 7.

40. Christy Carson, interview.

41. Claude Lévi-Strauss, *The Savage Mind* (Chicago: University of Chicago Press, 1966), 24.

42. John S. McClure, *Mashup Religion: Pop Music and Theological Invention* (Waco, TX: Baylor University Press, 2011), 1.

43. Ibid., 103.

44. Andrew Robinson, "In Theory / Bakhtin: Dialogism, Polyphony and Heteroglossia," July 29, 2011, *Ceasefire*, https://ceasefiremagazine.co.uk/in-theory-bakhtin-1/.

45. See Kathleen Hall Jamieson, *Packaging the Presidency: A History of Criticism of Presidential Campaign Advertising* (New York: Oxford University Press, 1992), 20.

46. "It Was a Very Good Year" was recorded by Sinatra for inclusion in his 1965 album, *September of My Years*. Released in anticipation of Sinatra's fiftieth birthday, the autumnal album includes other similarly age-tinted songs, including arranger Gordon Jenkins's "How Old Am I?" and Harold Arlen and Yip Harburg's "Last Night When We Were Young."

47. Benjamin, "The Storyteller," 83.

48. Ibid., 90.

49. Dolan, *Utopia in Performance*, 6.

50. Annette Martin, interview.

51. Longworth, *Caught in the Middle*, 4.

Chapter 6. Mezza Voce

1. Knapp, *American Musical*, 7.

2. Most, *Theatrical Liberalism*, 129. It is important to note that in *West Side Story* this sympathy falls along racial lines. In effect, a racial fantasy unfolds in this scenario: the Jets are a white gang who sing and dance to a jazz score, while the dark-skinned Sharks are shown to be incapable of keeping up with the vocal and choreographic chops the Jets demonstrate.

3. Kittler, *Gramophone, Film, Typewriter*, 27.

4. Anne Carson, "The Gender of Sound," in *Glass, Irony, and God* (New York: New Directions, 1995), 119.

5. See Nina Sun Eidsheim, "Race and the Aesthetics of Vocal Timbre," in *Rethinking Difference in Music Scholarship*, ed. Olivia Bloechl, Melanie Lowe, and Jeffrey Kallberg (New York: Cambridge University Press, 2015), 338–65; and Kheshti, *Modernity's Ear*.

6. Martha Feldman, "An Interstitial Voice: An Opening," in "Colloquy: Why Voice Now?" *Journal of the American Musicological Society* 68, no. 3 (2015): 658. See also Feldman, "Voice Gap Crack Break," in *The Voice as Something More: Essays toward Materiality*, ed. Martha Feldman and Judith T. Zeitlin (Chicago: University of Chicago Press, 2019), 188–208.

7. Michael Riedel, "How Broadway Emerged from Ruin to Become a Billion-Dollar Business," *New York Post*, June 12, 2011.

8. Lynne B. Sagalyn, *Times Square Roulette: Remaking the City Icon* (Cambridge: MIT Press, 2001), 310.

9. Ibid., 302.

10. Dave Malloy, "A Slushy in the Face: Musical Theater Music and the Uncool," *HowlRound*, December 12, 2011, https://howlround.com/slushy-face.

11. Ibid.

12. Adriana Nocco, writing for OnStageBlog.com, uses these words to describe Broadway's five "most distinctive female voices." According to Nocco's criteria, Menzel ranks at number three, ahead of Angela Lansbury and Ethel Merman and just behind Lena Hall and top-ranked Kristin Chenoweth.

13. Lauren Zuniga, "World's Tallest Hill," YouTube, July 15, 2012, https://www.youtube.com/watch?v=dswhhPtpdck.

14. "A Wicked Supercut of Elphaba's 'Defying Gravity,'" https://www.youtube.com/watch?v=qdjb2Xx6nyI, posted July 11, 2014. The website www.TheaterMania.com features several other supercuts, including "Don't Rain on My Parade" (*Funny Girl*), "Being Alive" (*Company*), "All That Jazz" (*Chicago*), "Some People" (*Gypsy*), and "Anything Goes" (*Anything Goes*).

15. Jonathan Burston, "Theatre Space as Virtual Place: Audio Technology, the Reconfigured Singing Body, and the Megamusical," *Popular Music* 17, no. 2 (1998): 205–206.

16. Jessica Sternfeld, *The Megamusical* (Bloomington: Indiana University Press, 2006), 4.

17. Ibid., 334.

18. Burston, "Theatre Space as Virtual Space," 206.

19. James R. Shortridge, *The Middle West: Its Meaning in American Culture* (Lawrence: University Press of Kansas, 1989), 33.

20. Wood, "Representing the Midwest," 14.

21. Frank Ragsdale, "Perspectives on Belting and Belting Pedagogy: A Comparison of Teachers of Classical Voice Students, Teachers of Nonclassical Voice Students, and Music Theatre Singers" (DMA diss., University of Miami, 2004), 47.

22. Ibid., 46.

23. "'The Triple-Threat' Philosophy." University of Cincinnati College-Conservatory of Music, https://ccm.uc.edu/areas-of-study/academic-units/musical-theatre.html.

24. "About," CCM Musical Theater Blog, https://ccmmt.wordpress.com/about/; emphasis added.

25. Rick Pender, "Retrospective: Forty Years of Musical Theatre Excellence," *CCM Village News Blog*, https://ccmpr.wordpress.com/2009/12/15/ccm-musical-theatre-a-retrospective/.

26. Nina Sun Eidsheim, *Sensing Sound: Singing and Listening as Vibrational Practice* (Durham, NC: Duke University Press, 2015); and Jennifer Stoever, *The Sonic Color Line: Race and the Cultural Politics of Listening* (New York: New York University Press, 2016).

27. Joan Melton, *Singing in Musical Theatre: The Training of Singers and Actors* (New York: Allworth Press, 2007), 133.

28. Kathryn Green, Warren Freeman, Matthew Edwards, and David Meyer, "Trends in Musical Theatre Voice: An Analysis of Audition Requirements for Singers," *Journal of Voice* 28, no. 3 (2014): 324–27. According to this website, this percentage comprised 59 of 1,238 total jobs from this period. Green and her coauthors conclude that while "traditional voice training remains indisputably valuable as a skill for the musical theatre singer . . . voice teachers and specialists must address CCM [Contemporary Commercial Music] styles of singing that currently dominate professional auditions in order to give musical theatre performers the best chance at success" (quote on p. 327).

29. Karen Hall, *So You Want to Sing Music Theater: A Guide for Professionals* (New York: Rowman and Littlefield, 2014), 59.

30. Ibid.

31. "The Demographics of the Broadway Audience 2018–2019," http://www.broadwayleague.com/index.php?url_identifier=the-demographics-of-the-broadway-audience.

32. Chris Geidner, "Patti LuPone Talks about Broadway's Problems" *MetroWeekly*, September 9, 2011, https://www.metroweekly.com/2011/09/patti-lupone-talks-about-broad/.

33. Riedel, "How Broadway Emerged."

34. Richard Zoglin, "Is Broadway Just for Tourists?" *Time*, January 2, 2013, https://entertainment.time.com/2013/01/02/is-broadway-just-for-tourists/.

35. Riedel, "How Broadway Emerged."

36. The microphone likewise contributed to a new vocal aesthetic, particularly among male voices. As Eric Salzman and Thomas Desi point out, the implementation of microphones in musical theater resulted in "a major reaction against the high, trained singing voices that had dominated for so long." Lower voices, no longer dependent on bodily projection, now came to dominate Broadway singing. Thus the bari-tenor displaced the primacy of higher vocal registers, for a time placing them "on the verge of extinction." Salzman and Desi, *The New Music Theater: Seeing the Voice, Hearing the Body* (New York: Oxford University Press, 2008), 24, 25n8.

37. Melton, *Singing in Musical Theatre*, 50.

38. Geidner, "Patti LuPone Talks about Broadway's Problems."

39. Burston, "Theatre Space as Virtual Space," 213.

40. Geidner, "Patti LuPone Talks about Broadway's Problems."

41. Ben Brantley, "How Broadway Lost Its Voice to 'American Idol,'" *New York Times*, March 27, 2005.

42. Ibid.

43. Eidsheim, "Race and the Aesthetics of Vocal Timbre." For a discussion of how the stethoscope amplified religious listening, see Schmidt, *Hearing Things*, 2–5.

44. James Q. Davies, "Voice Belongs," in "Colloquy: Why Voice Now?" *Journal of the American Musicological Society* 68, no. 3 (2015): 680.

Chapter 7. The Afterlives of Truth and Musicals

1. Michel de Certeau, *The Practice of Everyday Life*, trans. Steven Rendall (Berkeley: University of California Press, 1984), 93.

2. Matthew Causey, *Theatre and Performance in Digital Culture: From Simulation to Embeddedness* (London: Routledge, 2006), 15.

3. Maslon, *Broadway to Main Street*, 221.

4. Jorge Luis Borges, "On the Exactitude of Science," in *Collected Fictions*, trans. Andrew Hurley (New York: Penguin Books, 1998), 325. See also Lewis Carroll, *Sylvie and Bruno* (Mineola, NY: Dover Publications, 1988).

5. The practices of blackface, yellowface, and brownface are well documented, but some recent examples include Warren Hoffman, *The Great White Way: Race and the Broadway Musical* (New Brunswick, NJ: Rutgers University Press, 2014); Donatella Galella, "Feeling Yellow: Responding to Contemporary Yellowface in Musical Performance," *Journal of Dramatic Theory and Criticism* 32, no. 2 (2018): 67–77; and Dorinne Kondo's review essay of David Henry Hwang's musical *Soft Power*, "Soft Power: (Auto) ethnography, Racial Affect, and Dramaturgical Critique," *American Quarterly* 71, no. 1 (2019): 265–85. For a reading of queer minstrelsy onstage, see Drew Daniel, "'Why Be Something That You're Not?' Punk Performance and the Epistemology of Queer Minstrelsy," *Social Text* 31, no. 3 (116) (2013): 13–34.

6. Wilde, "Decay of Lying," 25–26.

7. See Arthur C. Danto, *After the End of Art: Contemporary Art and the Pale of History* (Princeton, NJ: Princeton University Press, 1997).

8. James Agee, "O My Poor Country I Have So Much Hated," in *The Collected Poems of James Agee* (New Haven, CT: Yale University Press, 1970), 157.

9. Roy Scranton, "Learning How to Die in the Anthropocene," *New York Times*, November 20, 2013.

10. Megan Garber, "'Edelweiss': An American Song for Global Dystopia," *The Atlantic*, November 23, 2015.

11. Frank, *What's the Matter with Kansas?*, 27.

12. Robert Simonson, "Mayor Giuliani Urges People to Help City by Attending Broadway Shows," *Playbill*, September 19, 2001.

13. Rebecca Morin and David Cohen, "Giuliani: 'Truth Isn't Truth,'" *Politico*, August 19, 2018, https://www.politico.com/story/2018/08/19/giuliani-truth-todd-trump -788161.

14. Garrison Keillor, "In Search of Lake Wobegon," *National Geographic*, December 2000, https://www.garrisonkeillor.com/national-geographic-in-search-of-lake-wobegon/. Keillor placed Lake Wobegon in central Minnesota and devised a clever explanation for its out-of-placeness: "If anyone asked why the town appeared on no maps, I explained that when the state map was drawn after the Civil War, teams of surveyors worked their way in from the four outer corners and, arriving at the center, found they had surveyed more of Minnesota than there was room for between Wisconsin and the Dakotas, and so the corners had to be overlapped in the middle, and Lake Wobegon wound up on the bottom flap."

15. David Whyte, *Consolations: The Solace, Nourishment, and Underlying Meaning of Everyday Words* (Langley, WA: Many Rivers Press, 2014), 117.

16. Twain, *On the Decay of the Art of Lying*, 11–12.

Bibliography

Agee, James. "O My Poor Country I Have So Much Hated." In *The Collected Poems of James Agee*, 157. New Haven, CT: Yale University Press, 1970.

Ahlquist, Karen. "Musical Assimilation and 'the German Element' at the Cincinnati Sängerfest, 1879." *Musical Quarterly* 94, no. 3 (2011): 381–416.

Albright, Daniel, ed. *Modernism and Music: An Anthology of Sources*. Chicago: University of Chicago Press, 2004.

Ariely, Dan. *The (Honest) Truth about Dishonesty: How We Lie to Everyone—Especially Ourselves*. New York: Harper Collins, 2012.

Ashon, Will. *Chamber Music: Wu-Tang and America (in 36 Pieces)*. New York: Faber & Faber Social, 2019.

Bakhtin, Mikhail. *The Dialogic Imagination*. Austin: University of Texas Press, 1983.

Barry, David, Ralph Bathurst, and Lloyd Williams. "Cadences at Waco: A Critique of 'Timing and Music.'" *Academic of Management Review* 28, no. 3 (2003): 367–68.

Benjamin, Walter. "The Storyteller: Reflections on the Works of Nikolai Leskov." In *Illuminations: Essays and Reflections*, edited by Hannah Arendt. New York: Schocken Books, 2007.

Bennion, Janet. *Polygamy in Primetime: Media, Gender, and Politics in Mormon Fundamentalism*. Boston: Brandeis University Press, 2012.

Boal, Augusto. *The Rainbow of Desire: The Boal Method of Theatre and Therapy*. London: Routledge, 1995.

Bok, Sissela. *Lying: Moral Choice in Public and Private Life*. New York: Vintage, 1999.

Borges, Jorge Luis. "On the Exactitude of Science." In *Collected Fictions*, translated by Andrew Hurley, 325. New York: Penguin Books, 1998.

Bourdieu, Pierre. *Masculine Domination*. Translated by Richard Nice. Stanford, CA: Stanford University Press, 2001.

Bradbury, Ray. *Dandelion Wine*. New York: Bantam Books, 1957.

Bradley, Ian. *You've Got to Have a Dream: The Message of the Musical*. Louisville, KY: Westminster John Knox Press, 2004.

Bradley, Martha Sonntag. *Kidnapped from That Land: The Government Raids on the Short Creek Polygamists*. Salt Lake City: University of Utah Press, 1993.

Brodsky, Seth. *From 1989; or, European Music and Modernist Unconscious*. Berkeley: University of California Press, 2017.

Bryant, Lei Ouyang. "Performing Race and Place in Asian America: Korean American Adoptees, Musical Theatre, and the Land of 10,000 Lakes." *Asian Music* 40, no. 1 (2009): 4–30.

Burston, Jonathan. "Theatre Space as Virtual Place: Audio Technology, the Reconfigured Singing Body, and the Megamusical." *Popular Music* 17, no. 2 (1998): 205–218.

Carroll, Lewis. *Sylvie and Bruno*. Mineola, NY: Dover Publications, 1988.

Carson, Anne. "The Gender of Sound." In *Glass, Irony, and God*, 119–37. New York: New Directions, 1995.

Cashner, Andrew A. *Hearing Faith: Music as Theology in the Spanish Empire*. Leiden: Brill, 2020.

——. "Playing Cards at the Eucharistic Table: Music, Theology, and Society in a Corpus Christi Villancico from Colonial Mexico, 1628." *Journal of Early Modern History* 18 (2014): 383–419.

Causey, Matthew. *Theatre and Performance in Digital Culture: From Simulation to Embeddedness*. London: Routledge, 2006.

Christensen, Clayton M. *Competing against Luck: The Story of Innovation and Customer Choice*. New York: Harper Business, 2016.

Clum, John. *Something for the Boys: Musical Theater and Gay Culture*. New York: Palgrave Macmillan, 2001.

Cohen-Cruz, Jan. *Local Acts: Community-Based Performance in the United States*. New Brunswick, NJ: Rutgers University Press, 2005.

Collins, Randall. *The Sociology of Philosophies: A Global Theory of Intellectual Change*. Cambridge, MA: Harvard University Press, 1998.

Couldry, Nick. *Why Voice Matters: Culture and Politics after Neoliberalism*. London: Sage Publications, 2010.

Daniel, Drew. "'Why Be Something That You're Not?' Punk Performance and the Epistemology of Queer Minstrelsy." *Social Text* 31, no. 3 (116) (2013): 13–34.

Danto, Arthur C. *After the End of Art: Contemporary Art and the Pale of History*. Princeton, NJ: Princeton University Press, 1997.

Davies, James Q. "Voice Belongs," in "Colloquy: Why Voice Now?" *Journal of the American Musicological Society* 68, no. 3 (2015): 677–81.

de Certeau, Michel. *The Practice of Everyday Life*. Translated by Steven Rendall. Berkeley: University of California Press, 1984.

Decker, Todd. *Music Makes Me: Fred Astaire and Jazz*. Berkeley: University of California Press, 2011.

Dick, Philip K. *Time Out of Joint*. Philadelphia: Lippincott, 1959.

Dinero, Dan. "A Big Black Lady Stops the Show: Black Women, Performances of Excess and the Power of Saying No." *Studies in Musical Theatre* 6, no. 1 (2012): 29–41.

Dolan, Jill. *Utopia in Performance: Finding Hope at the Theater*. Ann Arbor: University of Michigan Press, 2005.

Douglas, Mary. *Natural Symbols: Explorations in Cosmology*. London: Cresset Press, 1970.

———. *Purity and Danger: An Analysis of Concepts of Pollution and Taboo*. New York: Routledge, 1966.

Dowdle, Brett D. "'What Means This Carnage?': The Civil War in Mormon Thought." In *Civil War Saints*, edited by Kenneth L. Alford, 107–25. Provo, UT: Religious Studies Center, Brigham Young University, 2012.

Eagleton, Terry. *Culture and the Death of God*. New Haven, CT: Yale University Press, 2014.

Eidsheim, Nina Sun. "Race and the Aesthetics of Vocal Timbre." In *Rethinking Difference in Music Scholarship*, edited by Olivia Bloechl, Melanie Lowe, and Jeffrey Kallberg. New York: Cambridge University Press, 2015.

———. *Sensing Sound: Singing and Listening as Vibrational Practice*. Durham, NC: Duke University Press, 2015.

Eliade, Mircea. *Shamanism: Archaic Techniques of Ecstasy*. Princeton, NJ: Princeton University Press, 1951.

Ellis, Sarah Taylor. "Let's Do the Time Warp Again: Performing Time, Genre, and Spectatorship." In Wollman and Sternfeld, *Routledge Companion*, 273–82.

Erat, Sanjiv, and Uri Gneezy. "White Lies." *Management Science* 58, no. 4 (2012): 723–33.

Fauconnier, Gilles, and Mark Turner. *The Way We Think: Conceptual Blending and the Mind's Hidden Complexities*. New York: Basic Books, 2002.

Feldman, Martha. "An Interstitial Voice: An Opening," in "Colloquy: Why Voice Now?" *Journal of the American Musicological Society* 68, no. 3 (2015): 653–59.

———. "Voice Gap Crack Break." In *The Voice as Something More: Essays toward Materiality*, edited by Martha Feldman and Judith T. Zeitlin, 188–208. Chicago: University of Chicago Press, 2019.

Francis, Philip Salim. *When Art Disrupts Religion: Aesthetic Experience and the Evangelical Mind*. New York: Oxford University Press, 2017.

Frank, Thomas. *What's the Matter with Kansas? How Conservatives Won the Heart of America*. New York: Metropolitan Books, 2004.

Frommer, Myrna Katyz, and Harvey Frommer. *It Happened on Broadway: An Oral History of the Great White Way*. Lanham, MD: Taylor Trade Publishing, 2015.

Fukuyama, Francis. *The End of History and the Last Man*. New York: Free Press, 1992.

Galella, Donatella. "Feeling Yellow: Responding to Contemporary Yellowface in Musical Performance." *Journal of Dramatic Theory and Criticism* 32, no. 2 (2018): 67–77.

Gibson, J. J. *The Senses Considered as Perceptual Systems*. New York: Houghton Mifflin, 1966.

Ginsburg, Allen. "Wichita Vortex Sutra." In *Collected Poems, 1947–1997*, 402. New York: HarperCollins, 2010.

Girard, René. *Violence and the Sacred*. Baltimore: Johns Hopkins University Press, 1979.

Glassberg, David. "To Explain the City to Itself." In *American Historical Pageantry: The Uses of Tradition in the Early Twentieth Century*, 157–200. Chapel Hill: University of North Carolina Press, 1990.

Graff, Peter. "Music, Entertainment, and the Negotiation of Ethnic Identity in Cleveland's Neighborhood Theaters, 1914–1924." PhD diss., Case Western Reserve University, 2018.

Green, Kathryn, Warren Freeman, Matthew Edwards, and David Meyer. "Trends in Musical Theatre Voice: An Analysis of Audition Requirements for Singers." *Journal of Voice* 28, no. 3 (2014): 324–27.

Gullette, Margaret Morganroth. *Aged by Culture*. Chicago: University of Chicago Press, 2004.

Haenni, Sabine. *The Immigrant Scene: Ethnic Amusements in New York, 1880–1920*. Minneapolis: University of Minnesota Press, 2008.

Hall, Karen. *So You Want to Sing Music Theater: A Guide for Professionals*. New York: Rowman and Littlefield, 2014.

Harbert, Elissa. "Unlikely Subjects: The Critical Reception of History Musicals." In Wollman and Sternfeld, *Routledge Companion*, 312–22.

Hodder, Ian. *Entangled: An Archaeology of the Relationships between Humans and Things*. Hoboken, NJ: Wiley-Blackwell, 2012.

Hoffman, Warren. *The Great White Way: Race and the Broadway Musical*. New Brunswick, NJ: Rutgers University Press, 2014.

Holländer, Friedrich. "Münchhausen." In *Modernism and Music: An Anthology of Sources*, edited and with commentary by Daniel Albright, 349. Chicago: University of Chicago Press, 2004.

Hollander, John. *The Untuning of the Sky: Ideas of Music in English Poetry, 1500–1700*. Hamden, CT: Archon Books, 1993.

Huizinga, Johan. *Homo Ludens: A Study of the Play-Element in Culture*. New York: Routledge, 1980.

Ingalls, Monique M. *Singing the Congregation: How Contemporary Worship Music Forms Evangelical Community*. New York: Oxford University Press, 2018.

Jamieson, Kathleen Hall. *Packaging the Presidency: A History of Criticism of Presidential Campaign Advertising*. New York: Oxford University Press, 1992.

Jeffs, Brent W. *Lost Boy: The True Story of One Man's Exile from a Polygamist Cult and His Brave Journey to Reclaim His Life*. New York: Broadway Books, 2010.

Jenkins, Henry. *Textual Poachers: Television Fans and Participatory Culture*. New York: Routledge, 1992.

Jessop, Carolyn. *Escape*. New York: Broadway Books, 2007.

Johnson, Jake. *Mormons, Musical Theater, and Belonging in America*. Urbana: University of Illinois Press, 2019.

———. "Post-Secular Musicals in a Post-Truth World." In Wollman and Sternfeld, *Routledge Companion*, 265–72.

———. "*Promised Valley*, Integration, and the Singing Voice." In Johnson, *Mormons, Musical Theater, and Belonging*, 55–82.

Johnson, Jake, Masi Asare, Amy Coddington, Daniel Goldmark, Raymond Knapp, Oliver Wang, and Elizabeth Wollman. "Divided by a Common Language: Musical Theater and Popular Music Studies." *Journal of Popular Music Studies* 31, no. 4 (2019): 32–50.

Jung, Jiyoon. "The Right to See and Not to Be Seen: South Korean Musicals and Young Feminist Activism." *Studies in Musical Theatre* 14, no. 1 (2020): 37–50.

Kanellos, Nicolás. *A History of Hispanic Theatre in the United States: Origins to 1940*. Austin: University of Texas Press, 1990.

Kant, Immanuel. *Groundwork of the Metaphysics of Morals*, translated and edited by Mary Gregor and Jens Timmermann, with an introduction by Christine M. Korsgaard. New York: Cambridge University Press, 1998.

Kessler, Kelly. *Broadway in the Box: Television's Lasting Love Affair with the Musical*. New York: Oxford University Press, 2020.

Kheshti, Roshanak. *Modernity's Ear: Listening to Race and Gender in World Music*. New York: New York University Press, 2015.

Kimber, Marian Wilson. *The Elocutionists: Women, Music, and the Spoken Word*. Urbana: University of Illinois Press, 2017.

Kittler, Friedrich. *Gramophone, Film, Typewriter*. Translated by Geoffrey Winthrop-Young and Michael Wutz. Stanford, CA: Stanford University Press, 1999.

Knapp, Raymond. *The American Musical and the Performance of Personal Identity*. Princeton, NJ: Princeton University Press, 2006.

———. "History, 'The Sound of Music,' and Us." *American Music* 22, no. 1 (2004): 133–44.

———. "Popular Music contra German Idealism: Anglo-American Rebellions from Minstrelsy to Camp." In *Making Light: Haydn, Musical Camp, and the Long Shadow of German Idealism*, 137–220. Durham, NC: Duke University Press, 2018.

———. "Saving Mr. [Blank]: Rescuing the Father through Song in Children's and Family Musicals." In *Children, Childhood, and Musical Theater*, edited by Donelle Ruwe and James Leve, 59–79. New York: Routledge, 2020.

———. "'Waitin' for the Light to Shine': Musicals and Disability." In *The Oxford Handbook of Music and Disability Studies*, edited by Blake Howe, Stephanie Jensen-Moulton, Neil Lerner, and Joseph Straus. New York: Oxford University Press, 2015.

Knapp, Raymond, and Mitchell Morris. "Tin Pan Alley Songs on Stage and Screen before World War II." In *The Oxford Handbook of the American Musical*, edited by Raymond Knapp, Mitchell Morris, and Stacy Wolf, 81–96. New York: Oxford University Press, 2011.

Koegel, John. "Mexican Musical Theater and Movie Palaces in Downtown Los Angeles before 1950." In *The Tide Was Always High: The Music of Latin America in Los Angeles*, edited by Josh Kun, 46–75. Berkeley: University of California Press, 2017.

———. *Music in German Immigrant Theater: New York City, 1840–1940*. Rochester, NY: University of Rochester Press, 2009.

Kondo, Dorrine. "Soft Power: (Auto)ethnography, Racial Affect, and Dramaturgical Critique." *American Quarterly* 71, no. 1 (2019): 265–85.

Latour, Bruno. "Where Are the Missing Masses? A Sociology of a Few Mundane Artefacts." In *Shaping Technology/Building Society: Studies in Sociotechnical Change*, edited by W. E. Bijker and K. Law, 151–80. Cambridge: MIT Press, 1991.

Lerner, Ben. *The Topeka School*. New York: Farrar, Straus and Giroux, 2019.

Levine, Emma E., and Maurice E. Schweitzer. "Are Liars Ethical? On the Tension between Benevolence and Honesty." *Journal of Experimental Social Psychology* 53 (2014): 107–117.

———. "Prosocial Lies: When Deception Breeds Trust." *Organizational Behavior and Human Decision Processes* 126 (2015): 88–106.

Levine, Lawrence. *Highbrow/Lowbrow: The Emergence of Cultural Hierarchy in America*. Cambridge, MA: Harvard University Press, 1990.

Lévi-Strauss, Claude. *The Savage Mind*. Chicago: University of Chicago Press, 1966.

Lewis, C. S. *Mere Christianity*. New York: Harper Collins, 2009.

Longworth, Richard C. *Caught in the Middle: America's Heartland in the Age of Globalism*. London: Bloomsbury, 2008.

Loza, Steven. *Barrio Rhythm: Mexican American Music in Los Angeles*. Urbana: University of Illinois Press, 1993.

Magelssen, Scott. "Making History in the Second Person: Post-Touristic Considerations for Living Historical Interpretation." *Theatre Journal* 58, no. 2 (2006): 291–312.

Mangan, Michael. *Staging Ageing: Theatre, Performance, and the Narrative of Decline*. Chicago: University of Chicago Press, 2013.

Maslon, Laurence. *Broadway to Main Street: How Show Tunes Enchanted America*. New York: Oxford University Press, 2018.

Mason, Patrick Q. *The Mormon Menace: Violence and Anti-Mormonism in the Postbellum South*. New York: Oxford University Press, 2011.

McClure, John S. *Mashup Religion: Pop Music and Theological Invention*. Waco, TX: Baylor University Press, 2011.

McConachie, Bruce. "Falsifiable Theories for Theatre and Performance Studies." *Theatre Journal* 59, no. 4 (2007): 553–77.

McConkie, Bruce R. *Mormon Doctrine*. 2nd ed. Salt Lake City: Bookcraft, 1966.

McDonald, Laura. "The Sound of Musicals: Japan and Korea Have Embraced and Nurtured Western-Style Musicals: Can China Be Far Behind?" *American Theatre* (May/June 2017): 28–31, 58.

McPherson, Ben. "Baudrillard on Broadway: Bio-Musicals, the Hyperreal, and the Cultural Politics of *Simuloquism.*" *Journal of Interdisciplinary Voice Studies* 5, no. 1 (2020): 43–57.

Melton, Joan. *Singing in Musical Theatre: The Training of Singers and Actors.* New York: Allworth Press, 2007.

Merton, Thomas. *The Seven Storey Mountain.* 50th anniversary ed. 1948. New York: Harcourt, 1998.

Meyer, Moe. *The Politics and Poetics of Camp.* Edited by Moe Meyer. New York: Routledge, 1994.

Mondelli, Peter. "Offenbach's *Bouffonnerie,* Wagner's *Rêverie*: The Materiality and Politics of the Ineffable in Second Empire Paris." *Opera Quarterly* 32, nos. 2–3 (2016): 134–59.

Morris, Mitchell. "Kansas and the Prophetic Tone." *American Music* 18, no. 1 (2000): 1–38.

———. *The Persistence of Sentiment: Display and Feeling in Popular Music of the 1970s.* Berkeley: University of California Press, 2013.

Most, Andrea. *Making Americans: Jews and the Broadway Musical.* Cambridge, MA: Harvard University Press, 2005.

———. *Theatrical Liberalism: Jews and Popular Entertainment in America.* New York: New York University Press, 2013.

Nahshon, Edna, ed. *New York's Yiddish Theater: From the Bowery to Broadway.* New York: Columbia University Press, 2016.

Nemerov, Alexander. "Interventions: The Boy in Bed: The Scene of Reading in N. C. Wyeth's *Wreck of the 'Covenant.'*" *Art Bulletin* 88, no. 1 (2006): 61–68.

Pellegrini, Ann. "'Signaling through the Flames': Hell House Performance and Structures of Religious Feeling." *American Quarterly* 59, no. 3 (2007): 911–35.

Pisani, Michael V. *Music for the Melodramatic Theatre in Nineteenth-Century London and New York.* Iowa City: University of Iowa Press, 2014.

Preston, Katherine. *Opera for the People: English-Language Opera and Women Managers in Late 19th-Century America.* AMS Studies in Music. New York: Oxford University Press, 2017.

Ragsdale, Frank. "Perspectives on Belting and Belting Pedagogy: A Comparison of Teachers of Classical Voice Students, Teachers of Nonclassical Voice Students, and Music Theatre Singers." DMA diss., University of Miami, 2004.

Rao, Nancy Yunhwa. *Chinatown Opera Theater in North America.* Urbana: University of Illinois Press, 2017.

Regala, Jasmine, and Pamela Hogan. "A Conversation with Ted Neeley." *Fox Riverside Theater Foundation.* April 9, 2010.

Rodger, Gillian. *Just One of the Boys: Female-to-Male Cross-Dressing on the American Variety Stage.* Urbana: University of Illinois Press, 2018.

Rokem, Freddie. *Performing History.* Iowa City: University of Iowa Press, 2000.

Rosenzweig, Roy, and David Thelen. *The Presence of the Past: Popular Uses of History in American Life*. New York: Columbia University Press, 2000.

Sagalyn, Lynne B. *Times Square Roulette: Remaking the City Icon*. Cambridge: MIT Press, 2001.

Saltz, David Z. "Infiction and Outfiction: The Role of Theatrical Fiction in Theatrical Performance." In *Staging Philosophy: Intersections of Theater, Performance, and Philosophy*, edited by David Krasner and David Z. Saltz, 203–220. Ann Arbor: University of Michigan Press, 2006.

Salzman, Eric, and Thomas Desi. *The New Music Theater: Seeing the Voice, Hearing the Body*. New York: Oxford University Press, 2008.

Savran, David. "Broadway as Global Brand." *Journal of Contemporary Drama in English* 5, no. 1 (2017): 24–37.

Saxton, Alexander. "Blackface Minstrelsy and Jacksonian Ideology." *American Quarterly* 27, no. 1 (1975): 3–28.

Schmidt, Leigh Eric. *Hearing Things: Religion, Illusion, and the American Enlightenment*. Cambridge, MA: Harvard University Press, 2000.

Seller, Maxine, ed. *Ethnic Theatre in the United States*. New York: Greenwood Press, 1984.

Sexton, Anne. *The Awful Rowing toward God*. Boston: Houghton Mifflin, 1975.

Shklovsky, Viktor. "Art as Technique." In *Russia Formalist Criticism: Four Essays*, translated and with an introduction by Lee T. Lemon and Marion J. Reis. Lincoln: University of Nebraska Press, 1965.

Shortridge, James R. *The Middle West: Its Meaning in American Culture*. Lawrence: University Press of Kansas, 1989.

Singular, Stephen. *When Men Become Gods: Mormon Polygamist Warren Jeffs, His Cult of Fear, and the Women Who Fought Back*. New York: St. Martin's Press, 2008.

Slobin, Mark. *Tenement Songs: The Popular Music of the Jewish Immigrants*. Urbana: University of Illinois Press, 1982.

Smith, Daymon. "LDS Anthropologist Daymon Smith on Post-Manifesto Polygamy, Correlation, the Corporate LDS Church, and Mammon." *Mormon Stories* podcast, May 13, 2010. https://www.mormonstories.org/podcast/daymon-smith-on-correlation-the-corporate-lds-church-and-mammon/.

Sterne, Jonathan. "A Resonant Tomb." In *The Audible Past: Cultural Origins of Sound Reproduction*, 287–333. Durham, NC: Duke University Press, 2003.

Sternfeld, Jessica. *The Megamusical*. Bloomington: Indiana University Press, 2006.

Stevenson, Jill. "Embodying Sacred History: Performing Creationism for Believers." *TDR* 56, no. 1 (2012): 93–113.

"Still Kicking: The Fabulous Palm Springs Follies." Dir. Mel Damski. Santa Monica, CA: Little Apple Film Productions, 1997.

Stoever, Jennifer Lynn. *The Sonic Color Line: Race and the Cultural Politics of Listening*. New York: New York University Press, 2016.

Strausbaugh, John. *Black Like You: Blackface, Whiteface, Insult, and Imitation in American Popular Culture*. New York: Tarcher, 2006.

Sturman, Janet. *Zarzuela: Spanish Operetta, American Stage*. Urbana: University of Illinois Press, 1990.

Sylvan, Robin. *Traces of the Spirit: The Religious Dimensions of Popular Music*. New York: New York University Press, 2002.

Teasdale, Sara. *Flame and Shadow*. New York: Macmillan, 1920.

Thomas, Susan. *Cuban Zarzuela: Performing Race and Gender on Havana's Lyric Stage*. Urbana: University of Illinois Press, 2009.

Thompson, Michael, Richard Ellis, and Aaron Wildavsky. *Cultural Theory*. Boulder, CO: Westview Press, 1990.

Trilling, Lionel. *Sincerity and Authenticity*. Cambridge, MA: Harvard University Press, 1973.

Turner, Victor. "Liminality and Communitas." In *The Ritual Process: Structure and Anti-Structure*. New Brunswick, NJ: Aldine Transaction Press, 2008.

Twain, Mark. *On the Decay of the Art of Lying*. Portland, OR: Floating Press, 2008.

Ullom, Jeffrey. "Musicals in the Regional Theater." In Wollman and Sternfeld, *Routledge Companion*, 408–17.

Von Glahn, Denise. *The Sounds of Place: Music and the American Cultural Landscape*. Boston: Northeastern University Press, 2003.

Walden, Joshua S. "The 'Yidishe Paganini': Sholem Aleichem's Stempenyu, the Music of Yiddish Theatre, and the Character of the Shtetl Fiddler." *Journal of the Royal Music Association* 139, no. 1 (2014): 89–136.

Walker, Jessica. "Elder Stereotypes in Media and Popular Culture." www.agingwatch.com. October 30, 2010.

Walsh, Kirsten, and Adrian Currie. "Caricatures, Myths, and White Lies." *Metaphilosophy* 46, no. 3 (2015): 414–35.

Ward-Griffin, Danielle. "As Seen on TV: Putting the NBC Opera on Stage." *Journal of the American Musicological Society* 71, no. 3 (2018): 595–694.

Weber, Max. *Economy and Society*. New York: Bedminster Press, 1968.

Weiner, Isaac. *Religion Out Loud: Religious Sound, Public Space, and American Pluralism*. New York: New York University Press, 2013.

Westover, Jonas. *The Shuberts and Their Passing Shows: The Untold Tale of Ziegfeld's Rivals*. New York: Oxford University Press, 2016.

Westover, Tara. *Educated: A Memoir*. New York: Random House, 2018.

Whyte, David. *Consolations: The Solace, Nourishment, and Underlying Meaning of Everyday Words*. Langley, WA: Many Rivers Press, 2014.

Wilde, Oscar. "The Decay of Lying: An Observation." In *Intentions*. Auckland: Floating Press, 2009.

Willenbrink, Hank. "The Act of Being Saved: Hell House and the Salvific Performative." *Theatre Journal* 66, no. 1 (2014): 73–92.

Winner, Langdon. "Do Artifacts Have Politics?" *Daedalus* 109, no. 1 (1980): 121–36.

Wolf, Stacy. *Beyond Broadway: The Pleasure and Promise of Musical Theatre across America*. New York: Oxford University Press, 2019.

Wollman, Elizabeth L. *Hard Times: The Adult Musical in 1970s New York City*. New York: Oxford University Press, 2013.

——. *The Theater Will Rock: A History of the Rock Musical, From* Hair *to* Hedwig. Ann Arbor: University of Michigan Press, 2006.

Wollman, Elizabeth L., and Jessica Sternfeld, eds. *The Routledge Companion to the Contemporary Musical*. New York: Routledge, 2019.

Wood, Cara Leanne. "Representing the Midwest in American Stage and Film Musicals, 1943–1962." PhD diss., Princeton University, 2010.

Young, Steve, and Sport Murphy. *Everything's Coming Up Profits: The Golden Age of Industrial Musicals*. New York: Blast Books, 2013.

Zuniga, Lauren. "World's Tallest Hill." YouTube. July 15, 2012. https://www.youtube.com/watch?v=dswhhPtpdck.

Index

Abbey of Our Lady of Gethsemani, 66–67
Actor's Equity, 78–80, 90–91
Agee, James, 117
ageism, 69–70, 74, 76, 77
aging: as disability, 9–10, 72, 77; in popular culture, 68; in theatre, 9, 19, 48, 69–70. *See also* narrative of decline
Allen, Peter, 81
alternative facts. *See* post-truth
American Academy of Teachers of Singing, 106
American musical theater: adaptations of, 29, 31, 40, 43, 48; and age, 40, 69–71; and America, 42; conventions of the genre, 40, 97–99; and film, 22, 23, 31, 117–22; globally, 131n32; historiography, 17–19, 23–24; and history, 43–44, 47; industry, 107–9; and local communities, x, 23, 78, 97, 129n3; and politics, 33, 115, 122–25; and religion, 25–26, 35–38, 47, 51–52, 59–61, 63, 67, 132n34, 136n18; representation in, 112–13, 116; in schools, 17, 19, 34, 48, 79; violence in, 54–55, 62; voice in, 39, 44, 92–93, 95, 101–6, 109–11. *See also* blackface minstrelsy; burlesque; operetta; vaudeville

amplification, 96, 108, 141n36
Anderson Senior Follies, 72, 74
Annie, 15, 30, 40
Annie Get Your Gun, 15
anti-intellectualism, 51, 122
anti-Semitic, 43. *See also* fascism; Nazis
Anything Goes, 76
Applewhite, Marshall, 36
Ariely, Dan, 4, 60
Arthur, Bea, 70
Ashon, Will, 8–9
auditions, 96–97, 98, 115–16, 140n28
authenticity: of America, 10, 15, 122; and musicals, 9, 10, 14, 51, 62, 129n2; origins, 44; in religion, 53, 58–59, 60, 64; and the voice, 44–45, 93, 100–103, 107. *See also* honesty; lies
Autry, Gene, 105

Bakhtin, Mikhail, 29, 83
Beach Boys, The, 36
Beauty and the Beast, 108
belief: as hope, 14, 102; and musicals, 2, 25–26, 44, 113; in new worlds, 25, 47, 69, 125; and religion, 35–37; in voice, 9, 102, 110

belonging: in America, 32–33, 48, 77; in religion, 66, 94; through the stage, 30, 32–33, 46–47, 61, 86, 97; the voice and, 39, 92, 97, 106, 111

belting (singing): as identity, 103; gendered sounds of, 93–94; and the Middle, 104–5; qualities of, 96, 100–102; and truth, 100, 103; and vocal health, 106, 109. *See also* Broadway voice; vocal training

Benjamin, Walter, 70, 89–90

Bennion, Janet, 46

Bernstein, Leonard, 84

Best Exotic Marigold Hotel, The, 73

Best Little Whorehouse in Texas, The, 15

Big Love, 46

bio-musicals, 43

blackface minstrelsy, 8, 20, 23, 37, 115, 141n5

Blue Beard, 21, 32

Boal, Augusto, 71

Book of Mormon (musical), 116

Borges, Jorge Luis, 114

Boston, 20, 79

Bourdieu, Pierre, 18

Bradbury, Ray, 68

Bradley, Ian, 51

Branch Davidians, 36

Branson, Missouri: and Las Vegas, 54, 60, 61; region, 53–54, 56, 61; and Sight & Sound Theatres, x, 9, 51–53

Brantley, Ben, 109

bricolage, 81. *See also* mashup

Bridges of Madison County, The, 15

Broadway: and aging, 71; conventions, 2, 124; decentering, 2, 14, 17–18, 129n11; in the Middle, 79; performers, 10, 103, 107–9; as place, xii, 9, 112, 113, 126; and politics, 29, 44, 48, 114–15; and religion, 38; and technology, 22, 38, 129–30n11, 141n36; as tourist industry, 1, 23, 39, 53, 95–98, 106–7, 123. *See also* Broadway voice; Times Square

Broadway League, 106

Broadway voice, 95–99, 100, 105, 109–11, 139n12. *See also* vocal training

Brown, Nacio Herb, 82

brownface, 115, 141n5

burlesque, 20, 21, 69, 138n25

Burston, Jonathan, 98–99, 108

camp, 2, 14, 44

Campion, Carlotta, 70

Carousel, 19

Carson, Anne, 94

cartography. *See* maps

Cashner, Andrew A., 24

Cats, 98

Causey, Matthew, 113

CCM. *See* University of Cincinnati College-Conservatory of Music (CCM)

Chenoweth, Kristin, 139n12

Chess, 98

Chitty Chitty Bang Bang, 27, 39–41, 42

Christensen, Clayton M., 17

Christianity, 51–52, 61. *See also* evangelical Christianity

Cincinnati, 23. *See also* University of Cincinnati College-Conservatory of Music (CCM)

City Beautiful, 21

Civic Center Music Hall, 78, 88

Cohen-Cruz, Jan, 79

Collins, Randall, 11

Colorado City, AZ, 29, 33, 39, 41, 126

color-blind casting, 45. *See also* representation

combinatory culture, 82–83. *See also* mashup

community theater, 17, 78, 79, 90

Couldry, Nick, 80

Crawford, Michael, 118

Creation Museum, The, 56–57, 66

Crosby, Bing, 22

cruise ships, 17

cult leaders, 36

Currie, Adrian, 45

Dallas, Texas, 72

Daniel in the Lion's Den, 54

Danto, Arthur C., 116

Daunno, Damon, 103, 105

Davies, James Q., 110

deception. *See* lies

de Certeau, Michel, 112

Deseret (opera), 32

Deseret, or a Saint's Afflictions, 32

Detroit, 118

dialogism, 83

Dick, Philip K., 69, 120

disability, 10, 72, 77

Disney, 41, 60, 95, 107, 122–23
divahood, 70, 136–37n6
Dolan, Jill, 3, 90
Douglas, Mary, 4–6
Drake, Alfred, 103–5
Dust Bowl, 15, 22

Eagleton, Terry, 37, 47, 59
egalitarianism, 5–7, 45
Eidsheim, Nina Sun, x, xi, 94, 101, 110
Eliade, Mircea, 2
Ellis, Sarah Taylor, 69
Elphaba, 98
equity theater. *See* Actor's Equity
ethnicity: depictions on stage, 8, 44,
    139n2; in the Middle, 11, 16
ethnic theater, 10, 23, 69, 130–31n24
evangelical Christianity, 9, 35, 51, 54–59,
    61, 65–66
Evita, 43
exoticism, 15, 75, 99

Fabulous Palm Springs Follies, 72
fantasy: of the Middle, 15; and race,
    139n2; and reality, 58–59, 91, 113; in
    religion, 60, 61; through the stage,
    2–3, 8, 28, 47, 64, 113–14; values of,
    8, 56, 90, 117, 120, 122–23; the voice
    and, 44, 92, 106, 109–11. *See also* lies;
    post-truth
fascism, 41, 43, 120
fatalism, 5–7, 47
Fauconnier, Giles, 58
Feldman, Martha, 94
Fiddler on the Roof, 41–42, 116
5th Dimension, 86
film musicals: adaptations, 27, 33, 38–39,
    41, 103, 137n7; and Broadway, 17, 129–
    30n11; distributed throughout America,
    19, 22, 31
Fiorello!, 43
Follies, 70
42nd Street, 70
Fourth Wall Political Theater, 36
Fourth Wall Repertory Company, 36
Francis, Philip Salim, 35, 60
Frank, Jason, 45
Frank, Thomas, 15, 122–23
Freed, Arthur, 82
Frye, Jud, 7, 8, 28, 55, 128n16

Fukuyama, Francis, 47, 116
fundamentalism: and art, 35–37, 47; and
    mashup, 38, 83; in Mormonism, 28,
    33–34, 39, 43; and theater, 9, 29, 30, 36,
    37, 46–47; and whiteness, 37
Fundamentalist Church of Jesus Christ
    of Latter-day Saints (FLDS), 28–31,
    33–34, 38–39, 42, 49, 133n13

Gaither, Bill and Gloria, 61–62
Garland, Judy, 17, 22
Gershwin, George, 84
Gigi, 85
Gilbert and Sullivan Society (Tulsa), 78
Ginsburg, Allen, 15
Girard, René, 7, 56
Giuliani, Rudy, 123
Glassberg, David, 21, 79
Glee, 29, 81–83, 97
Goffman, Erving, 68
Grease, 70, 92
Great Passion Play, 21
Grey Gardens, 71
Grid-Group model of cultural theory. *See*
    Douglas, Mary
Guittard, Laurence, 103–5
Gullette, Margaret Morganroth, 71, 73
Guthrie, Woody, 15
Guys and Dolls, 70

Haenni, Sabine, 23
Hair, 86
Hallo Witnessing, 56
Hamilton, 44–45, 55, 114
Hammerstein, Oscar, 2, 51. *See also* Rodg-
    ers and Hammerstein
Happiest Millionaire, The, 38, 42
Harbert, Elissa, 43
Heaven's Gate, 36
Hell Houses, 56–57
Hello, Dolly!, 118–19
Herman, Jerry, 118
heteroglossia, 29
Higgins, Henry, 70
Hill, Harold, 7
history musicals, 43, 47, 60
Ho, Don, 85
Hodder, Ian, 19
Holländer, Friedrich, 2
Hollander, John, 25

Hollywood, 1, 2, 22, 38, 115. *See also* Los Angeles
honesty: in musicals, 8; and purity, 4; and the voice, 44, 93–94, 102–4
Huizinga, Johan, 2–3

immigration, 11, 20, 23, 45, 114–15. *See also* migration
Indian Territory, 87. See also *Oklahoma!*
industrial musicals, 23
infiction, 63–64
Ingalls, Monique M., 65
In the Heights, 115
Into the Woods, 48

Jackman, Hugh, 103, 105
Jeffs, Brent W., 34
Jeffs, Warren, 30, 34–35, 36, 39, 42
Jersey Boys, 43
Jessop, Carolyn, 30, 42
Jessop, Merril, 30–31, 39
Jesus Christ: in Christian worship, 58–59; and deception, 60; depictions of, 32, 51, 54, 137n4; in Mormonism, 34; as scapegoat, 7, 56
Jesus Christ Superstar, 51, 70
Jonah, 54
Judaism, 23, 61–62, 66, 134n26, 136n18

Kanellos, Nicolás, 23–24
Keillor, Garrison, 124
Kelly, Gene, 82
Kennedy, Lisa, 73
Kermode, Frank, 37
Kheshti, Roshanak, 94
King and I, The, 33, 55
King of the Entire World, The, 36
Kirkpatrick Theater, 78, 81
kitsch, 17. *See also* camp
Kittler, Friedrich, 25, 93
Knapp, Raymond, x–xi, 8, 20–22, 40–43, 71, 92
Koegel, John, x, 23, 24
Koresh, David, 36
Kramnick, Isaac, 45
Kristeva, Julia, 59

Lane, Bobbie Burbridge, 72
Lansbury, Angela, 139n12

Las Vegas, 54, 60–61
Laurey (character), 6–7, 55
Lerner, Alan Jay. *See* Lerner and Loewe
Lerner, Ben, 48
Lerner and Loewe, 32, 85
Les Misérables, 98
Levine, Emma E., 4
Levine, Lawrence, 29, 79
Lévi-Strauss, Claude, 81
Lewis, C. S., 51
Lewis, Jerry, 34
lies: and creativity, 4–5, 8, 60, 122–24; to deliver from post-truth, 7, 91, 123, 126; the end of, 10, 113–17, 125–26; and imagining new worlds, 3–4, 70, 91, 95, 97; musicals as, 1, 8, 12, 29, 45–46, 113; out of place, 5–7; prosocial, 4–5, 8, 44, 52, 111, 117; religion and, 9, 25, 29, 47, 52, 60; and the voice, 109
Light Opera of Oklahoma (LOOK), 77–78
Little Night Music, A, 71
Loewe, Frederick. *See* Lerner and Loewe
Longworth, Richard C., 16, 91
Los Angeles, 20, 23, 24
Lost Boys, 34
LoVetri, Jeannette, 108
LuPone, Patti, 106, 109
Lyric Theatre of Oklahoma, 77–81, 89–91

MacRae, Gordon, 103
Magelssen, Scott, 45
Malloy, Dave, 96
Mangan, Michael, 72–73
Man in the High Castle, The, 119–22
Manson, Charles, 36
maps, 9, 112–17, 120–22, 124–25, 142n14
Martin, Annette, 72, 74, 76, 90
Marx, Groucho, 34
Mary Poppins, 40
mashup: and language, 29, 132n2; in the Oklahoma Senior Follies, 81–82, 84–86; and religion, 82–84
Maslon, Laurence, 22, 28, 113
Mason, Patrick, 32
McClure, John, 82
McConachie, Bruce, 58
McConkie, Bruce R., 34
McLain, Curly, 6–7, 55, 103–5
megamusical, 95, 98–99

Menzel, Idina, 96, 98, 103
Merman, Ethel, 103
Merton, Thomas, 50, 66–67
Meyer, Moe, 62–63
mezza voce, 94–95, 99, 103. *See also* vocal training
microphone. *See* amplification
Middle, the (concept): America's fantasies of, 15–16, 122; between values, 12–13, 29, 38, 47, 66, 70, 73, 86, 97; musicals in, 14, 18, 19, 21–26, 96, 112, 118; power of, 93, 94, 111, 119, 126; voices and, 102–3, 104–6, 109, 114
Middle, the (place). *See* Midwest
middlebrow, 12, 20, 48, 75
middle-class, 16, 33, 44, 46, 87. *See also* belonging
Midwest, 15–16, 23, 59–62, 89–91, 95
migration, 16, 87
Miranda, Lin-Manuel, 45, 114, 115
Mondelli, Peter, 77
Mormonism: and blackface, 130n23; fundamentalism in, 30–35, 43, 46; and Jews, 134n26; and theater, 13, 20, 21, 31, 116. See also *Re-Sound of Music, The*
Mormons, The, 32
Morris, Mitchell, x, xi, 8
Morrow, Karen, 100
Moses, 53, 54
Most, Andrea, x, 7, 92
Muny, The, 21
Murphy, Sport, 23
museums, 56–57. *See also* Creation Museum, The
Music Man, The, 7, 8
My Fair Lady, 70
myth: of America, 3, 33, 109; and caricatures, 45–46; in religious texts, 57–58, 61, 65; and theater, 24, 37; among white communities, 11

narrative of decline, 10, 71–73, 75–77, 86–87, 89–90
Nazis, 31, 41–43, 117, 120
NBC Opera Company, 32, 132n8
Neeley, Ted, 70, 137n7
Nemerov, Alexander, ix, 17
Newton, Saul B., 36
Nietzsche, Friedrich, 47, 59

Noah, 54
non-Equity theater. *See* Actor's Equity

Obama, Barack, 114
off-Broadway, 78, 129n11
Offenbach, Jacques, 21, 32
Oklahoma!: in the American imagination, 15; and identity, 7, 128n16; in media, 28; productions of, 19; and reconciliation, 6–8, 55; and the state of Oklahoma, 84; voices in, 103–5
Oklahoma City: land run, 87; MAPS (Metropolitan Area Projects), 78, 88; modern development, 87, 89; origins, 87–88; theater, 9, 72, 77–81, 89–91; Thunder, 88
Oklahoma City University, xi, 99
Oklahoma Senior Follies: and local theater, 80–81, 90–91; and mashup, 81–82, 84–86; origins, 69–70, 72, 74; as a Ziegfeld revue, 75–77
Olsson, Jeanette, 119–21
One and Only, Genuine, Original Family Band, The, 41, 42
On the Town, 84
operetta, 20–21, 32, 46, 69, 77
outfiction, 63–64

Pageant and Masque of St. Louis, The, 21
pageantry, 17, 21, 79
Paint Your Wagon, 32–33
Palm Springs, California, 72
Palo Duro Canyon State Park, 21
passaggio, 104–6. *See also* mezza voce
Pei, I. M., 87
Pellegrini, Ann, 56
Pence, Mike, 114
Phantom of the Opera, The, 98, 99
Pippin, 71
Pisani, Michael, 20
Pixar, 118
place: and memory, 15–16, 48, 79, 87; in religion, 25, 32, 38; stories out of, 1, 4–5, 49, 68, 112, 118–19; and theater, 7, 12, 68, 79, 90, 112–13, 126. *See also* belonging; re-place; utopia
polygamy: legal aspects of, 133n13, 134n38; and Mormonism, 33–34, 133n12; on stage, 31–32, 33; public perception of, 33, 46

Porter, Cole, 51
posthuman, 117–22
post-truth, 5, 19, 26, 47, 113–17
Poteau, OK, 97
Prairie Home Companion, A, 124
Preston, Katherine, 20
Pride of Oklahoma Marching Band, 84, 85
prosocial lies. *See* lies
Pyle, John Howard, 33. *See also* Short Creek Raid

Quartet, 73
queer minstrelsy, 115

radio broadcasts: among the FLDS, 30, 34, 39; reaching the Middle, 30, 48–49; of musicals, 18, 22; in politics, 83–84
Ramona Pageant, 21
Rao, Nancy Yunhwa, 24
regional theater, xii, 10, 53, 78–79, 96. *See also* community theater; pageantry
religion: and deception, 7, 25; and mashup, 38, 82; and musicals, 2, 19, 20, 25, 32, 50, 51; in popular music, 132n38; and sound, 25, 59; and unreality, 52, 60; and violence, 56; and whiteness, 37. *See also* belief
re-place, 10, 13, 18–19, 24, 112
representation: and maps, 113; in media, 46; on stage, 9, 10, 20, 115–17; and politics, 110
Re-Sound of Music, The, 27–31, 38–42, 46. See also *Sound of Music, The*
Rice, Thomas, 37
Richard Rodgers Theatre, 45, 126
Riedel, Michael, 106–7
River City, Iowa, 7, 8
Robinson, Andrew, 83
Rockford, IL, 72
Rocky Horror Picture Show, The, 69
Rodgers and Hammerstein, 84, 87, 103, 119
Rodgers, Jimmie, 105
Rodgers, Richard, 27, 41, 85. *See also* Rodgers and Hammerstein
Rokem, Freddie, 45
rural America: and immigration, 16; musical theater in, 9, 30, 53, 97; urban fascination with, 13–15, 18, 66, 124

Sagalyn, Lynne B., 95

Saltz, David Z., 22, 63–64
Samson, 9, 54–55, 57–58, 61–67
Satie, Erik, 36, 37
Saunders, Mary, 100
Saxton, Alexander, 20
scapegoat, 7–8, 56
Schmidt, Leigh Eric, 25
Schweitzer, Maurice E., 4
Scriabin, Alexander, 36, 37
Senior Follies movement, 9, 69, 72, 74, 76–77, 90–91
Seven Brides for Seven Brothers, 19
1776, 43
Sexton, Anne, 38, 125
shamanism, 2. *See also* religion
Sherman Brothers, 27, 41
Shklovsky, Viktor, 60
Shore, Dinah, 22
Short Creek Raid, 32–33
Shortridge, James, 99
Sight & Sound Theatres: in Branson, Missouri: x, 9, 51, 61; and fiction, 51–52, 63–67; in Lancaster, PA, 51, 53; production values, 52, 53–55, 67; and religious values, 51–52, 53, 56–57, 58–61, 63
Sinatra, Frank, 22, 86, 138n46
Singular, Stephen, 34
Sister Wives, 46
Smith, Daymon, 32
Smith, Joseph, 33, 37
Smith, Joseph F., 34
Smith, Luther Ely, 21
Sondheim, Stephen, 48, 70, 71
Sontag, Susan, 44
Sound of Music, The: adaptations of, 9, 27–31, 41–42, 119; and aging, 70; and history, 42–43; in religious settings, 19; the voice in, 39–40
South Pacific, 36
State Fair, 15
Steinbeck, John, 15
Sterne, Jonathan, 69
Sternfeld, Jessica, 98–99
Stevenson, Jill, 56
St. Louis Municipal Opera Theatre. *See* Muny, The
Stoever, Jennifer, 101
Streisand, Barbra, 103
Stritch, Elaine, 70

Sullivan, Ed, 22
summer stock theater, 21, 115–16

Teasdale, Sara, 13
television: and aging, 73, 137n10; appropriation in, 62; and the FLDS, 34, 41, 46; and musicals, 17, 18, 19, 29, 117, 129–30n11; and opera, 32; series, 29, 81, 97, 121
Texas Outdoor Musical, 21
textual poaching, 29, 38, 39, 42, 43, 132n2
Third Reich, 120. *See also* fascism; Nazis
Thomas, Susan, 24
Thompson, Lydia, 21
Times Square: gentrification of 95–96, 123; and the Middle, 10, 22–23, 107; myth of centrality, 12, 17–18. *See also* Broadway
Tina: The Tina Turner Musical, 43
Tirado, Romualdo, 24
Titanic, 43
Trilling, Lionel, 44
triple threat, 100–101. *See also* vocal training
Trump, Donald, 123
truth. *See* authenticity; lies; post-truth
Turner, Mark, 58
Turner, Victor, 37, 73
Twain, Mark, 4, 125–26

University of Cincinnati College-Conservatory of Music (CCM), 99, 100–101, 107
Utah Territory, 21
utopia: as deception, 5, 7, 13, 142n14; in film, 118; and theater, 3, 7, 13, 90, 97, 112–13

Van Dyke, Dick, 27
vaudeville, 20, 21, 69
villancico, 24, 131n30
vocal coaching. *See* vocal training
vocal health. *See* belting
vocal training: costs of, 106–9; industry demands of, 95–96, 100, 107; in the Middle, 10, 21, 95–97, 100–102; rhetoric of honesty surrounding, 93–94, 100, 101–2; and style, 104–5; and the vocal coach, 10, 100, 101–2, 111. *See also* belting

voice: and authenticity, 44, 93–94, 104; and belonging, 39, 69, 89–91, 92–93, 111; as a convention in musicals, 44, 92–95; and democracy, 110–11; as emblem of identity, 44, 74, 79–81, 94, 101–2, 109–10. *See also* vocal training
Voice Foundation, 106
voix mixte, 104–5. *See also* mezza voce; vocal training
Von Glahn, Denise, 54
von Trapp, Maria: character of, 27–28, 30–31, 38–41; the person, 43, 45

Wagner, Richard, 36
WALL-E, 118–19
Walsh, Kirsten, 45
Wanderer, or a Mormon Wooing, The, 32
Weber, Max, 7
Weiner, Isaac, x, 59
Westover, Jonas, 75, 137–38n25
Westover, Tara, 30
West Side Story, 70, 92, 139n2
whiteness: as depicted on stage, 23, 44, 64, 115, 139n2; and ethnicity, 23; in the Middle, 16; and migration, 16, 23, 87; among musical theater communities, 10–11, 15, 50, 106; in religion, 37, 46. *See also* ethnicity
Whyte, David, ix, 125
Wicked, 97–99
Wilde, Oscar, 3, 116–17
Willenbrink, Hank, 56–57
Wilson, Dennis, 36
Wilson, Meredith, 123
Wizard of Oz, The, 15, 22
Wolf, Stacy, x, 2
Wood, Cara, 15

Yearning for Zion Ranch, 30
yellowface, 115, 141n5
Young, Brigham, 32, 33, 35, 133n11
Your Hit Parade, 22

zarzuela, 24, 131n29
Ziegfeld *Follies*, 9, 75, 76, 81
Zuniga, Lauren, 97

JAKE JOHNSON is an associate professor of musicology at Oklahoma City University and the author of *Mormons, Musical Theater, and Belonging in America*.

MUSIC IN AMERICAN LIFE

Only a Miner: Studies in Recorded Coal-Mining Songs   *Archie Green*
Great Day Coming: Folk Music and the American Left   *R. Serge Denisoff*
John Philip Sousa: A Descriptive Catalog of His Works   *Paul E. Bierley*
The Hell-Bound Train: A Cowboy Songbook   *Glenn Ohrlin*
Oh, Didn't He Ramble: The Life Story of Lee Collins, as Told to Mary Collins
   Edited by Frank J. Gillis and John W. Miner
American Labor Songs of the Nineteenth Century   *Philip S. Foner*
Stars of Country Music: Uncle Dave Macon to Johnny Rodriguez   *Edited by Bill C. Malone
   and Judith McCulloh*
Git Along, Little Dogies: Songs and Songmakers of the American West   *John I. White*
A Texas-Mexican *Cancionero*: Folksongs of the Lower Border   *Américo Paredes*
San Antonio Rose: The Life and Music of Bob Wills   *Charles R. Townsend*
Early Downhome Blues: A Musical and Cultural Analysis   *Jeff Todd Titon*
An Ives Celebration: Papers and Panels of the Charles Ives Centennial
   Festival-Conference   *Edited by H. Wiley Hitchcock and Vivian Perlis*
Sinful Tunes and Spirituals: Black Folk Music to the Civil War   *Dena J. Epstein*
Joe Scott, the Woodsman-Songmaker   *Edward D. Ives*
Jimmie Rodgers: The Life and Times of America's Blue Yodeler   *Nolan Porterfield*
Early American Music Engraving and Printing: A History of Music Publishing
   in America from 1787 to 1825, with Commentary on Earlier and Later
   Practices   *Richard J. Wolfe*
Sing a Sad Song: The Life of Hank Williams   *Roger M. Williams*
Long Steel Rail: The Railroad in American Folksong   *Norm Cohen*
Resources of American Music History: A Directory of Source Materials from Colonial
   Times to World War II   *D. W. Krummel, Jean Geil, Doris J. Dyen, and Deane L. Root*
Tenement Songs: The Popular Music of the Jewish Immigrants   *Mark Slobin*
Ozark Folksongs   *Vance Randolph; edited and abridged by Norm Cohen*
Oscar Sonneck and American Music   *Edited by William Lichtenwanger*
Bluegrass Breakdown: The Making of the Old Southern Sound   *Robert Cantwell*
Bluegrass: A History   *Neil V. Rosenberg*
Music at the White House: A History of the American Spirit   *Elise K. Kirk*
Red River Blues: The Blues Tradition in the Southeast   *Bruce Bastin*
Good Friends and Bad Enemies: Robert Winslow Gordon and the Study of American
   Folksong   *Debora Kodish*
Fiddlin' Georgia Crazy: Fiddlin' John Carson, His Real World, and the World of
   His Songs   *Gene Wiggins*
America's Music: From the Pilgrims to the Present (rev. 3d ed.)   *Gilbert Chase*
Secular Music in Colonial Annapolis: The Tuesday Club, 1745–56   *John Barry Talley*
Bibliographical Handbook of American Music   *D. W. Krummel*
Goin' to Kansas City   *Nathan W. Pearson Jr.*

"Susanna," "Jeanie," and "The Old Folks at Home": The Songs of Stephen C. Foster from His Time to Ours (2d ed.)   *William W. Austin*

Songprints: The Musical Experience of Five Shoshone Women   *Judith Vander*

"Happy in the Service of the Lord": Afro-American Gospel Quartets in Memphis   *Kip Lornell*

Paul Hindemith in the United States   *Luther Noss*

"My Song Is My Weapon": People's Songs, American Communism, and the Politics of Culture, 1930–50   *Robbie Lieberman*

Chosen Voices: The Story of the American Cantorate   *Mark Slobin*

Theodore Thomas: America's Conductor and Builder of Orchestras, 1835–1905   *Ezra Schabas*

"The Whorehouse Bells Were Ringing" and Other Songs Cowboys Sing   *Collected and Edited by Guy Logsdon*

Crazeology: The Autobiography of a Chicago Jazzman   *Bud Freeman, as Told to Robert Wolf*

Discoursing Sweet Music: Brass Bands and Community Life in Turn-of-the-Century Pennsylvania   *Kenneth Kreitner*

Mormonism and Music: A History   *Michael Hicks*

Voices of the Jazz Age: Profiles of Eight Vintage Jazzmen   *Chip Deffaa*

Pickin' on Peachtree: A History of Country Music in Atlanta, Georgia   *Wayne W. Daniel*

Bitter Music: Collected Journals, Essays, Introductions, and Librettos   *Harry Partch; edited by Thomas McGeary*

Ethnic Music on Records: A Discography of Ethnic Recordings Produced in the United States, 1893 to 1942   *Richard K. Spottswood*

Downhome Blues Lyrics: An Anthology from the Post–World War II Era   *Jeff Todd Titon*

Ellington: The Early Years   *Mark Tucker*

Chicago Soul   *Robert Pruter*

That Half-Barbaric Twang: The Banjo in American Popular Culture   *Karen Linn*

Hot Man: The Life of Art Hodes   *Art Hodes and Chadwick Hansen*

The Erotic Muse: American Bawdy Songs (2d ed.)   *Ed Cray*

Barrio Rhythm: Mexican American Music in Los Angeles   *Steven Loza*

The Creation of Jazz: Music, Race, and Culture in Urban America   *Burton W. Peretti*

Charles Martin Loeffler: A Life Apart in Music   *Ellen Knight*

Club Date Musicians: Playing the New York Party Circuit   *Bruce A. MacLeod*

Opera on the Road: Traveling Opera Troupes in the United States, 1825–60   *Katherine K. Preston*

The Stonemans: An Appalachian Family and the Music That Shaped Their Lives   *Ivan M. Tribe*

Transforming Tradition: Folk Music Revivals Examined   *Edited by Neil V. Rosenberg*

The Crooked Stovepipe: Athapaskan Fiddle Music and Square Dancing in Northeast Alaska and Northwest Canada   *Craig Mishler*

Traveling the High Way Home: Ralph Stanley and the World of Traditional Bluegrass Music   *John Wright*

Carl Ruggles: Composer, Painter, and Storyteller   *Marilyn Ziffrin*

Never without a Song: The Years and Songs of Jennie Devlin, 1865–1952
  Katharine D. Newman
The Hank Snow Story   *Hank Snow, with Jack Ownbey and Bob Burris*
Milton Brown and the Founding of Western Swing   *Cary Ginell,*
  with special assistance from Roy Lee Brown
Santiago de Murcia's "Códice Saldívar No. 4": A Treasury of Secular Guitar Music from
  Baroque Mexico   *Craig H. Russell*
The Sound of the Dove: Singing in Appalachian Primitive Baptist Churches
  Beverly Bush Patterson
Heartland Excursions: Ethnomusicological Reflections on Schools of Music
  Bruno Nettl
Doowop: The Chicago Scene   *Robert Pruter*
Blue Rhythms: Six Lives in Rhythm and Blues   *Chip Deffaa*
Shoshone Ghost Dance Religion: Poetry Songs and Great Basin Context   *Judith Vander*
Go Cat Go! Rockabilly Music and Its Makers   *Craig Morrison*
'Twas Only an Irishman's Dream: The Image of Ireland and the Irish in American
  Popular Song Lyrics, 1800–1920   *William H. A. Williams*
Democracy at the Opera: Music, Theater, and Culture in New York City, 1815–60
  Karen Ahlquist
Fred Waring and the Pennsylvanians   *Virginia Waring*
Woody, Cisco, and Me: Seamen Three in the Merchant Marine   *Jim Longhi*
Behind the Burnt Cork Mask: Early Blackface Minstrelsy and Antebellum American
  Popular Culture   *William J. Mahar*
Going to Cincinnati: A History of the Blues in the Queen City   *Steven C. Tracy*
Pistol Packin' Mama: Aunt Molly Jackson and the Politics of Folksong   *Shelly Romalis*
Sixties Rock: Garage, Psychedelic, and Other Satisfactions   *Michael Hicks*
The Late Great Johnny Ace and the Transition from R&B to Rock 'n' Roll
  James M. Salem
Tito Puente and the Making of Latin Music   *Steven Loza*
Juilliard: A History   *Andrea Olmstead*
Understanding Charles Seeger, Pioneer in American Musicology   *Edited by Bell Yung*
  and Helen Rees
Mountains of Music: West Virginia Traditional Music from *Goldenseal*
  Edited by John Lilly
Alice Tully: An Intimate Portrait   *Albert Fuller*
A Blues Life   *Henry Townsend, as told to Bill Greensmith*
Long Steel Rail: The Railroad in American Folksong (2d ed.)   *Norm Cohen*
The Golden Age of Gospel   *Text by Horace Clarence Boyer; photography by Lloyd Yearwood*
Aaron Copland: The Life and Work of an Uncommon Man   *Howard Pollack*
Louis Moreau Gottschalk   *S. Frederick Starr*
Race, Rock, and Elvis   *Michael T. Bertrand*
Theremin: Ether Music and Espionage   *Albert Glinsky*
Poetry and Violence: The Ballad Tradition of Mexico's Costa Chica   *John H. McDowell*
The Bill Monroe Reader   *Edited by Tom Ewing*

Music in Lubavitcher Life   *Ellen Koskoff*
Zarzuela: Spanish Operetta, American Stage   *Janet L. Sturman*
Bluegrass Odyssey: A Documentary in Pictures and Words, 1966–86   *Carl Fleischhauer*
    and Neil V. Rosenberg
That Old-Time Rock & Roll: A Chronicle of an Era, 1954–63   *Richard Aquila*
Labor's Troubadour   *Joe Glazer*
American Opera   *Elise K. Kirk*
Don't Get above Your Raisin': Country Music and the Southern Working Class
    Bill C. Malone
John Alden Carpenter: A Chicago Composer   *Howard Pollack*
Heartbeat of the People: Music and Dance of the Northern Pow-wow   *Tara Browner*
My Lord, What a Morning: An Autobiography   *Marian Anderson*
Marian Anderson: A Singer's Journey   *Allan Keiler*
Charles Ives Remembered: An Oral History   *Vivian Perlis*
Henry Cowell, Bohemian   *Michael Hicks*
Rap Music and Street Consciousness   *Cheryl L. Keyes*
Louis Prima   *Garry Boulard*
Marian McPartland's Jazz World: All in Good Time   *Marian McPartland*
Robert Johnson: Lost and Found   *Barry Lee Pearson and Bill McCulloch*
Bound for America: Three British Composers   *Nicholas Temperley*
Lost Sounds: Blacks and the Birth of the Recording Industry, 1890–1919   *Tim Brooks*
Burn, Baby! BURN! The Autobiography of Magnificent Montague   *Magnificent*
    Montague with Bob Baker
Way Up North in Dixie: A Black Family's Claim to the Confederate Anthem
    Howard L. Sacks and Judith Rose Sacks
The Bluegrass Reader   *Edited by Thomas Goldsmith*
Colin McPhee: Composer in Two Worlds   *Carol J. Oja*
Robert Johnson, Mythmaking, and Contemporary American Culture   *Patricia R.*
    Schroeder
Composing a World: Lou Harrison, Musical Wayfarer   *Leta E. Miller and Fredric Lieberman*
Fritz Reiner, Maestro and Martinet   *Kenneth Morgan*
That Toddlin' Town: Chicago's White Dance Bands and Orchestras, 1900–1950
    Charles A. Sengstock Jr.
Dewey and Elvis: The Life and Times of a Rock 'n' Roll Deejay   *Louis Cantor*
Come Hither to Go Yonder: Playing Bluegrass with Bill Monroe   *Bob Black*
Chicago Blues: Portraits and Stories   *David Whiteis*
The Incredible Band of John Philip Sousa   *Paul E. Bierley*
"Maximum Clarity" and Other Writings on Music   *Ben Johnston, edited by Bob Gilmore*
Staging Tradition: John Lair and Sarah Gertrude Knott   *Michael Ann Williams*
Homegrown Music: Discovering Bluegrass   *Stephanie P. Ledgin*
Tales of a Theatrical Guru   *Danny Newman*
The Music of Bill Monroe   *Neil V. Rosenberg and Charles K. Wolfe*
Pressing On: The Roni Stoneman Story   *Roni Stoneman, as told to Ellen Wright*
Together Let Us Sweetly Live   *Jonathan C. David, with photographs by Richard Holloway*

Live Fast, Love Hard: The Faron Young Story   *Diane Diekman*
Air Castle of the South: WSM Radio and the Making of Music City   *Craig P. Havighurst*
Traveling Home: Sacred Harp Singing and American Pluralism   *Kiri Miller*
Where Did Our Love Go? The Rise and Fall of the Motown Sound   *Nelson George*
Lonesome Cowgirls and Honky-Tonk Angels: The Women of Barn Dance
    Radio   *Kristine M. McCusker*
California Polyphony: Ethnic Voices, Musical Crossroads   *Mina Yang*
The Never-Ending Revival: Rounder Records and the Folk Alliance   *Michael F. Scully*
Sing It Pretty: A Memoir   *Bess Lomax Hawes*
Working Girl Blues: The Life and Music of Hazel Dickens   *Hazel Dickens*
    and Bill C. Malone
Charles Ives Reconsidered   *Gayle Sherwood Magee*
The Hayloft Gang: The Story of the National Barn Dance   *Edited by Chad Berry*
Country Music Humorists and Comedians   *Loyal Jones*
Record Makers and Breakers: Voices of the Independent Rock 'n' Roll Pioneers
    John Broven
Music of the First Nations: Tradition and Innovation in Native North America
    Edited by Tara Browner
Cafe Society: The Wrong Place for the Right People   *Barney Josephson,*
    with Terry Trilling-Josephson
George Gershwin: An Intimate Portrait   *Walter Rimler*
Life Flows On in Endless Song: Folk Songs and American History   *Robert V. Wells*
I Feel a Song Coming On: The Life of Jimmy McHugh   *Alyn Shipton*
King of the Queen City: The Story of King Records   *Jon Hartley Fox*
Long Lost Blues: Popular Blues in America, 1850–1920   *Peter C. Muir*
Hard Luck Blues: Roots Music Photographs from the Great Depression   *Rich Remsberg*
Restless Giant: The Life and Times of Jean Aberbach and Hill and Range Songs
    Bar Biszick-Lockwood
Champagne Charlie and Pretty Jemima: Variety Theater in the
    Nineteenth Century   *Gillian M. Rodger*
Sacred Steel: Inside an African American Steel Guitar Tradition   *Robert L. Stone*
Gone to the Country: The New Lost City Ramblers and the Folk Music Revival
    Ray Allen
The Makers of the Sacred Harp   *David Warren Steel with Richard H. Hulan*
Woody Guthrie, American Radical   *Will Kaufman*
George Szell: A Life of Music   *Michael Charry*
Bean Blossom: The Brown County Jamboree and Bill Monroe's Bluegrass
    Festivals   *Thomas A. Adler*
Crowe on the Banjo: The Music Life of J. D. Crowe   *Marty Godbey*
Twentieth Century Drifter: The Life of Marty Robbins   *Diane Diekman*
Henry Mancini: Reinventing Film Music   *John Caps*
The Beautiful Music All Around Us: Field Recordings and the American
    Experience   *Stephen Wade*
Then Sings My Soul: The Culture of Southern Gospel Music   *Douglas Harrison*

The Accordion in the Americas: Klezmer, Polka, Tango, Zydeco, and More!
Edited by Helena Simonett

Bluegrass Bluesman: A Memoir   *Josh Graves, edited by Fred Bartenstein*

One Woman in a Hundred: Edna Phillips and the Philadelphia Orchestra
Mary Sue Welsh

The Great Orchestrator: Arthur Judson and American Arts Management
James M. Doering

Charles Ives in the Mirror: American Histories of an Iconic Composer   *David C. Paul*

Southern Soul-Blues   *David Whiteis*

Sweet Air: Modernism, Regionalism, and American Popular Song   *Edward P. Comentale*

Pretty Good for a Girl: Women in Bluegrass   *Murphy Hicks Henry*

Sweet Dreams: The World of Patsy Cline   *Warren R. Hofstra*

William Sidney Mount and the Creolization of American Culture   *Christopher J. Smith*

Bird: The Life and Music of Charlie Parker   *Chuck Haddix*

Making the March King: John Philip Sousa's Washington Years, 1854–1893
Patrick Warfield

In It for the Long Run   *Jim Rooney*

Pioneers of the Blues Revival   *Steve Cushing*

Roots of the Revival: American and British Folk Music in the 1950s   *Ronald D. Cohen
and Rachel Clare Donaldson*

Blues All Day Long: The Jimmy Rogers Story   *Wayne Everett Goins*

Yankee Twang: Country and Western Music in New England   *Clifford R. Murphy*

The Music of the Stanley Brothers   *Gary B. Reid*

Hawaiian Music in Motion: Mariners, Missionaries, and Minstrels   *James Revell Carr*

Sounds of the New Deal: The Federal Music Project in the West   *Peter Gough*

The Mormon Tabernacle Choir: A Biography   *Michael Hicks*

The Man That Got Away: The Life and Songs of Harold Arlen   *Walter Rimler*

A City Called Heaven: Chicago and the Birth of Gospel Music   *Robert M. Marovich*

Blues Unlimited: Essential Interviews from the Original Blues Magazine
Edited by Bill Greensmith, Mike Rowe, and Mark Camarigg

Hoedowns, Reels, and Frolics: Roots and Branches of Southern Appalachian
Dance   *Phil Jamison*

Fannie Bloomfield-Zeisler: The Life and Times of a Piano Virtuoso
Beth Abelson Macleod

Cybersonic Arts: Adventures in American New Music   *Gordon Mumma,
edited with commentary by Michelle Fillion*

The Magic of Beverly Sills   *Nancy Guy*

Waiting for Buddy Guy   *Alan Harper*

Harry T. Burleigh: From the Spiritual to the Harlem Renaissance   *Jean E. Snyder*

Music in the Age of Anxiety: American Music in the Fifties   *James Wierzbicki*

Jazzing: New York City's Unseen Scene   *Thomas H. Greenland*

A Cole Porter Companion   *Edited by Don M. Randel, Matthew Shaftel,
and Susan Forscher Weiss*

Foggy Mountain Troubadour: The Life and Music of Curly Seckler   *Penny Parsons*

Blue Rhythm Fantasy: Big Band Jazz Arranging in the Swing Era   *John Wriggle*
Bill Clifton: America's Bluegrass Ambassador to the World   *Bill C. Malone*
Chinatown Opera Theater in North America   *Nancy Yunhwa Rao*
The Elocutionists: Women, Music, and the Spoken Word   *Marian Wilson Kimber*
May Irwin: Singing, Shouting, and the Shadow of Minstrelsy   *Sharon Ammen*
Peggy Seeger: A Life of Music, Love, and Politics   *Jean R. Freedman*
Charles Ives's *Concord*: Essays after a Sonata   *Kyle Gann*
Don't Give Your Heart to a Rambler: My Life with Jimmy Martin, the King
    of Bluegrass   *Barbara Martin Stephens*
Libby Larsen: Composing an American Life   *Denise Von Glahn*
George Szell's Reign: Behind the Scenes with the Cleveland Orchestra
    Marcia Hansen Kraus
Just One of the Boys: Female-to-Male Cross-Dressing on the American Variety
    Stage   *Gillian M. Rodger*
Spirituals and the Birth of a Black Entertainment Industry   *Sandra Jean Graham*
Right to the Juke Joint: A Personal History of American Music   *Patrick B. Mullen*
Bluegrass Generation: A Memoir   *Neil V. Rosenberg*
Pioneers of the Blues Revival, Expanded Second Edition   *Steve Cushing*
Banjo Roots and Branches   *Edited by Robert Winans*
Bill Monroe: The Life and Music of the Blue Grass Man   *Tom Ewing*
Dixie Dewdrop: The Uncle Dave Macon Story   *Michael D. Doubler*
Los Romeros: Royal Family of the Spanish Guitar   *Walter Aaron Clark*
Transforming Women's Education: Liberal Arts and Music in Female Seminaries
    Jewel A. Smith
Rethinking American Music   *Edited by Tara Browner and Thomas L. Riis*
Leonard Bernstein and the Language of Jazz   *Katherine Baber*
Dancing Revolution: Bodies, Space, and Sound in American Cultural
    History   *Christopher J. Smith*
Peggy Glanville-Hicks: Composer and Critic   *Suzanne Robinson*
Mormons, Musical Theater, and Belonging in America   *Jake Johnson*
Blues Legacy: Tradition and Innovation in Chicago   *David Whiteis*
Blues Before Sunrise 2: Interviews from the Chicago Scene   *Steve Cushing*
The Cashaway Psalmody: Transatlantic Religion and Music in Colonial
    Carolina   *Stephen A. Marini*
Earl Scruggs and Foggy Mountain Breakdown: The Making of an American
    Classic   *Thomas Goldsmith*
A Guru's Journey: Pandit Chitresh Das and Indian Classical Dance in Diaspora
    Sarah Morelli
Unsettled Scores: Politics, Hollywood, and the Film Music of Aaron Copland and
    Hanns Eisler   *Sally Bick*
Hillbilly Maidens, Okies, and Cowgirls: Women's Country Music, 1930–
    1960   *Stephanie Vander Wel*
Always the Queen: The Denise LaSalle Story   *Denise LaSalle with David Whiteis*
Artful Noise: Percussion Literature in the Twentieth Century   *Thomas Siwe*

The Heart of a Woman: The Life and Music of Florence B. Price   *Rae Linda Brown,*
    edited by Guthrie P. Ramsey Jr.
When Sunday Comes: Gospel Music in the Soul and Hip-Hop Eras   *Claudrena N. Harold*
The Lady Swings: Memoirs of a Jazz Drummer   *Dottie Dodgion and Wayne Enstice*
Industrial Strength Bluegrass: Southwestern Ohio's Musical Legacy
    Edited by Fred Bartenstein and Curtis W. Ellison
Soul on Soul: The Life and Music of Mary Lou Williams   *Tammy L. Kernodle*
Unbinding Gentility: Women Making Music in the Nineteenth-Century South
    Candace Bailey
Punks in Peoria: Making a Scene in the American Heartland   *Jonathan Wright*
    and Dawson Barrett
Homer Rodeheaver and the Rise of the Gospel Music Industry   *Kevin Mungons*
    and Douglas Yeo
Americanaland: Where Country & Western Met Rock 'n' Roll   *John Milward,*
    with Portraits by Margie Greve
Listening to Bob Dylan   *Larry Starr*
Lying in the Middle: Musical Theater and Belief at the Heart of America   *Jake Johnson*

The University of Illinois Press
is a founding member of the
Association of University Presses.

———————————————

University of Illinois Press
1325 South Oak Street
Champaign, IL 61820-6903
www.press.uillinois.edu